DON PEDRO CALDERÓN
DE LA BARCA

LA GRAN COMEDIA,

GVÁRDATE

DE LA AGVA MANSA

❧ BEWARE OF STILL WATERS ❧

DON PEDRO CALDERÓN
DE LA BARCA

LA GRAN COMEDIA,

GVÁRDATE

DE LA AGVA MANSA

BEWARE OF STILL WATERS

A Translation with
Introduction and Notes by
DAVID M. GITLITZ

Trinity University Press

Library of Congress Cataloging in Publication Data

Calderón de la Barca, Pedro, 1600-1681.
  Guárdate de la agua mansa : la gran comedia = Beware
of still waters.

  Translation of: Guárdate de la agua mansa. I. Gitlitz,
David M. (David Martin) II. Title. III. Title: Beware
of still waters.
PQ6292.G8G57 1984   862'.3   84-224
ISBN 0-939980-04-5 cloth
ISBN 0-939980-08-8 paper

Photographs courtesy of the Department of Drama, the University of Nebraska-Lincoln, and used with permission. They were taken during the production of *Beware of Still Waters* at the University of Nebraska-Lincoln in October 1981. The director was Rex McGraw, scenic designer Tom Umfrid, costume designer Janice Stauffer, and lighting designer Greg Kemery.
Originally published as *Guárdate de la agua mansa* from the *Octava parte de comedias del célebre poeta español Don Pedro Calderón de la Barca* (Madrid, 1684).

Manufactured in the United States of America
Printed by Best Printing Company
Bound by Custom Bookbinders

CONTENTS

Introduction   vii
  The Epithalamium   vii
  The Play: Antecedents, Characters, Plot   ix
  This Translation   xv
  Metrical Structures   xix
Text and Translation of *Guárdate del agua mansa*   1

INTRODUCTION

The Epithalamium

The summer of 1648 was not a felicitous time at the Spanish court, for it was clear to king and commoner alike that the 150-year-old Iberian empire in Europe was slipping into ruin: Philip IV's troops battled the French in Flanders and Cataluña, pricked at the Portuguese on Spain's western frontier and were pricked in turn by the Neapolitans in Italy. The Low Countries continued to fester. The Hapsburg union still held, but Austria and Spain found themselves increasingly impotent against the Protestant north and west. Now the protracted, exhausting, devastating wars of religion were coming to an end, and with them Spain's long-held dream of a Catholic Europe united under the banners of Spain. The peace of Westphalia, in October 1648, stripped Spain of her territories in Holland for which so much Spanish blood had been shed, and Philip's spirits sank to a new low.

His queen, Isabel of Bourbon, had died in 1644; their only son, Baltasar Carlos, had followed her to the grave two years later. Philip's other son, the bastard Juan de Austria, could never assume the throne. Spain had no heir, and weak-willed, sensual Philip, whose bed was seldom empty but whose spirit was wracked with obsessive bouts of repentance[1] and melancholy, would have to wed. His search committee cast no further than the Austrian court where Ferdinand III, soon to be the Holy Roman Emperor, offered in the person of his daughter Mariana both consolation and a strengthened Hapsburg alliance. No matter that in 1648 Philip was forty-three and Mariana was only fourteen. No matter that she previously had been betrothed to Philip's own son, the recently deceased Baltasar Carlos. No matter even that she was Philip's own niece, the daughter of Philip's sister María and Ferdinand III.[2] Philip would have a new wife and Spain, with God's help, would have an heir. Catholic Europe hoped fervently that the marriage would signal a change in Spain's fortunes; thus the Hapsburg nations and their allies feted the teenaged queen as if she represented at once the culmination of European greatness and the new beginning of Catholic hegemony. Even in such a ceremonious age as the seventeenth century, the spectacles of 1648 and 1649 were remarkable.

When the prospective queen's entourage left Vienna on November 13, 1648, it was in no hurry. Historians speculate that one probable reason was that Mariana may not yet have reached puberty.[3] Surely another was that her snail-gaited passage afforded the vassal and allied states opportunity to substantiate with costly pageantry their loyalty to Ferdinand and Philip. Whatever the reason, the journey from her father's palace to her uncle's bed took Mariana nearly a year.

In Trent, where she was met by the Duke of Nájera and Maqueda and his retinue of 170 courtiers, the festivals lasted several days. In Milan, what with balls and masques, tournaments and state dinners, not to mention the countless parades through streets festooned with arches, the queen's party delayed two months. When she finally set sail for Spain, it was in the company of nineteen galleys of the Duke of Tursis, twenty-one warships of the Mediterranean Armada, and five thousand marines, none of whom were able to quell the rough weather that plagued the twelve-day crossing. From the Spanish port of Denia, where the Admiral of Castile replaced Tursis (who had been accused of insufficient attention to pomp), the queen's train set out with measured pace for the court.

Since custom dictated that whatever town hosted a royal wedding was forever exempt from paying taxes, the insignificant village of Navalcarnero, twenty-nine kilometers southwest of Madrid, was where Philip chose to meet his new wife. After the wedding ceremony, and two days of bullfights and performances by theatrical companies brought out from Madrid, the couple proceeded to the monastery palace of the Escorial, whose vast expanse was lit for the occasion with eleven thousand candles. They honeymooned there for three weeks and then moved to the Buen Retiro to prepare for their triumphant entry into Madrid.

If the rest of Europe had spent millions on the wedding, Madrid would spend tens of millions. While the king and queen rested in the Retiro, entertained by dances and plays, the city transformed itself into a fantasy of wood, stone, canvas, and papier maché. An ersatz Mount Parnassus rose on the Prado, statued with all the famous Spanish poets since Roman times. Legions of Spanish monarchs graced another construction. Arches, both floral and allegorical, spanned Madrid's principal streets: the Carrera de San Jerónimo, Atocha, the Calle Mayor, the Gradas de San Felipe, the Puerta del Sol, and Platerías. The Fountain of San Salvador was buried under a rocky crag which teemed with live birds and animals. The Plaza de Santa María held a complex allegory of the Spanish conquest of America. Emblems, devices, poems, and mottos were inscribed on every bare surface by Spain's most talented fashioners of spectacle, among whom—if we are to believe Juan de Vera Tassis[4]—figured the king's favorite playwright, Don Pedro Calderón de la Barca.[5]

When at last, on November 15, a year and two days after Mariana had left Vienna, Philip and his bride finally crossed the city to the royal palace, it must have seemed to madrileños to be the apotheosis of pageantry. Their awe permeates the some thirty contemporary descriptions, each of which vies with the others to heap accolade on hyperbole.[6]

Even if Calderón did not design the arches, there is no doubt that he contributed to the wedding festivities. His most prominent work is the extensive wedding poem, or epithalamium, found in *Beware of Still Waters*, a play which undoubtedly was composed[7] to be performed for the royal audience shortly after the momentous events themselves. Calderón's narration of the wedding festivities occupies the central portion of each act of the play. In the first act (verses 451-690) Don Juan praises Mariana's virtues and alludes to her extreme youth:

> The reason why they chose to wait
> was for the tenderness
> of childhood to pass gaily by,
> until she should ingress
> into the bright domain of youth; (499-503)

In elegant images he traces her journey from Trent to Milan, and then vividly paints for our ears the queen's ocean voyage. In the second act (verses 1242-1489), Don Félix explains Madrid's preparations for the royal entrance. The jousts, the masked balls, the concerts, the exquisite liveries, and the bullfights take shape before our eyes in Félix's words. Calderón pulls out all the stops as he fulfills his promise to dazzle us with synesthetic effects:

> Prosopopoeia is the trope
> that makes impossible
>   events seem real, when ideas
> clothed with form appear,
> and silently fill up the eye,
> or loudly fill the ear. (1324-29)

In the third act (verses 3011-3174), Clara and Eugenia chronicle the processions themselves: they detail the queen's costume; the arches with allegorical representations of the monarchy; the four elements; the Hapsburg possessions in Europe, Asia, Africa, and America; and Hymen, the god of marriage. Even after three centuries these descriptions are so vivid that when they are over we can exclaim with Don Alonso that "everything my eyes were keen to see my ears have heard you tell" (3177-78).

The epithalamium is central in but not central to Calderón's play, which is a lighthearted comedy of intrigue and love. Nonetheless, the play and wedding poem are admirably stitched together. The narration of Mariana's journey to Spain has a thematic parallel in Don Pedro's and Don Juan's journeys to Madrid in search of their lady loves. In the second act, Félix describes Madrid's preparations for the wedding just as he and his two friends are creating a strategem to help them meet Clara and Eugenia. And the final act's recreation of the royal entry processions, performed as a stately duet by the two sisters, both symbolizes their competition for mates and is a prelude to the finale in which Clara, as omnipotent mistress of ceremonies, artfully manipulates all of the play's characters in her own triumphant procession to marriage.

If it were not so obvious that *Beware of Still Waters* was written for the royal audience, one would be tempted to read another meaning into the play. Don Alonso wants to marry off a troublesome, perhaps even licentious, daughter and chooses a cousin from the north as her mate; Spain, which would be delighted to see playboy King Philip safely wed, sends off for his niece from Vienna. Loose-mannered Eugenia, of course, turns out to be only a noisy rill; are we meant to be reminded that the king, in spite of his well-known obsessive sexual escapades, is a man of depth and substance? Landless Don Alonso would cement an alliance with the wealthy Asturian branch of his family; Spain, weak and nearly bankrupt, had much to gain from strengthening ties with the soon-to-be Holy Roman Emperor Ferdinand III. Might Calderón be suggesting that Philip and his advisors were as crassly mercenary as Don Alonso? Worse yet, the northern cousin, Don Toribio, turns out to be a dolt, haughty, ignorant and simple, whom Don Alonso eventually has to send packing. What then are we to think of the queen? Anecdotes about her insolence, her willfulness, her shameless disregard for the proprieties of Spanish courtly customs were already circulating widely in Madrid.[8] Surely Calderón was not hinting that Mariana would turn out to be another Don Toribio, vain and unadaptable to courtly ways. The body of the play is too silly to be taken seriously, and the epithalamium is too sincerely fawning for any of these speculations to be taken as fact. And yet despite the play's glittering veneer, a patina of disaffection shines through. Or, to adapt Calderón's own metaphor, beneath the crystaline mirror of the still waters of his art runs a current of mordant irony.

The Play: Antecedents, Characters, Plot

The playwrights of Calderón's day, who were known in Spanish simply as *poetas*, made their reputations on the quality of their verses, the memorability of their characters, their deft handling of incident, and their ability to evoke emotion. Plots, on the other hand, belonged to the public domain. Theatrical *poetas* felt no scruples in liberally borrowing plotlines from their immediate predecessors or even their contemporaries. Thus it is not surprising, nor is it in any way deleterious to our appreciation of *Beware of Still Waters*, to discover that much of its plot is adapted from one of Don Antonio Hurtado de Mendoza's dozen surviving plays, *Cada loco con su tema, o el montañés indiano*. From this source Calderón took his principal characters: the rich, widowed nobleman just returned to Madrid from the Indies with two marriageable daughters; the grotesquely proud and doltish nephew summoned from a hamlet in the Montaña region of northern Spain to wed his choice of the daughters; and the pair of rival suitors who have come to Madrid to woo the girls. From Hurtado, Calderón also took several incidents and descriptions: the bringing of the papal dispensation from Rome; the truncated duel in the street in front of the girls' house; the ludicrous portrayal of the country bumpkin's clothes; and a verbal joke or two.

But a close comparison of the two works turns up more differences than similarities and increases our admiration for Calderón's craft. With the exception of some of the broadly comic scenes, Hurtado's play is sluggish, lacking clearly defined or convincingly motivated characters, prosaic in verse, and largely devoid of the comic tension which Calderón created by incremental clashes of will and mistaken motives and identities. For example, the two daughters in Hurtado's play project no sense of rivalry. The elder, Leonor, is a fluffy-headed social climber, obsessed with the shame she will suffer if she is forced to wed a gentleman so poor that, unable to afford a horse, his boots will track up her reputation with the redolent mud of Madrid's Calle Mayor; she is as devoid of good sense, or backbone, as a cantaloupe. The younger daughter, Isabel, is courted by three gallants (one of them an effeminate dandy) and an outlandishly proportioned *montañés* as well. Throughout most of the play Isabel seems as fickle as a weathervane; she never undergoes the crises and subsequent evolution that characterizes Eugenia in *Beware of Still Waters*. Hurtado's noble suitors are largely insipid, and while the nameless bumpkin cousin[10] blusters comically about his honor, he exhibits little of the prideful stupidity and hyperbolic oafishness that make Calderón's Toribio such a scene-stealing delight.

For all its loose ends, and there are several,[11] Calderón's play is much more finely crafted than that of Antonio Hurtado de Mendoza. Calderón's characters, for example, are solid enough that their attitudes, motives, and decisions are for the most part consistent and believable. Don Alonso, the gout-ridden, loyal civil servant, recently returned from Mexico to find his daughters ripe for marriage, is a convincing paternal tyrant, moved both by the wish to acquire his brother's estates through marriage of daughter to cousin, and by the urgency he feels to marry off his teenage volcano before she erupts all over his honor. His loving concern for his two daughters shines through his strictness with them. In the course of the play, Don Alonso's values do not change significantly, but his attitude toward Don Toribio does. Indeed, the rapidity of this shift is one weakness in the play: since already by early in act 2 Don Alonso recognizes his cousin's imbecility (v. 1578), it is hard to understand why he continues to favor the suit.

Don Toribio Quadradillos is a classic *figurón*, a pretentiously exaggerated stereotypical character who is held up to ridicule, whose designs are eventually thwarted, and who provides the principal comic interest in the play, usurping one of the traditional functions of the *gracioso*, or comic foil. The twin touchstones of Toribio's character are his inflated sense of personal worth and his lack of intellect. Because he is from the Montaña, the northern mountainous region of Asturias and Santander which reputedly was never invaded by Moors nor settled by Jews, he is proud of his unsullied bloodlines as well as his status as an *hidalgo*, which puts him on the ladder of Spanish nobility, albeit on the lowest rung. The emblem of these attributes are the certificates of *hidalguía* which Toribio carries with him wherever he goes as a kind of talisman; in his mind the power of these letters patent is so great that Toribio feels they can even be substituted for the Bible in the swearing of an oath (v. 2826). In Toribio's mind the logical consequence of his position as a lesser deity is that everything he receives—and more—is his due: the polite hypocrisies of social grace are either lost on him or cause him offense. He will not stoop to saying thank you, nor can he be bothered to conform to the code of courtly dress. In fact, if the costume department's imagination is half as fertile as Calderón's, Toribio's entrance at the end of act 1 should stop the show. Toribio's other characteristic is a lack of sophistication bordering on imbecility. In a society in which lovers regularly exchange sonnets, Toribio cannot read and will not learn. Some of the play's funniest scenes build on Toribio's incomprehension of a word like *filis* (knack), or his misunderstanding of what was then a common artifact such as a farthingale in act 2.

The three *galanes*, who in the course of the play's complexities become rivals for the two daughters, have characters familiar to Calderón's audience. Don Juan, an impetuous soldier who has already slain one rival, wants shelter with his friend in Madrid until his pardon is confirmed. He knows that his beloved is in Madrid, and he will risk anything to see her. Don Pedro, a university student who has also come to Madrid for love, would hide for a few days to evade his father and further his suit. Their accommodating friend, Don Félix, a confirmed bachelor who disdains love and seems at the same time bored with the loose pleasures of court, is the most interesting of the three, for his character develops parallel to that of Clara. His initial interest in the women is that they live next door. But then Clara captures his attention, and we see him grapple first with his sense of loyalty to his friends and then with his own philosophy of bachelorhood before at last he commits himself to love and wins Clara's hand. In the fashion of Calderón's theater, the characters of Juan and Pedro seem to have been deliberately flattened in order to leave the audience free to focus on Félix who has a strong and engaging personality: a keen mind, a flair for lyricism, and a courtly finesse that contrasts nicely with Toribio's lack thereof.

Left to right, Doña Eugenia, Don Alonso, Don Toribio, and Doña Clara.

But it is the two daughters who are at the play's core. Calderón presents them to us from the very first as opposites. Eugenia, wild and sassy (except to her father, of course), thinks only of having a good time. She goes into raptures about the gaiety of the street: she craves riding in coaches for the same reason my generation frequented drive-in movies. For Eugenia, a party would not be a party without the exotic and costly drink grown popular since the conquest of Mexico: hot chocolate. Eugenia's sister and her duenna are scandalized by her behavior, while her father is so upset when he learns of it that he makes his top priority getting her married and safely removed to cousin Toribio's mountain village. Yet in the course of the play we learn that Eugenia is really more imprudent than immoral, more enamored of being thought naughty than of doing wrong. As she says to her sister, in a rare moment of self-analysis at the end of act 2:

> women like me, if no one draws
> the line, seem loose, and to enjoy
> themselves; but yet they don't destroy
> themselves. It's all a game. This kind
> of puppy love, let me remind
> you, is nothing but a lot of
> noise (v. 2363-69).

Thus, in the end, we are not surprised when Eugenia capitulates to her father's will, volunteering to marry whomever he elects for her (v. 3465).

Clara, in contrast with her sister, is presented initially as the "imitator/here on this earth of Heaven's peace" (v. 151): kind to her servants, grateful for the comforts of her father's house, and soft-spoken, except when she yields to the temptation to preach. But of course Calderón is setting us up for the major character change of the play, for once the defenses of Clara's heart have been breached, she changes before our eyes into a shrewd puppetrix of love. She thwarts her sister's attempts to recover a love note, she ably hides Don Félix and misdirects the household who are searching for him, she bamboozles Toribio at her whim, she enlists her duenna's aid in order to communicate with her lover, and in the play's penultimate scene she in turn sequesters Toribio, Eugenia, and Félix on diverse balconies and then retrieves them and sets them against the other characters as it suits her purpose.

Clara and Eugenia, of course, incarnate the play's metaphoric title. Eugenia is the mountain rill, flashy, attractive, but essentially shallow, and so noisily obvious that she poses no real threat. Clara, on the other hand, presents a still, clear, crystalline exterior which reflects the approved values of seventeenth-century Spain; yet underneath runs a current of spunk, so that with both will and wit Clara flaunts society's mores to win her heart's desire.

Clara is not what she initially seems to be, and as though to reinforce this central tenet, the plot of *Beware of Still Waters* turns on a device common in cloak and dagger *comedia*: mistaken identity. When the sisters first appear on the balcony, Juan and Pedro each privately confide to their friend Félix that they are in love with one of the young women. Félix has himself been taken with one of the sisters—as yet unidentified—and we, the audience, speculate on the rich possibilities for confusion (vv. 749-58). If either Juan or Pedro loves the one who has attracted Félix, then either friendship or Félix's incipient romance would have to be sacrificed. Or, worse, if Juan and Pedro both love the same woman, they will undoubtedly clash, and with that Félix's friendship, and perhaps even his honor, will be caught in the middle. We are

Doña Clara and Doña Eugenia.

left in suspense until the beginning of the second act when the three gallants encounter the sisters in the street. Now Juan and Pedro each reveal covertly that they love Eugenia, the one who holds the handkerchief. But before Félix can turn around to identify her, Eugenia passes the handkerchief to her sister Clara, and with that gesture precipitates a snarl of comic errors that is not unraveled until the final scene.

Thematically related to the principal confusion are two comic subplots involving Toribio. In the first, he misinterprets the word *filis*, or knack for love, which Eugenia says he does not have. Thinking that a *filis* must be an artifact rather than a character trait, Toribio goes whirling off to purchase one or have one brought from his family estates. In the second instance, Toribio thinks the farthingale which Eugenia uses to support her wide skirt is really a ladder on which some man climbs to visit her in her chamber.

Confusion is the play's dominant mode, and there the major lines of the play converge: confusion as the result of Toribio's simplemindedness and malicious desire to expect the worst; confusion as the offspring of Clara's wit and artful deceiving; and

Don Alonso, Don Toribio, and the farthingale.

confusion loosed from the gilded arabesques of Calderón's description of the royal wedding. All these combine, harmoniously, to dazzle the baroque audience.

Dazzling harmonious combination might be a good way of describing Calderón's work in general. Artists of the mid-seventeenth century, whom we are accustomed to labeling baroque, appreciated unity in a way fundamentally different from both earlier and later generations. At the core of their artifacts, of course, there were themes, motifs, and patterns of construction basic to art across the ages; but baroque artists made certain that the core was sumptuously arrayed. In the firm conviction that more is more, these artists eschewed simplicity in favor of complex sight lines and lavish surface decoration. To embellish was literally to beautify by ornamental additions. In *Beware of Still Waters*, the epithalamia are superb examples of descriptions enhanced through the accumulation of sensory stimuli.

Another dominant feature of the baroque is the creation of tension through dramatic juxtaposition of opposites. Styles were set against one another like a form of counterpoint: thus we find long and short meters, high and low diction, allusive and straightforward language, verse and prose, music and cacophony. Moral dilemmas were advanced through dialectic (see, for example, vv. 1769-1836). Oxymorons and paradoxes abounded (vv. 585-6, 3161-62); chiasmi, both visual (vv. 659-66) and conceptual (vv. 3177-78) were rife. In the hands of a master like Calderón, these diverse and opposing strands of melody generally resolved themselves into a final harmonious chord: we find the lovers wed, the dolts sent packing, the wicked punished, and all questions answered.

A third notable feature is the baroque's fascination with allusive language. The most commonplace things or events or relationships were habitually linked to external referents through metaphor or simile. Although *Beware of Still Waters* is not nearly as rich or as cohesive in imagery as are some of Calderón's more finely crafted plays,[12] it nevertheless shares the baroque predilection for allusion. Alonso considers his daughters two pieces of his soul (v. 10), and for Brígida they are two suns (v. 116); repeatedly the monarchs are eagles and demigods. Some metaphors startle us with their vivid freshness: the queen's galley is a "wandering metropolis of sail" (v. 656). Others are extended so far from their original equation that they are in danger of breaking with the strain (vv. 508-11, 656-66). Modern mortals coexist with mythologi-cal figures: Hymen is summoned to bless the marriage (v. 1290); Venus fires darts across the royal galley's bows (v. 607). In the baroque, royalty and commoners alike indulged their taste for allusiveness in elaborate allegorical spectacles: masques, pag-eants, and in this play a procession that winds through symbolic arches festooned with emblematic devices, living statues, tableaus, and hieroglyphics.

This play, then, like the constructs which lined the route of the wedding procession, and like so many works of the baroque, is an amalgam of genres, motifs, and styles. Seen one way it is a classic *comedia de enredo*, a play of deception or entanglement. In another it is a *comedia de figurón* in which Don Toribio, both larger and stranger than life, is the chief comic impediment to love. In another it is a finely developed study of character, in particular of Clara's evolution from submissive prude to choreographer of her own destiny. In another it is social satire, skewering the bourgeois *indiano*, the doltish old-Christian *montañés*, gossipy servants, heavy-handed duennas, and the fop-pish gallants of the court. And lastly it is a gift, presented by Calderón to the king and new queen of Spain on the occasion of their wedding.

This Translation

This project was born in the spring of 1978 when the University of Nebraska-Lincoln began planning for the 1981 tercentenary of Calderón's death. Rex McGraw, the director of the University Department of Theater Arts, agreed to stage a

Left to right, Don Pedro, Don Félix, Don Juan, Doña Eugenia, and Doña Clara.

Calderón play if I would translate one that had not been performed previously in English.[13] Since Calderón is best known to English-speaking audiences for his honor plays and his philosophical plays, McGraw suggested that we do a comedy and, further, that I either provide a wealthy angel or else choose a play with a small cast and few scene changes. A year and a half later, when he thought the project had long since been safely forgotten, I handed him plot outlines of a half-dozen suitable comedies. McGraw took one look at the epithalamia that anchor the center of each of the acts of *Beware of Still Waters* and recoiled with horror: "There is no way these descriptions can be staged for a modern audience!" Five minutes later he had made up his mind: "Let's do that one."

For me the difficulties inherent in getting the intricacies of Calderón's verse safely transubstantiated into English presented a similar challenge.[14] Golden Age Spanish *comedias* were always written within the constraints of strict patterns of both meter and rhyme. Most lines were the traditionally Spanish octosyllables, while a few were in the more refined Italian hendecasyllables. From the days when Lope de Vega established the conventions, a half-century before *Beware of Still Waters*, particular meters were reserved for certain kinds of speeches: ballads, or *romances* (octosyllables with assonant rhyme in the even-numbered verses), were used for narration; sonnets were reserved for soliloquies; dialogue was often cast in *redondillas* (octosyllabic quatrains rhyming *abba, cddc,* . . .). While additional forms were occasionally used by playwrights, Calderón preferred a limited palate: 97.5 percent of the lines in *Beware of Still Waters* are *romances* and *redondillas*. A schema of the metrical structures of the Spanish play and my English equivalents is appended to this introduction.

Although Calderón accepted the Lopean constraints, it is clear that he found their rhythms oppressive, for he strove to superimpose a more natural prosodic rhythm

Doña Clara, Doña Eugenia and Don Félix.

Doña Clara, Don Pedro, and Doña Eugenia.

over the formalities of the verse. In conversational passages he did this by using large numbers of run-on lines, by allowing a sentence—or sometimes an entire speech—to end in midline, and by letting the rhymes fall on normally unstressed words. On the other hand, in highly rhetorical speeches, such as love plaints or richly embellished narrative passages or philosophical soliloquies, Calderón took pains to have the prosodic and poetic rhythms coincide, thus stressing the formal nature of those passages.

I have tried to do the same.[15] In the passages of everyday dialogue, I have used run-on lines, non-stressed rhyme words, and randomly placed full stops. While keeping to octosyllabic verse, I have deliberately not let any regular pattern of scansion establish itself. To contrast with this straightforward speech I have set the formal passages, notably the long epithalamia, into an English ballad form which emphasizes both meter and rhyme.

A note about method may be in order. In the course of translating I found that I had to vary strategy according to the sense of each passage. Most dialogue I was able to translate in the order in which the lines are spoken. But whenever a pun or some other verbal device was paramount, I had to begin with it, work out its ramifications, and then elaborate from it in both directions. The "knack" (v. 1967) and the "farthin-gale" (v. 2923) are the most notable examples. The same procedure was required whenever some striking image imposed itself on a scene, or whenever a climax was underscored by language. The complexities of the wedding narrations required that I sketch out a prose version before attempting the ballad form. In the low style I tried, following Calderón, to let words fall as far as possible in the order of natural speech. But where Calderón gave free rein to anaphora, hyperbaton, and other deforming artifices of rhetoric, I did the same. It is clear that tangled syntax, interminable sentences, and complex images demand an almost superhuman effort on the part of the modern listener to maintain the thread of sense, but I felt that I would falsify the aesthetic experience if I took away that pleasure by simplifying. The baroque mind obviously enjoyed the struggle to apprehend an entire skein of thought without breaking the thread; language addicts of our day do not return week after week to the *New York Times* crossword puzzle because it is easy.

In spite of what I just said, the playability of the translation was always a concern.[16] My two pre-teenage daughters, Deborah and Abigail, kindly consented to let me try out the text on them. In fact they demanded it, emerging each morning from their tent on the shore of Mexico's Lake Pátzcuaro to see if I had finished another scene so they could find out what happened next. If there was any passage they could not understand, or I could not easily explain to them, I rewrote it. When the first longhand draft was complete, Linda Davidson, who typed it, honed a number of problem spots. Then Rex McGraw, who directed the production for the University of Nebraska-Lincoln (and, by the way, maintained audience interest throughout the 648-line epithalamium), combed the text for inconsistencies of meaning and for awkward combinations of words or rhythms. Last, I owe a debt of gratitude to the actors who began plying me with questions at the initial read-through of the play and kept on questioning through rehearsals and through eleven performances in Lincoln, one in Cedar Falls, Iowa, and a final performance at the Seventh Chamizal Golden Age Drama festival in El Paso, Texas. It is the long and conscientious production process that deserves the credit for whatever polish this translation may have; its weaknesses, of course, are my own. Pedro speaks for me, as well as for Calderón, when in the last scene he begs: "que perdonéis/de mis faltas los yerros."

Metrical structures

	Verses	Spanish meter		English meter
I.	1-218	romance	a-o	octosyllabic couplets
	219-450	redondillas		octosyllabic quatrains: abba
	451-690	romance	i-a	ballad meter: epithalamium I
	691-758	redondillas		octosyllabic quatrains: abba
	759-914	romance	a-o	octosyllabic couplets
	915-1109	romance	e-o	octosyllabic couplets
II.	1110-1241	romance	e-a	octosyllabic couplets
	1242-1489	romance	e-a	ballad meter: epithalamium II
	1490-1663	romance	e-a	octosyllabic couplets
	1664-1968	redondillas		octosyllabic quatrains: abba
	1969-2237	romance	i-a	octosyllabic couplets
	2238-2265	romance	e-e	ballad meter: letter
	2266-2409	romance	e-e	octosyllabic couplets
III.	2410-2597	romance	e-e	octosyllabic couplets
	2598-2767	redondillas		octosyllabic quatrains: abba
	2768-2856	heptasílabo;		
		endecasílabos	pareados	pentameter: couplets
	2857-2982	romance	e-e	octosyllabic couplets
	2983-3010	redondillas		octosyllabic quatrains: abba
	3011-3174	romance	a-a	ballad meter: epithalamium III
	3175-3266	redondillas		octosyllabic quatrains: abba
	3267-3496	romance	e-o	octosyllabic couplets pentameter: couplet

Notes

1. See Philip's well-known correspondence with Sor María de Agreda, for example. *Cartas de la madre Sor María de Agreda y del Rey Don Felipe IV,* ed. F. Silvela (Madrid: Sucesores de Rivadaneyra, 1885-86).

2.

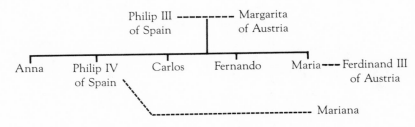

3. Martin Hume, *The Court of Philip IV* (New York: Putnam, 1907), p. 142. See verses 499-503.

4. For descriptions of the wedding see José Amador de los Ríos, *Historia de la Villa y Corte de Madrid,* vol. III (Madrid, 1863), pp. 391-93; Martin Hume, *The Court of Philip IV;* Martin Hume, *Queens of Old Spain* (New York: McClure, Phillips, 1906), pp. 364-66; Emilio Cotarelo y Mori, *Ensayo sobre la vida y obras de Don Pedro Calderón de la Barca,* BRAE 9 (1922), pp. 607-12. References to contemporary sources are given by Cotarelo.

5. Don Pedro Calderón de la Barca (1600-1681) — poet, soldier, courtier, playwright, fighter of duels in his youth and in his maturity one of Europe's most sublime religious polemicists — typifies the literary brilliance of Hapsburg Spain. Calderón was trained at a Jesuit grammar school, and later at the University of Salamanca. By the age of 20 he had both won his first major poetic competition and killed his first rival. After his plays began to be produced beginning in 1623, he enlisted with the famed Spanish *tercios* and fought in Italy, Flanders, and later with distinction in the Cataluña wars of 1640-42. By the 1630s he was King Philip IV's favorite playwright, penning works at his sovereign's command, and winning both popular fame and elevation to the coveted Order of Santiago. Although in 1651, shortly after the completion of *Beware of Still Waters,* he entered the Church, he continued to write for the theater, especially the one-act religious allegorical plays known as *autos sacramentales.*

Among Calderón's best-known plays are comic plays such as *Casa con dos puertas mala es de guardar (The House with Two Doors)* and *La dama duende (The Phantom Lady);* plays about the effects of honor such as *El pintor de su deshonra (The Painter of His Dishonor)* and *El médico de su honra (The Physician of His Honor);* religious plays such as *El mágico prodigioso (The Wonder Working Magician);* costumbristic plays such as *El alcalde de Zalamea (The Mayor of Zalamea);* and Calderón's philosophical masterpiece, *La vida es sueño (Life is a Dream).*

For additional material in English, see Everett W. Hesse, *Calderón de la Barca* (New York: Twayne, 1967), which contains a selected bibliography and a list of Calderón plays which have been translated into English. See also D. W. Cruickshank and John Varey, *The Comedias of Calderón* (London: Tamesis, 1973); Bruce Wardropper, *Critical Essays on the Theatre of Calderón* (New York: New York University, 1965); Frederick A. de Armas, *et al., Critical Perspectives on Calderón de la Barca* (Lincoln, Nebraska: Society for Spanish and Spanish American Studies, 1981).

6. Cited by Cotarelo, p. 608. Modern palates tend not to savor these descriptions. Hume calls them merely "ceremonies and pomp which would be tedious to relate" (*Queens of Old Spain,* p. 364). Cotarelo passes over them with a nod: "Mucho espacio sería necesario para enumerar simplemente los adornos de las calles" (p. 607).

7. Or resurrected. This play, as will be discussed later, is not very tightly crafted. One might imagine that Calderón, pressured by the king to prepare something for the wedding,

took *Beware of Still Waters* from his drawer, revised it slightly, inserted the freshly composed epithalamium, and sent it off, hoping that no one would notice the paste and staples.

8.   Martin Hume relates how Mariana scoffed at the palace dwarfs and buffoons, laughed loudly in public, and even walked on her own legs instead of letting herself be carried, all of which shocked the court. *The Court of Philip IV,* p. 414.

9.   I am indebted to Vern Williamsen for this datum.

10.   In spite of the subtitle of Hurtado's play, it is the father, not the *montañés,* who comes from the Indies.

11.   For example, Don Alonso's attack of the gout (v. 2327) is not adequately prepared. The secret marriage, which occurred prior to the action of the play, is not mentioned, or even hinted at, until the final lines: it is clearly an afterthought, a device to bring the work to a swift conclusion.

12.   For a full discussion of this technique, see my *La estructura lírica de la comedia de Lope de Vega* (Madrid: Albatros, 1980).

13.   Edward Fitzgerald, he of the *Rubaiyyat of Omar Khayyam,* in 1853 adapted six of Calderón's plays into English, among them *Beware of Smooth Waters,* whose length he proudly cut by nearly one-third on the grounds that "dramatic Spanish passion is still bombast to English ears, and confounds otherwise distinct outlines of character." (New York: E. P. Dutton and Co., 1928), p. 45. Edwin Honig, whose translations of Calderón are surely the most successful to date, characterizes Fitzgerald's work in this way: "Fitzgerald used a stock but modified form of Elizabethan diction, cutting long speeches, altering and adding lines as he saw fit, and generally polishing crude surfaces with his own debonair intelligence. The effect is something like a series of Restoration plays with just a hint of the taste of the Spanish to suggest how much verbal mediocrity had to be applied to reduce the original to innocuousness in English." *Calderón, Four Plays* (New York: Hill and Wang, 1961), p. xxiv.

14.   For my text of the play, I have used the *Octava parte de comedias del célebre poeta español Don Pedro Calderón de la Barca* (Madrid, 1684).

15.   Although I translated from the *Octava parte,* in this edition I have modernized the spelling and punctuation. The Spanish text is based on the 1917 Menéndez Pidal text, *Teatro Selecto de Calderón de la Barca* (Madrid, 1917), rigorously corrected to the Octava parte. It has been necessary to make certain changes which are indicated in the text in the following manner: punctuation, capitalization, and accentuation have been modernized or corrected without notation or explanation; the Spanish text reproduces the stage directions as in the *Octava parte* while, for the sake of clarification, some additional stage directions are given in my English version; when an obvious error in the Old Spanish has garbled the text, I have corrected it, but where the Old Spanish differs significantly from clarified, updated versions, I have gone with the sensible version and have footnoted with asterisk the seventeenth-century Spanish.

16.   The passages supercharged with rhetoric were relatively easy, for my grammar, as Calderón's, could be bent to fit into the rigid parameters of rhyme and octosyllabic rhythm. Much more difficult were the passages where, even with the same fettering constraints, the goal was limpid, natural-sounding speech. These passages had to be accessible to the untrained ears of modern audiences.

DON PEDRO CALDERÓN DE LA BARCA

LA GRAN COMEDIA,

GVÁRDATE

DE LA AGVA MANSA

 BEWARE OF STILL WATERS

Personas

Doña Clara, *dama*

Doña Eugenia, *dama*

Brígida, *criada*

Mari-Nuño, *dueña*

Hernando, *criado*

Don Félix, *galán*

Don Juan de Mendoza, *galán*

Don Pedro, *galán*

Don Toribio Quadradillos

Don Alonso, *viejo*

Otáñez, *escudero, vejete*

Characters

Donā Clara, *lady*

Doña Eugenia, *lady*

Brígida, *maid*

Mari-Nuño, *duenna*

Hernando, *servant*

Don Félix, *gallant*

Don Juan de Mendoza, *gallant*

Don Pedro, *gallant*

Don Toribio Quadradillos

Don Alonso, *father*

Otáñez, *old servant*

Jornada Primera

[Salen don Alonso y Otáñez.]

OTÁÑEZ
Una y mil veces, señor,
vuelvo a besarte la mano.

D. ALONSO
Y yo una y mil veces vuelvo
a pagarte con los brazos.

OTÁÑEZ
¿Posible es que llegó el día
para mí tan deseado,
como verte en esta corte?

D. ALONSO
No lo deseabas tú tanto
como yo; pero ¿qué mucho,
si en dos hijas dos pedazos
del alma me estaban siempre
con mudas voces llamando?

OTÁÑEZ
Aun en viéndolas, señor,
mejor lo dirán tus labios.
¡Oh si mi señora viera
este día!

D. ALONSO
No mi llanto
ocasiones con memorias
que siempre presentes traigo.
Téngala Dios en el cielo;
que a fe que he sentido harto
su muerte; que desde el día
que su Majestad, premiando
mis servicios, en el reino
de Méjico me dio el cargo
de que vengo, a no más ver
me despedí de sus brazos.
No quiso pasar conmigo
a Nueva España, no tanto
por los temores del mar,
como porque en tiernos años
dos hijas eran estorbo
para camino tan largo.
Criándolas quedó en casa:
fue Dios servido que al cabo
de tantos años faltó.
A cuya causa, abreviando
yo con mi oficio, dispuse
volver para ser reparo
de su pérdida; que no
estaban bien sin amparo
de padre y madre.

Act I

A room in Don Alonso's house
[Don Alonso and Otáñez enter.]

OTÁÑEZ   My lord! A thousand times I kiss
              your hand to demonstrate my bliss.

ALONSO   A thousand times, then, find your place
              and your reward in my embrace.

OTÁÑEZ   Can that great day have come to pass   5
              that I've hoped for so, when at last
              you are here at court, as before?

ALONSO   You cannot have hoped for it more
              than I did; but then, who could do
              otherwise? Because in those two   10
              daughters, two pieces of my soul
              called to me to make my heart whole.

OTÁÑEZ   Ah, but when you see them, my lord,
              your lips will double their reward.
              If but my dear lady this day   15
              had lived to see!

ALONSO   Please don't dismay
              me by recalling memories
              that will always disturb my peace.
              God preserve her with him above,
              for, by my faith, my lasting love   20
              has felt her death; for since the day
              the king decided to repay
              my service with that Mexican
              post, my absence from her began.
              She did not want to cross with me   25
              to New Spain, not because the sea
              terrified her, rather because
              the girls' tender age gave her pause,
              thinking the trip too great a strain.
              So to raise them she stayed in Spain.   30
              And now the good Lord, after all
              these years, has decided to call
              her to him. And thus I cut short
              my duties, so I could transport
              myself here at once to protect   35
              them from straying; for I suspect
              that two young girls should not be left
              of both of their parents bereft.

---

23 Mexican post: as an officer in the colonial administration
26 New Spain: Mexico

OTÁÑEZ   Es muy justo
señor, en ti ese cuidado;
pero si alguno pudiera
no tenerle, eras tú. Es llano,
porque el día que faltó
mi señora, ambas se entraron
seglares en un convento,
sin más familia ni gasto
que a Mari-Nuño y a mí,
donde en Alcalá han estado
con sus tías hasta hoy,
que obedientes al mandato
tuyo, vuelven a la corte.
Y habiéndolas yo dejado
ya en el camino, no pude
sufrir del coche el espacio;
y así, por verte, señor,
me adelanté.

D. ALONSO   Unos despachos
que para su Majestad
traje, demás del cuidado
de tener puesta la casa,
tiempo ni lugar me han dado
de ir yo por ellas, demás
que el camino es tan cosario,
que perdona la fineza,
pues es venir de otro barrio.
¿Cómo vienen?

[Dentro]
Voces   Para, para.

OTÁÑEZ   Ya parece que han llegado:
ellas lo dirán mejor.

D. ALONSO   A recibirlas salgamos.

OTÁÑEZ   Excusado será, pues
están ya dentro del cuarto.

[Salen doña Clara, doña Eugenia, y Mari-Nuño, de camino.]

CLARA   Padre y señor, ya que el cielo,
enternecido a mí llanto,
me ha concedido piadoso
la dicha de haber llegado
adonde, puesta a tus pies,
merezca besar tu mano,
cuanto desde hoy viva, vivo
de más; pues no me ha dejado

OTÁÑEZ

My lord, with your rapid return
you demonstrate your just concern.   40
But if ever man could appear
without such care, it's you. That's clear,
because the day my lady died,
your two daughters went to reside
in a convent; their family   45
was just Mari-Nuño and me;
and they have lived with those kind aunts
until now, when obedience
to your command they demonstrate
by returning to court with great   50
speed. But still their coach creeps along,
and I, unwilling to prolong
the journey, rushed ahead to greet
you, my lord, and my joy complete.

ALONSO

Some letters for his majesty   55
that I brought from New Spain with me,
together with my eagerness
to prepare the house, I confess,
have not permitted me to go
for them personally. Although   60
there was no reason to go my-
self, that road is so crowded. Why,
it's like walking from shop to shop.
Tell me: how are they?

Voices
[Offstage]   Stop! Hey, stop!

OTÁÑEZ

Well, why not ask them yourself, for   65
they have just arrived at your door.

ALONSO

Come, let us go welcome those two
girls.

OTÁÑEZ   No. Here they come into
the house this very instant. Look!

[Enter Clara, Eugenia and Mari-Nuño, in traveling clothes.]

CLARA

Father, lord: it seems Heaven took   70
compassion on my sad laments
and has granted me the immense
grace of being able to greet
you where, kneeling here at your feet,
I am allowed to kiss your hand;   75
each new day I live will expand
my life beyond all I deserve;

ya que pedirle, si no es
sólo el eterno descanso.

EUGENIA   Yo, padre y señor, aunque
logre en estas plantas cuanto
me prometió mi deseo,
más que pedir me ha quedado
al cielo, y es que tal dicha
dure en tu edad siglos largos;
porque esto del morir, no
lo tengo por agasajo.

D. ALONSO   No en vano, mitades bellas
del alma y vida, no en vano
al corazón puso en medio
del pecho el cielo, mostrando
que con dos afectos puede
comunicarse en dos brazos.
Alzad del suelo; llegad
al pecho, que enamorado
vuelva a engendraros de nuevo.

CLARA   Hoy puedo decir que nazco,
pues hoy nuevo ser recibo.

EUGENIA   Dices bien, que tal abrazo
infunde segunda vida.

D. ALONSO   Entrad, no quedéis al paso:
tomaréis la posesión
desta casa en que os aguardo,
para que seáis dueños della,
hasta que piadoso el hado
traiga a quien merezca serlo
de dos tan bellos milagros;
si bien en mí, esposo, padre
y galán tendréis, en tanto
que os vea como deseo.
¡Brígida!

[Sale Brígida.]

BRÍGIDA   Señor.

D. ALONSO   Su cuarto
enseña a tus amas.

BRÍGIDA   Todo
limpio está y aderezado;
pero ¿qué mucho es, si tales
dueños espera, el estarlo
como un cielo, con dos soles?

	for God keeps nothing in reserve	
	for me now but my last reward:	
	rest with my everlasting Lord.	80
EUGENIA	And I, father and lord, although	
	I find here at your feet the glow	
	of joy promised by my desire,	
	even so there is a higher	
	boon I ask of God and that is	85
	that such good luck endure endless	
	years, for this business of dying	
	does not seem so satisfying.	
ALONSO	It was not in vain, my two sweet,	
	lovely halves of soul, I repeat,	90
	'twas not in vain God set my heart	
	in my chest, where it can impart	
	its dual affection equally	
	in these arms that draw you to me.	
	Please, rise up from the ground: draw near	95
	this breast that, filled with most sincere	
	love, engenders you both anew.	
CLARA	I can say these arms give me new	
	being and my old life erase.	
EUGENIA	How right you are, from such embrace	100
	my new life will originate.	
ALONSO	Come in, come in, daughters. Don't wait	
	there in the door; come, take possession	
	of this house, in which your discretion	
	shall make you true masters, until	105
	most generous fate shall fulfil	
	your destiny with masters who	
	shall merit such wonders as you.	
	But you shall both retain in me	
	father and husband, 'til I see	110
	you one day well provided for.	
	Brígida! Brígida!	

[Brígida enters.]

BRÍGIDA	My lord.
ALONSO	Show your two mistresses their room.

BRÍGIDA	It's all clean and in freshest bloom.	
	But that's not much, for two such ones	115
	it's a heaven waiting for two suns.	

| CLARA | ¡Feliz yo que a ver alcanzo
este día, aunque a pension
de haber, Eugenia, dejado
las paredes del convento! |

[Vase.]

| EUGENIA | ¡Feliz yo, pues he llegado
a ver calles de Madrid,
sin rejas, redes, ni claustros! |

[Vase.]

| MARI-NUÑO | Ya, señor, que el alborozo
de dos hijas ha dejado
algún lugar para mí,
merezca también tu mano. |

| D. ALONSO | Y no con menor razón
que ellas, el alma y los brazos,
pues por vuestra buena ley,
en lugar de madre os hallo.
Y ya que ausentes las dos,
solos, Mari-Nuño, estamos,
decidme sus condiciones;
que como las dos quedaron
niñas, mal puedo hacer juicio
que no sea temerario,
para que prudente y cuerdo
pueda, como maestro sabio,
gobernar inclinaciones
que pone el cielo a mi cargo. |

| MARI-NUÑO | Con decir, señor, que son
hijas tuyas, digo cuanto
puedo decir; mas porque
no presumas que te hablo
sólo al gusto, aunque de entrambas
la virtud y ejemplo es raro,
de lo general verás
que a lo particular paso.
doña Clara, mi señora,
mayor en cordura y años,
es la misma paz del mundo,
no se ha visto igual agrado
hasta hoy en mujer. Pues ¿qué
su modestia y su recato?
Apenas cuatro palabras
habla al día: no se ha hallado
que haya dicho con enojo
a crïada ni a crïado
en su vida una razón: |

CLARA   What a happy day! Though the cost,
                        Eugenia, was that I have lost
                        the sheltering walls of the convent.

EUGENIA   As for me, I'm doubly content   120
                        to look at the streets of Madrid
                        free from those cloisters, screens and grids.

[Exit Clara, Eugenia, Brígida, and Otáñez.]

MARI-NUÑO   Well, my lord, and now that the pleasure
                        of seeing the daughters you treasure
                        has left some small place here for me   125
                        may I kiss your hand?

ALONSO   Certainly,
                        and with no less reason than they
                        take my arms and soul too, I pray.
                        Let me fold you in my embrace,
                        for you have filled their mother's place.   130
                        And now that the two girls have gone,
                        Mari-Nuño, and we're alone,
                        tell me what kind of girls they are,
                        because when I left for the far
                        Indies, they were so young that any   135
                        judgment I'd make would be so many
                        wild guesses; yet, prudent and wise,
                        I must, like a teacher, advise
                        and govern the wants of those fair
                        maidens Heaven puts in my care.   140

MARI-NUÑO   By telling you, my lord, that they
                        are both daughters of yours, I say
                        as much as I can say; but so
                        that you will not assume I show
                        you only what you want to hear,   145
                        although the two of them are clear
                        models of virtue, I'll tell you
                        what differentiates the two.
                        My lady Doña Clara, greater
                        in years and wisdom, is imitator   150
                        here on this earth of Heaven's peace.
                        It's impossible to increase
                        her pleasantness. Her modesty's
                        as great as her propriety.
                        In a whole day she barely says   155
                        a dozen words. In all her days
                        no one can ever show that she
                        has spoken one rude word to me,
                        to her servants or to her maids.

es, en fin, ángel humano,
que a vivir solo con ella,
pudiera uno ser esclavo.
doña Eugenia, mi señora,
aunque en virtud ha igualado
sus buenas partes, en todo
lo demás es al contrario.
Su condición es terrible,
no se vio igual desagrado
en mujer, dará, señor,*
una pesadumbre a un santo.
Es muy soberbia y altiva,
tiene a los libros humanos
inclinación, hace versos;
y si la verdad te hablo,
de recibir un soneto
y dar otro, no hace caso.
Pero no por eso . . .

D. ALONSO   Basta,
que en eso habéis dicho harto.
Yo os estimo, como es justo,
que, prevenido del daño,
sepa adónde he de poner
desde hoy desvelo y cuidado.
Y así, aunque en edad menor,
sea primera en estado;
que el marido y la familia
son los médicos más sabios
para curar lozanías,
flores de los verdes años.
Desde el día que llegué,
a la montaña he enviado
por un sobrino, que hijo
es de mi mayor hermano;
y en él quiero de mis padres
y abuelos el mayorazgo
aumentar: pobre es, yo rico,
y es bien que el caudal fundamos
de la sangre y de la hacienda,
porque conservemos ambos
el solar de Cuadradillos
con más lustre. Así, en llegando,
será Eugenia esposa suya:
veamos si el nuevo cuidado
enmienda las bizarrías
de los verdores lozanos.

*en mujer: dirá, señor,

And to conclude, I am afraid   160
she's an angel; one could become
a slave to labor in her home.
My lady Doña Eugenia has
beauty quite as praiseworthy as
her virtue, but then everything   165
else about her's unflattering.
Her manner is so negative
that no woman has ever lived
who was more unpleasant, my lord.
She would drive a saint overboard.   170
She is proud and imperious;
She just reads trash, not religious
books; she even composes verses,
and if you'd know the truth, far worse is
she's not bothered at all to get   175
a love sonnet, or write one. Yet
that is no reason to . . .

ALONSO   Enough!
My head is reeling with this stuff.
I thank you for shedding such light
on this; you give me the foresight   180
to be able to know just where
to place my watchfulness and care.
Though she's the younger, none the less,
let her be the first to profess
marriage. Husband and family   185
are the wisest doctors, you'll see,
for curing the exuberance,
the bloom and folly of youth's dance.
The very day that I arrived
I thought of someone, and contrived   190
that down from the Mountains would come
here to Madrid my brother's son.
With him I intend to add to
all the estates that were my due
from my parents and my grandparents.   195
If either one of us inherits
it should be both. I'm rich, he's poor;
joined together we can assure
the union of lands and bloodlines,
so that our ancestral home shines   200
with more lustre. When he gets here
from Quadradillos, we will cheer
him as our Eugenia's intended.
Her outrageous ways will be ended,
and her responsibilities   205
as wife will cool youth's revelries.

---

191 Mountains: Asturias, a region in northern Spain
202 Quadradillos: a fictitious Asturian town

[Sale Otáñez.]

OTÁÑEZ   Un hombre espera allí fuera.

D. ALONSO   ¿Quién es? Que ese breve espacio
                  tardaré, a las dos decid.
                  ¿Versos? ¡Gentil cañamazo!
                  ¿No fuera mucho mejor
                  un remiendo y un hilado?

[Vase.]

OTÁÑEZ   ¿Qué le has dueñado a señor,
                  que es lo mismo que chismeado,
                  que ya va tan desabrido?

MARI-NUÑO   ¿Ahora sabes, mentecato,
                  que apostatara una dueña,
                  si supiera callar algo?

[Vanse.]

[Sale don Félix, vistiéndose, y Hernando.]

HERNANDO   ¡Bravas damas han venido,
                  señor, a la vecindad!

D. FÉLIX   El agasajo, en verdad,
                  perdonara por el ruido,
                  pues dormir no me han dejado.

HERNANDO   La una es dada.

D. FÉLIX   ¿Qué importó,
                  si a la una duermo yo,
                  que haya dado o no haya dado?
                  Mas ¿qué género de gente
                  es?

HERNANDO   De lo muy soberano:
                  Las hijas de aqueste indiano,
                  que compró el jardin de enfrente,
                  que dicen, señor, que lleno
                  de riquezas para ellas,
                  a solamente ponellas
                  viene en estado.

D. FÉLIX   Eso es bueno.
                  ¿Son hermosas?

HERNANDO   Yo las vi
                  al apearse, y a fe
                  que por tales las juzgué.

[*Otáñez enters.*]

OTÁÑEZ	There is a man waiting outside.
ALONSO	I see. Did you tell the girls I'd be there in a moment or two? Sonnets?! There's needlepoint for you! Some mending or a spinning wheel would suit her far better, I feel.

210

[*He exits.*]

OTÁÑEZ	What gossip have you told my lord? What wild scandal have you explored, to make him leave so out of sorts?

215

MARI-NUÑO	You know what, my foolish consort? I'd stop my gossip in a minute if there wasn't such pleasure in it.

[*They exit.*]

[*A room in Don Félix's house*]
[*Don Félix, dressing, and Hernando*]

HERNANDO	Two really gorgeous women, sir, have moved into the neighborhood.

220

FÉLIX	Thanks for the good news; but I would forego them to forego the stir, because their noise won't let me sleep.
HERNANDO	But it's one o'clock.
FÉLIX	I don't care; when I sleep is my own affair. I like to keep the hours I keep. But what sort of ladies are they, anyway?

225

HERNANDO	La crème de la crème, daughters of this American who bought the house across the way: which, sir, they say by his design was filled with riches just for them; they say he comes here to condemn them to marriage.

230

FÉLIX	That's really fine. Are they beautiful?
HERNANDO	I confess when I saw them, believe me, sir, I certainly thought that they were.

235

---

229 American: returnees from the Indies were all presumed to be wealthy

D. Félix	¿Hermosas y ricas?
Hernando	Sí.
D. Félix	Buenas dos alhajas son:
	dirémoslas al momento
	todo nuestro pensamiento,
	por gozar de la ocasión,
	por estar cerca de casa;
	que estoy cansado de andar
	lo que hay desde aquí al lugar.
Hernando	Un vejete cuanto pasa*
	me dijo: y al padre igualo
	al hombre de más valor,
	pues dice que por su honor
	matara al Sofí.
D. Félix	Eso es malo;
	que aunque yo no soy Sofí,
	en extremo me pesara
	que para que él me matara,
	por él me muriera aquí.
	Y de las hijas, ¿qué dijo?
	Que escudero que empezó
	a hablar, nada reservó.
Hernando	Diversas cosas colijo
	de ambas que apruebo y condeno,
	porque hay del pan y del palo.
	Una es callada.
D. Félix	Eso es malo.
Hernando	Otra es risueña.
D. Félix	Eso es bueno.
	Para la alegre, por Dios,
	habrá sonetazo bello;
	y para la triste aquello
	de "ojos, decídselo vos."
Hernando	Alegre o triste, me holgara
	de verte, señor, un día,†
	con una galantería,
	que decirla te costara
	desvelo.
D. Félix	¿A mí? Harto fuera
	que alabarse, vive el cielo,
	de que me costó un desvelo
	ninguna mujer pudiera.

*Hernando   lo que hay desde aqui al lugar,
           un vejete cuanto pasa

†diviertas, señor, un día

FÉLIX	Beautiful and wealthy too?
HERNANDO	Yes.
FÉLIX	Those are the best two ornaments.

FÉLIX
Those are the best two ornaments.
Let's go right over there and give   240
them warm welcome, and say we live
down the street, by coincidence.
I am pleased that they live so near,
for I am getting tired of walking.

HERNANDO
Just a while ago I was talking   245
to some geezer who bent my ear
about what's happening there; he
said that no man alive is braver
than their father, who would not quaver,
for honor, to kill the Sophí.   250

FÉLIX
That's bad. Though I'm not the Sophí,
it would still bother me a lot
if I were to be stabbed or shot
because he thought that I was he.
About the girls what did he say?   255
For once a squire begins to yak,
there's no way he will hold things back.

HERNANDO
I picked up things which both dismay
me and fill me with great delight,
for there's both happy news and sad.   260
One is very quiet.

FÉLIX
                                        That's bad.

HERNANDO
The other's full of laughs.

FÉLIX
                                        All right!
For the jolly sister, by Jove,
spicy sonnets will do the trick;
and for the sad one I will pick   265
lines like: "Eyes, you tell her my love."

HERNANDO
Jolly or sad, I wish I could
see you, sir, just once ill at ease;
I'd like to hear some gallantries
true enough to cost you a good   270
night's sleep to fashion.

FÉLIX
                                        Me? That might
make news to talk about, God's blood!,
if some sweet flower of maidenhood
could make me spend a sleepless night!

---

250 Sophí the Turkish sultan
266 "Eyes, you tell her my love": ("Ojos, decídsela vos"):
    presumably a popular love song of the day

Eso no, pues sabe Dios
que si las hiciere ya
algún terrero, será
por estar cerca y ser dos.
Aunque a cualquiera me inclina
ya fuerza más poderosa.

HERNANDO   Será ser rica y hermosa.

D. FÉLIX   No es sino el estar vecina,
que es mayor perfección, pues
[*Llaman.*]   nada la iguala.
                                    Mas dí,
                  ¿Llaman a la puerta?

HERNANDO   Sí.

D. FÉLIX   Ve y mira, Hernando, quién es.

[Sale don Juan, en traje de camino.]

D. JUAN   Yo soy, don Félix; que estando
la puera abierta, no fuera
bien que más me detuviera.

D. FÉLIX   Mal llamar ha sido, cuando
sabéis que puertas y brazos
están siempre para vos
de una suerte.

D. JUAN   Guárdeos Dios,
que ya sé que destos lazos
el estrecho nudo fuerte
que en nuestras almas está,
sin romperle, no podrá
desatárnosle la muerte.

D. FÉLIX   Seáis bien venido; que aunque
en la jornada de Hungría,
que veníades sabía,
no tan presto os esperé.

D. JUAN   Fuerza adelantarme ha sido
para un negocio, en razón,
don Félix, de mi perdón.

D. FÉLIX   ¿Habéisle ya conseguido?

D. JUAN   Sí, y habiendo perdonado
la parte, gozar quisiera
del indulto que se espera

	No, God knows, that would never do,	275
	for if I'm off to serenade	
	them from the street, I am afraid	
	it's because they're here, and they're two.	
	Though there is a most powerful	
	force that draws me to either one.	280

HERNANDO   That they're rich, and a paragon
of beauty?

FÉLIX   They're accessible,
which puts them beyond all compare,
since there's nothing like at-hand-ness.
Say, is that someone knocking?

HERNANDO   Yes.   285

FÉLIX   Hernando, go see who is there.

[Don Juan enters, in traveling clothes.]

JUAN   Hello, Don Félix; it's I, who
when I saw the door open wide
thought, why should I wait outside?

FÉLIX   Good friend, there is no need for you   290
to knock, because you know my door
is always open and my arms
as well.

JUAN   May God keep you from harm,
for I know the interior
cords which our two souls tightly bind   295
are tied with such a knot that death
may cut them with our final breath,
but she cannot make them unwind.

FÉLIX   Welcome, dear friend, welcome; although
I knew from Hungary you'd come   300
when your assignment there was done,
I thought your trip would be more slow.

JUAN   I had to travel at top speed
on some business that is connected,
Félix, as you may have suspected,   305
with my pardon.

FÉLIX   Did you succeed?

JUAN   Yes, and since I've been pardoned by
the parties, I hope to receive
part of the general reprieve

---

300 Hungary: prior to the Peace of Westphalia, which ended the Thirty Years War, Spanish
troops were engaged throughout central Europe

306 pardon: Don Juan has evidently slain a rival; strangely, this incident has
little bearing on the plot

por las bodas; y así, he dado
prisa a venir, para que,
en vuestra casa escondido,
me halle a todo prevenido.

D. FÉLIX   Dicha es mía. Y ¿cómo fue?

D. JUAN   Ya sabéis que por la muerte,
Félix, de aquel caballero,
fui a Italia. Pues, lo primero,
dispuso mi buena suerte
ser ocasión que el señor
duque excelso y generoso
de Terranova famoso,
iba por embajador
a Alemania. Acomodado
con él a Alemania fui;
y hallándose allá de mí
bien servido y obligado,
a España escribió, porque
conocimiento tenía
con la parte: y así un día,
sin saberlo yo, me hallé
con el perdón, en un pliego
que de su mano me dio.

D. FÉLIX   El lance fue tal, que erró
la parte en no darle luego,
pues fue casual la pendencia
que dio la conversación.

D. JUAN   Esa es, Félix, la opinión
común; pero mi impaciencia
de mayor causa nacía,
que la que ocasiona el juego.

D. FÉLIX   Eso es lo que yo no llego
a saber.

D. JUAN   Pues yo servía
(ya que decirlo no importa)
a una dama rica y bella
para casarme con ella;
y no con suerte tan corta
que esperanzas no tuviese;
aunque me las dilataba
que ausente su padre estaba,
y la madre no quisiese
tratar su estado sin él.
En este tiempo entendí
servirla el muerto; y así,

	given for the wedding. That's why	310
	I came so quickly, to sit	
	hidden here in your house until	
	I profit from the king's good will.	
Félix	That's great! Can you talk about it?	
Juan	You are aware that when I killed	315
	that gentleman, Félix, I had	
	to go to Italy. And glad	
	I was to find that they had filled	
	the German ambassadorship	
	with the famous and noble lord,	320
	Duke of Terranova, adored	
	for his kindness and statesmanship.	
	I lodged myself with him and went	
	to Germany, and there I served	
	him most faithfully, as he deserved.	325
	And therefore to Spain the duke sent	
	a petition, because somehow	
	he knew one of the parties; and	
	one day, without my having planned	
	it, and without my knowing how,	330
	a pardoning certificate	
	he placed with his hand in my own.	
Félix	You'd think the parties would have shown	
	you pardon long since, for the weight	
	of that sad incident was slight,	335
	really a minor altercation.	
Juan	That's the common interpretation,	
	Don Félix, but in fact the fight	
	was not about the cards, or sport,	
	but something much more serious.	340
Félix	You know that makes me curious.	
Juan	Don Félix, I was paying court	
	(there's no need to conceal it now)	
	to a lady both beautiful	
	and rich; I wished to marry, full	345
	of confidence she would allow	
	my suit one way or another,	
	though she endlessly drew it out,	
	since her father was not about,	
	and there was no way her mother	350
	would deal with such things without him.	
	About then I chanced to discover	
	my rival hoped to be her lover	

---

321 Duke of Terranova: Diego de Aragón y Tagliaria, Philip IV's ambassador to Germany

ocasionado de aquel
lance que el juego nos dio,
con capa de otros desvelos
venganza tomé a mis celos,
con que todo se perdió;
pues fueran necios engaños,
confiado de mi estrella,
pensar hoy que aun viva en ella
memoria de tantos años.

D. FÉLIX   Vos estáis bien persuadido;
que en Madrid, cosa es notoria
que en las damas, la memoria
vive a espaldas del olvido.
Su favor y su desdén
ya en ningún estado no
hizo fe: ¡bien haya yo,
que en mi vida quise bien!

D. JUAN   ¿Todavía dese humor?

D. FÉLIX   Sí, pues aunque ellas son bellas,
me quiero a mí más que a ellas;
y así tengo por mejor,
a la que me ha de engañar,
engañarla yo primero;
que yo por amigo quiero
al gusto, más no al pesar.
Y para que no se crea
que lo es para vos mi humor,
ni para mí vuestro amor,
otra la plática sea.
¿Cómo en la jornada os ha ido?

D. JUAN   Como a quien viene de ver
darse poder a poder
desempeños a partido;
porque tal autoridad,
pompa, aparato y riqueza
como ostentó la grandeza
de una y otra majestad,
el día que la hija bella
del águila soberana,
generosamente ufana
trocó el Norte por la estrella

as well. And so, weighed down with grim
thoughts, I endeavored that the game   355
should conceal my true rivalry;
thus I avenged my jealousy
and lost everything, to my shame.
For I'm certain it would be sheer
idiocy, or faith in my   360
lucky star to suppose that I
might now, after so many years,
be remembered.

FÉLIX   That's a good guess.
For in Madrid it is well known
that women's memory is prone   365
to be drowned by forgetfulness.
In any case, both her disdain
and her favor have in no way
kept faith with you. And so I say,
lucky me, to avoid love's pain!   370

JUAN   You mean, you haven't changed your mind?

FÉLIX   No. For as lovely as they are,
I love myself much more by far,
which is the reason why I find
that the women who would deceive   375
me I prefer to deceive first.
For to be frank, my friend, I thirst
for pleasure. I'd rather not grieve.
But I don't want to persuade you
your style of love is best for me,   380
Juan, or that my humor could be
suitable for you. Let's pursue
some other theme. How was the trip?

JUAN   Like you'd expect: for I've just come
from an epithalamium   385
where two monarchs tried to outstrip
each other in splendor. Such pomp,
such magnificence, such display!
Two monarchs on one wedding day,
each one of them vying to swamp   390
the other in grandeur. You should
have seen the daughter of that regal,
haughty, and most generous eagle
exchange her North Star for the good

---

385 epithalamium: wedding celebration or wedding poem; see the introduction
    for historical background

393 eagle: Ferdinand III of Austria (1608-57) of the Hapsburg dynasty whose escutcheon
    was topped by an eagle

394 north star: metaphorically, the guidance of her father, a north European

	del hispano (en cuya acción, llanto a gozo competido, dejó del águila el nido por el lecho del león), no la vio otra vez el día.
D. Félix	De paso no estoy contento de oirla.
D. Juan	Pues estadme atento, porque a la relación mía los afectos cortesanos paguéis.
D. Félix	Yo os la ofrezco brava.
D. Juan	Deudora Alemania estaba . . .

[Sale don Pedro, vestido de color.]

D. Pedro	Don Félix, bésoos las manos.
D. Félix	Seáis, don Pedro, bien venido. Por esta puerta en un punto hoy se entra el bien todo junto. Pues, ¿qué venida esta ha sido? ¿Acabóse el curso?
D. Pedro	No.
D. Félix	Pues ¿qué os trae?
D. Pedro	Yo os lo diré.
D. Juan	Si yo embarazo, me iré.
D. Pedro	No, caballero; que yo, hallándoos con Félix, fío mucho de vos, porque arguyo que basta que amigo suyo seáis, para ser señor mío. Demás, que aquí es mi venida (que en decirlo no hago nada) una dama celebrada, que a mi amor agradecida pude en Alcalá servir: vino hoy a Madrid, y a vella vengo, don Félix, tras ella.
D. Félix	¿Y qué más?

	Heaven of Castille (by which deed,	395

Heaven of Castille (by which deed,   395
—and while tears did her joy contest,—
she surrendered her eagle's nest
for a lion's bed) and indeed
that day never saw her again.

FÉLIX   That was all much too fast for me,   400
             I fear.

JUAN   The virtuosity
             with which I strive to entertain
             your whole attention shall demand.

FÉLIX   Every ounce I have you shall get.

JUAN   Well then, Germany was in debt . . .   405

[Enter Don Pedro, dressed in red.]

PEDRO   Don Félix: let me kiss your hand.

FÉLIX   Welcome, Don Pedro, please come in.
             Today this door has proved to be
             the gate through which good comes to me
             all at once. But, where have you been?   410
             Have your courses finished yet?

PEDRO   No.

FÉLIX   Well, what brings you?

PEDRO   It is like this.

JUAN   If I'm in the way, I'll dismiss
             myself.

PEDRO   No, good sir, please don't go;
             it is enough for me that you   415
             are here with Félix to confide
             in you, for I'd be gratified
             if I could count you my friend, too.
             Anyway, the reason I came
             (I guess it is not necessary   420
             to hide) is the extraordinary
             lady I love. She feels the same
             for me. In Alcalá I paid
             court to her. Today she arrived
             here; and, Don Félix, I contrived   425
             to follow.

FÉLIX   What else?

---

423 Alcalá: site of the great Spanish Renaissance university, the Complutense
    (now the University of Madrid)

D. PEDRO   Que por huir
de mi padre, aquí escondido
dos días habré de estar.

D. FÉLIX   Albricias me podéis dar
de haber a tiempo venido,
que en ella don Juan también
puede haceros compañía.

D. JUAN   Será gran ventura mía
que en mí conozcáis a quien
serviros desea.

D. PEDRO   Los cielos
os guarden.

D. FÉLIX   Pues vive Dios
que no habéis de hablar los dos
tocados de amor y celos.
Haz que nos den de comer,

[A Hernando.]

y pues no hemos de salir
de casa, por divertir
el tiempo que puede haber,
la relación me decid,
don Juan, de la real jornada.

D. JUAN   Con calidad, que acabada,
la prevención de Madrid
diréis después.

D. FÉLIX   Soy contento.

D. PEDRO   Yo vengo a buena ocasión,
que una y otra relación
nueva es para mí.

D. JUAN   Oid atento.
Deudora Alemania estaba
a España de la más rica,
de la más hermosa prenda,
desde el venturoso día
que María nuestra infanta,
generosamente altiva,
trocó la española alteza
por la majestad de Hungría.

PEDRO   To evade
                 my father I would like to hide
                 a couple of days here with you.

FÉLIX   Then you can give thanks to your true
                 good fortune that you coincide   430
                 with Don Juan, who is staying here
                 too, and can keep you company.

JUAN   How fortunate that is for me;
                 for you know I am your sincere
                 and devoted servant.

PEDRO   Sir, may   435
                 God keep you.

FÉLIX   By the stars above
                 just think how endless talk of love
                 and jealousy will fill each day!

[To Hernando, who exits.]

                 Have them bring us something to eat.
                 Gentlemen: Since we shall not leave   440
                 the house, perhaps we can relieve
                 the tedium, if you would treat
                 us to your description, Don Juan,
                 of the royal festivities.

JUAN   I shall, if Don Félix agrees   445
                 to tell us what Madrid has done
                 to welcome them.

FÉLIX   Alright, I will.

PEDRO   Well, I got here conveniently,
                 for both these descriptions will be
                 new for me.

JUAN   Hear me, and be still.   450
                   Germany became Spain's debtor
                 for the richest ornament
                 and the loveliest young lady
                 from that day when Heaven sent
                   Queen María, our dear princess,   455
                 with proud liberality
                 to give up the crown of Spain
                 to gain the crown of Hungary.

---

451 Germany: Germany, Austria, Hungary are names used interchangeably to refer
    to the Austro-Hungarian Empire

Deudora Alemania estaba
(otra vez mi voz repita)
de tanto logro al empeño,
de tanto empeño a la dicha,
sin esperanzas de que
pudiese su corte invicta
desempeñarse con otra
de iguales méritos digna,
hasta que piadoso el cielo
ilustró su monarquía
de quien, si no la excedió,
pudo al menos competirla,
para que nos restituya
en Mariana su hija
tan una misma beldad,
que parece que es la misma.
Pues si de las dos esferas
vamos corriendo las líneas,
y en florida primavera
le dimos la maravilla,
la maravilla nos vuelve
en primavera florida,
que apenas catorce abriles
bebió del alba la risa.
Si la real sangre de Austria
sus hojas tiñó en la tiria
púrpura, en ella también
quiso que esotras se tiñan.
Si prudencia, si virtud,
si ingenio y partes divinas
la dimos, ésas nos vuelve,
porque de todas es cifra.
Después de capitulado
el Rey, que mil siglos viva,
se dilataron las bodas
más tiempo del que quería
la ansia de los españoles;
mas no fueran conocidas
las dichas, si no vinieran
con su pereza las dichas.
Fue causa a la dilación
esperar que la festiva
tierna edad de la niñez
creciese, hasta ver que hoy pisa
de la juventud la margen:
¡Buen defecto es el de niña,
pues se va, aunque ella no quiera,
enmendando cada día!

Germany became Spain's debtor
(I repeat what I just stated),   460
obligated with such interest
and with luck so obligated
  that the German court could never
hope to meet the obligation
with a girl of equal merit,   465
grace, nobility and station
  'til at last Heaven took pity
and set everything aright
with one who (if not surpassing)
shone with as intense a light,   470
  so that they their pledge could honor
in her daughter, Maryanne;
who is so like her in beauty
they are cut to the same plan.
  Then, if we should trace Heaven's lines   475
as they loop and unfold,
we'd see how in the bloom of spring
we gave our Mary-gold,
  and golden Mary they returned
when spring puts flowers on;   480
who barely fourteen Aprils
has tasted the laugh of dawn.
  If the royal blood of Austria's
petals are dipped in Tyre's
purple, then she dipped theirs as well,   485
as royal blood requires.
  If we gave prudence, virtue, wit
and grace and charm divine,
these very things she gives us back:
in her all these combine.   490
  After their king capitulated
(ever may he reign!),
the wedding was delayed much longer
than the men of Spain
  would wish; but then, good fortune   495
cannot be appreciated
unless it drags its feet and is
long time anticipated.
  The reason why they chose to wait
was for the tenderness   500
of childhood to pass gaily by,
until she would ingress
  into the bright domain of youth;
and youth's a fine disease:
for every day it cures itself,   505
whether or not you please.

---

484 Tyre: town in Asia Minor known for its purple dye

Llegó, pues, el deseado
de que feliz se despida
el águila generosa
del real nido que la abriga,
porque saliendo a volar,
el cuarto planeta diga
que imperial águila es, puesto
que de hito en hito le mira.
Y porque no sin decoro
deje la corte que habita,
llegó la nueva a Madrid,
de que allí el Rey se despida
de su hermana, hasta la entrega,
mezclando el llanto y la risa;
que siempre en bodas de infanta
el pesar y el alegría
se equivocan, hasta que
de gala el dolor se vista,
saliendo de ellas casada.
Ferdinando, rey de Hungría
y Bohemia, ínclito joven,
que no vanamente aspira
que heredada la elección,
Roma su laurel le ciña,
en nombre del Rey con ella
se desposa, y ejercita
tan amante sus poderes,
que sin perderla de vista,
hasta Trento la acompaña
con la pompa más lucida,
con el fausto más real
que vio el sol; pues a porfía
españoles, alemanes
y italianos, con su vista
se compitieron de suerte,
que era gloriosa la envidia,
porque unos y otros hicieron
en costosas libreas ricas,
tratable el oro en sus venas,
fácil la plata en sus minas,
agotando de una vez
todo el caudal a las Indias.
Y porque por mar y tierra
halle siempre prevenida
quien por la tierra y el mar
de parte del Rey la sirva,

At long last came the longed-for day
when this most high-born eagle
with happiness would bid farewell
to that sheltering regal   510
    nest, and then rising high in flight,
the fourth planet shall cry
that she's an imperial eagle
looking him straight in the eye.
    Since she'd not leave the court   515
without pomp, for decorum's sake,
they wrote to Madrid that the king
from his sister would take
    his leave, until they'd be rejoined,
thus mixing smiles and tears: 520
for when a princess marries,
rampant joy mingles with fears,
    until the day when grief puts on
the bright clothes of relief
to know that they are finally wed.   525
King Ferdinand, whose fief
    is Hungary and Bohemia,
which he inherited,
who hopes that Rome the laurel wreath
shall place upon his head,   530
    stood for our king as these two were
betrothed, and quickly found
himself so full of love that she
to him was tightly bound
    until they came at last to Trent   535
with utmost pageantry,
and the most regal processions
that the sun shall ever see.
    Spaniards, Germans, and Italians
fought each other for her glance: 540
and thus envy was transmuted
to show extravagance,
    because every single one in wealthy
liveried designs
made flexible the veins of gold,   545
and soft the silver mines,
    and siphoned all for their display
that Indies called her own.
And so that earth and ocean
should in all seasons be known   550
    to be prepared, he gave who serves
him best on both the sea:

---

512 fourth planet: Venus
529 laurel wreath: crowning him Holy Roman Emperor
535 Trent: city in northern Italy known for the Council (1545-63)
    that condemned the Reformation

el cargo del mar al Duque
de Tursis (de esclarecida
generosa casa de Oria,
siempre afecta y siempre fina
a esta corona) le dio,
porque de nuevo repita
en servicios y finezas
obligaciones antiguas.
La Reina estuvo en Milán
detenida algunos días,
por ocasión de que el mar
embarazó con sus iras
de España el pasaje; pero
¿quién de su inconstancia fía,
que no motive de culpa
lo que no es más que desdicha?
Del mar y del viento, en fin,
las condiciones esquivas
o vencidas o templadas
(aténgome a que vencidas),
llegó el día de embarcarse;
y apenas la vio en su orilla
el mar, cuando convocó
todo el coro de sus ninfas
para que corriendo a tropas
la campaña cristalina,
tan sólo en ella dejaran
aquella inquietud tranquila,
que no bastando a temerla,
baste a hermosearla y lucirla.
Entró la Reina en la Real,
cuya popa era encendida
brasa de oro, que a despecho
de tanta agua, estaba viva.
La chusma, toda de tela
nácar y plata vestida
con camisolas de holanda,
que su gala es estar limpias,
velamen, jarcias y velas
a su modo guarnecidas
de mil colores, formaban
un pensil, a quien matizan
de flores los gallardetes
y las flámulas, que heridas
del aire que las tremola
y el agua que las salpica,

and thus the noble duke of Tursis
holds the admiralty.
    (The ducal house is Oria,   555
defenders of the crown,
always faithful, always loving.)
With this present, new renown
    the king would claim from this great lord
whose service speaks his praise.   560
The queen found herself in Milán
detained for several days,
    because the sea, with its wild raging,
caused the trip to Spain
to be too dangerous. (But then,   565
how many men complain
    of her faithless inconstancy
and call their luck her fault?)
At last the rough condition
of the wind and waves did halt   570
    (who knows if by themselves, or did
Her Highness intervene?).
The day came to set sail, and when
the sea beheld the queen
    approach she called out to her troop   575
of nymphs to come and race
across the crystaline expanse,
and mar it with no trace
    of chaos, but the barest touch
of tranquil restlessness,   580
which, insufficient to cause fear,
shimmers with loveliness.
    The queen boarded her flagship,
whose tall afterdeck burned hotter
than golden coals, and was alive   585
with flame, despite the water.
    Decked out in pearly white and silver
garments were the crew,
wearing ruffled shirts of linen,
clean as if they all were new.   590
    The sails and all the rigging
which, festooned beyond compare,
with their thousand vibrant colors,
formed a hanging garden, where
    the gay pennants gleamed like flowers; 595
and the streamers, shuddering
from the wind that hoists their colors
and the whitecaps' splattering,

---

553 Duke of Tursis: admiral of the Spanish navy
567 her: refers to the sea
671 Denia: a seaport in the province of Alicante

venganza daban al aire
y el agua de la ojeriza
que tenían con las salvas,
por ver que de ver las quitan
las negras nubes de humo
que dejó la artillería,
la más pura, la más bella,
la más noble y más divina
Vénus que sobre la espuma
flechas de constancia vibra.
Aquí al compás de las piezas,
clarines y chirimías,
a leva tocó la Real,
cuya seña, obedecida,
aún primero que escuchada
fue de todos, con tal prisa,
que a un mismo tiempo la boga
arrancó; y siendo la grita
segunda salva vocal,
nos pareció, cuando se iba
de la tierra, una vistosa
primavera fugitiva.
Cuarenta galeras fueron
las que siguieron su quilla,
que más que rompen las olas,
las encrespan y las rizan.
El golfo tomó la nao,
aún sin tocar en las islas
Mallorca, Ibiza y Cerdeña;
no a causa de la enemiga
oposición de los puertos
de Francia; que bien podía,
viniéndose tierra a tierra,
tomar puerto en sus marinas,
porque en las enemistades
de las coronas, militan
en la campaña las armas,
y en la paz la cortesía;
y así, con salvoconducto
general en sus milicias,
Francia esperó a nuestra reina.
¡Qué bien lidian los que lidian
para vencer cuando vencen,
aún menos que cuando obligan!
Mas no puedo detenerme
en referir las festivas
demonstraciones que Francia
la tenía prevenidas.

took their vengeance on the breezes
and the water for the grudge   600
that they held against the cannons
for their loud salutes which smudge,
   with their roiling ebon clouds, that view
which by all rights should shine:
of the purest, the most lovely,   605
the most noble, most divine
   Venus who darts of constancy
hurls out across the foam.
Then to trumpets and to oboes
and to loud guns' metronome   610
   the queen's flagship played "Hoist anchor!",
and the signal was obeyed
before the piping reached the ears
of the crew, who delayed
   not one instant in applying   615
their backs to their oars; their shout
was a second salutation;
and we thought when she sailed out
   in the bay she was a gallant springtime
fleeing from the land.   620
Trailing her keel, forty galleys
proudly followed her command:
   rather than break through the waves
they sliced them into curly piles.
Thus the ship set out across the gulf,   625
without touching the isles
   of Mallorca, or Ibiza,
or Sardinia: not because
the threat of their French enemy
gave them the slightest pause: 630
   for by visiting each country
they could well have taken port
in French harbors; for when kingdoms
are not friends, then they resort
   to their arms only in battle: 635
they wage peace with courtesies.
Thus by ordering a general
safe conduct through her seas,
   France our queen prepared to welcome.
How well warriors wage war   640
to win all when they would conquer:
to oblige us, how much more!
   Yet I must not halt my story
to tell all the revelries
or respectful demonstrations   645
that France organized to please
   the queen. The ship set out across

El golfo tomó la nao,
trayendo siempre benigna
en los vientos y los mares
la fortuna, porque mira
que con sólo este festejo
que hace a España, se desquita
de otras penas que le debe
la vanidad de su envidia.
En fin, con serena paz
la vaga ciudad movida,
ya del remo que la impele,
ya del viento que la inspira,
los mares sulca de España,
y de sus campos divisa
los celajes, que quisieran
que el mar en sus ondas frías
huéspedes los admitiese,
porque una vez se compitan
golfos de verde esmeralda
con montes de nieve riza.
Ya el mar saluda a la tierra,
ya la tierra al mar se humilla,
siendo la primera que
sus reales plantas pisan,
Denia. ¡Oh tú, mil veces tú
felice, pues en tu orilla
hoy de la concha de un tronco
sacas la perla más rica!
Querer que yo diga ahora
la majestad de las vistas,
el séquito de su corte,
las galas, las bizarrías,
el amor de sus vasallos,
de sus reinos la alegría,
no es posible, si no es que
con la voz de todos diga
que este repetido lazo,
en quien de esposa y sobrina
el nudo apretó dos veces,
con propagada familia,
para bien común de España
venturosos siglos viva.

D. FÉLIX   No tuve gusto mayor.
                    Estad ahora vos atento.
                    Con el general contento
                    digno a su lealtad . . .

[Sale Hernando.]
HERNANDO   Señor.

the gulf, fanned by benign
currents and winds of Fortune,
whose vain, dangerous design   650
    for Spain, sprung from her envy
of our wealth and our success,
with this one great festive act
is worthy of our thankfulness.
    At last, with calm, this wandering   655
metropolis of sail,
which at times the oars push forward
and at times the winds avail,
    plows the fertile seas of Spain,
and watches piled up high above   660
her fields soft clouds, which in the cold
waves of the sea would love
    to be welcomed as guests, which would
in competition throw
deep gulfs of emerald green   665
against high peaks of curly snow.
    And now the sea salutes the land;
now land bows to the sea,
being the very first to kiss
the feet of royalty   670
    Denia. Oh happy, happy shore
where first she makes landfall;
for from a shell of tree you take
the richest pearl of all!
    Good friends, to ask me to relate   675
the splendor of that view,
the parades, the ostentation,
the rich and courtly retinue,
    the true love of all her vassals,
and the joy of all her realms,   680
is too much, for our united
joyous cheering overwhelms
    my voice. So come and join me then
in toasting with great pride
this queen who first as niece, then wife,   685
is doubly to us tied:
    Thus with her family and heirs
may Heaven's power ordain
she live a hundred happy years
for the common good of Spain!   690

FÉLIX   Bravo! I've never had greater
                    pleasure. Now lend attentive ear
                    to my description. With great cheer,
                    the multitudes showed they were . . .

[Hernando enters.]
HERNANDO   Sir.

D. Félix   ¿Qué dices?

Hernando   Que las dos bellas
               damas que al barrio han venido
               a la ventana han salido,
               y desde esta puedes vellas.

D. Félix   Perdone la relación,
               pues dice a voces la fama:
               "Antes que todo es mi dama,"
               y después habrá ocasión
               para ella; que ver deseo
               qué cosa son mis vecinas.
               ¡Vive Dios, que son divinas!

[Mirando hacia dentro.]

D. Juan   Veámoslas todos.

[Llega don Juan a mirar.]

                                    ¡Que veo!
               Ella es.

[Llega don Pedro.]

D. Pedro   Pues las visteis vos,
               a mí me dejad llegar.

D. Félix   A fe que hay bien que admirar
               en cualquiera de las dos.

D. Pedro

               ¿Qué es lo que veo? Ella es. ¡Cielos!
               Gran dicha ha sido venir
               a vuestro barrio a vivir.

D. Juan
[Aparte.]   (Disimulen mis desvelos.)
               Bizarra cualquiera es.

D. Pedro
[Aparte.]   (Finja mi pena amorosa.)
               Cualquiera es dellas hermosa.

D. Félix   ¿Oyen vuesarcedes? Pues
               bizarras y hermosas son,
               quítense de aquí, porque
               son muy tiernos para que
               les dé mi jurisdicción.
               A su dama cada uno,
               pues están enamorados:
               déjenme con mis cuidados,

FÉLIX	Eh? What's that you say?	
HERNANDO	That the two	695

beauties who moved here recently
have stepped out on their balcony
and from here you have a good view.

FÉLIX   Let me skip my descriptive rhyme
for now, for fate sings loud and clear: 700
"Before my life shall come my dear."
Besides, I'm sure there will be time
to hear it later. For I'm hot
to see how bright these neighbors shine.

[Félix looks offstage.]

My God! I think they are divine!   705

JUAN   Let us look too. Give me a spot!

[Juan looks offstage.]
[Aside]   (What's this? It's she!)

PEDRO   You've had your turn.
Let me have a look at them too.

[Pedro looks offstage.]

FÉLIX   Both of them are well worth the view,
I think. They both a prize could earn.   710

PEDRO
[Aside]   (What's that? Heavens! It's she! I know.)
For me it was certainly good
luck to move to this neighborhood.

JUAN
[Aside]   (I hope my worries do not show.)
Each one of them is exquisite.   715

PEDRO
[Aside]   (I hope I hide my love and grief.)
Both of them are beyond belief.

[Exit Hernando.]

FÉLIX   Do you hear that, my good friends? It
seems both are lovely and a prize.
You're too young for them anyway;   720
for me to allow you to pay
court to them would be most unwise.
The two of you give me a pain.
Don't you have ladies of your own?
Pay court to them, leave these alone.   725

---

701 "Before my life . . ." ("Antes que todo es mi dama"): presumably the title of a popular song

sin alabarme ninguno
bellezas ni bizarrías;
que aquestas damas, les digo
que son cosas de un amigo.

D. JUAN

¡Qué poco mis alegrías
duraron! Ya se quitaron
de la ventana.

[Aparte.]   Porqué
yo llore su ausencia fue.*
La primer cosa que hallaron,
¡cielos! mis penas, ha sido
dellas la causa. ¡Ay de mí!

D. PEDRO

La primer cosa que vi,
es por la que aquí he venido.

HERNANDO   La mesa espera, señor.

[Vase Hernando.]

D. FÉLIX   Vamos a comer, que aunque
tan enamorado esté,
tengo más hambre que amor.

D. JUAN

Aunque de burlas habláis,
sabed que de mi fortuna
una es la causa.

[Vase.]

D. FÉLIX
                                        Adiós, una.

D. PEDRO   Aunque tan de humor estáis,
por sí y por no, sabed que
una de las dos, por Dios,
es la que sigo.

[Vase.]

D. FÉLIX   Adiós, dos.
¡Qué corta mi dicha fué!
Si no es que una misma sea
(que aún peor que esto sería)
la que uno y otro quería.

*Yo llore su ausencia: y fue

Don't keep trying to entertain
me with talk of their loveliness.
So, gentlemen, I recommend
you leave these beauties to your friend.

JUAN
[Aside]   (What a short time my happiness   730
                         lasted!)

[Aloud]   Now they have gone away
                         from the window.

[Aside]   (Her absence was
                         planned to make me grieve; and it does.
                         My God, the first thing my dismay
                         has found in Madrid is the flame   735
                         which is its cause. What shall I do?)

PEDRO
[Aside]   (The first thing I see in my new
                         home is the reason why I came!)

[Hernando enters.]

HERNANDO   Sir, the table is ready now.

[Hernando exits.]

FÉLIX   Then let's go and eat, for although   740
                         love's passion sets me all aglow,
                         I am hungrier still, I vow.

JUAN
[Aside to Félix.]   Although, my friend, you talk in jest,
                         you should know that one of those two
                         is my love.

[Juan exits.]

FÉLIX
[Aside]   (Number one, adieu.)   745

PEDRO   Even though you joke, it is best
                         you be aware that one of those
                         girls is the one I love.

[Pedro exits.]

FÉLIX   How brief
                         my joy has been, how great my grief!
                         First the first, now the second goes.   750
                         Unless perhaps the two are one
                         and the same: that would be far worse.

¡Plegue a Dios que no se vea
empeñado en los desvelos
de dos amigos mi honor,
y pague celos y amor
quien no tiene amor ni celos.

[Vase, y salen doña Clara y doña Eugenia.)

CLARA   Por cierto, casa y adorno,
                          todo, Eugenia, está extremado.

EUGENIA   A mí no me ha parecido
                          sino de la corte el asco.

CLARA   ¿Por qué?

EUGENIA   Cuanto a lo primero,
                          porque éste, Clara, es el barrio
                          donde de la corte habitan
                          los pájaros solitarios.
                          A los Pozos de la Nieve
                          casa mi padre ha tomado:
                          ¡Fresca vecindad! Agosto
                          le agradezca el agasajo.

CLARA   Por la quietud y el jardín
                          lo haría.

EUGENIA   ¡Lindos cuidados!
                          ¿Quietud y jardín? Para eso
                          Yuste está juntico a Cuacos.
                          Pero en Madrid, ¿qué quietud
                          hay como el ruido? y ¿qué cuadro,
                          aunque con más tulipanes
                          que trajo extranjero mayo,
                          como una calle que tenga
                          gente, coches y caballos,
                          llena de lodo el invierno,
                          llena de polvo el verano,
                          donde una mujer se esté
                          de la celosía en los lazos,
                          al estribo de un balcón,
                          a todas horas paseando?
                          pues ¿qué los adornos?

Both in love with one? What a curse
that would be. I hope to God none
of my friends' loving lunacy   755
pulls my honor into their plan!
Jealous love should not hurt a man
who feels no love, nor jealousy.

[Félix exits.]

A room in Don Alonso's house
[Clara and Eugenia]

CLARA   The house and everything inside
                   it, Eugenia, fill me with pride.   760

EUGENIA   Not me. I think it is a sort
                   of stinking cesspool of the court.

CLARA   But why say that?

EUGENIA   Where can I start?
                   This street is in the dullest part
                   of Madrid, where old men live.   765
                   He had to buy a primitive
                   house out here by the Icy Wells
                   where no one but an ice man dwells!
                   What chilly neighbors! In the hot
                   days of August we'll like this spot.   770

CLARA   We'll enjoy the tranquility
                   and the garden.

EUGENIA   You might, not me!
                   Garden, tranquility! That's why
                   Yuste and Cuacos stultify
                   so close together. But Madrid?   775
                   Who wants tranquility amid
                   such excitement? A boulevard
                   is what I'd like. Who wants a yard,
                   even with more tulips than May
                   and twenty Dutchmen could array?   780
                   I want a street teeming with men,
                   women, coaches, horses. A fen
                   in wintertime, mud everywhere;
                   in summer, dust choking the air
                   where a woman can sit and see   785
                   what goes on from the privacy
                   of her balcony, hid behind
                   the shutters where no one can find
                   her with their eyes. Don't talk to me
                   of furniture.

---

767 Icy Wells (Los Pozos de la Nieve): a district in then suburban Madrid near the modern
    Glorieta de Bilbao
774 Yuste, Cuacos: two mountain villages southwest of Madrid; Charles V retired to a small
    monastery in Yuste in 1556

CLARA   ¿No es
de terciopelo este estrado
y sillas y con su alfombra,
de granadillo y damasco
estas camas, los tapices
de buena estofa, y los cuadros
de buen gusto, y el demás
menaje, Eugenia, ordinario,
limpio y nuevo? Pues ¿qué quieres?

EUGENIA   Buenos son; pero diez años
de Indias son mucho mejores.
Yo pensaba que el adagio
de tener el padre alcalde,
era niño comparado
con la suma dignidad
de tener el padre indiano.
Fuera de que entre estas cosas
que tú me encareces tanto,
la mejor cuadra y mejor
alhaja es la que no hallo.

CLARA   ¿Cuáles son?

EUGENIA   Coche y cochera,
que ella en invierno y verano
es la mejor galería,
y el más hermoso trasto.
¿Qué Indias hay donde no hay coche?
¡Aquí de Dios y sus santos!
¡Que ensayados trae, no ha escrito,
muchos pesos? Pues veamos,
si no han de hacer su papel,
¿Para qué se han ensayado?

CLARA   ¿Ni aún a tu padre reserva
la sátira de tus labios?
¡Jesús mil veces!

EUGENIA   ¡Mala hija!
Vivir quisiera mil años,
sólo por ver si me logro.

CLARA   Advierte, Eugenia, que estamos
ya en la corte, y que el despejo,
el brío y el desenfado
del buen gusto, aquí es delito;
que aquí dan los cortesanos
estatua al honor, de cera,
y a la malicia, de mármol.

CLARA   Our balcony   790
and drawing room are decorated
with velvet chairs, accentuated
with rugs, couches with coverlets
from Damascus, fine cabinets,
beautiful, costly tapestries,   795
all these tasteful paintings that please
the eye; and, sister, all the rest
new, clean, and in order. You jest
if you ask for more.

EUGENIA   They're alright,
but ten years in the Indies might   800
have done better. That line about
"your father the mayor" no doubt
is only kid stuff when it is
compared to one who has made his
pile in the Indies. Anyway,   805
in this long list of things you say
are so perfect, the very best
you did not put with all the rest.

CLARA   What's that?

EUGENIA   Why, a coach and a team:
in any season that's my dream   810
of the best way to see the town:
that's the jewel for this drab crown.
It's no Indies without a coach.
Didn't our father himself broach
the subject of just how much money   815
he would bring home with him? It's funny
how after rehearsing that play,
now that it's real, he will not pay.

CLARA   Hold your tongue! How can you use
such language? How can you abuse   820
your father?

EUGENIA   What pomposity!
I'd like to live a century,
just to see how much I could get!

CLARA   Eugenia, you know etiquette
reigns here at court, that any breech   825
in good taste, or licentious speech
or behavior, here are all sins.
At court virtuous honor wins
a flimsy statue made of wax,
while boorish malice never lacks   830

---

802 "your father the mayor" ("tener el padre alcalde"): a proverb indicating
    special protection or privilege

No digo que no sea bueno
lo galante y lo bizarro;
pero ¿qué importa si no
lo parece? Y no es tan malo
no ser bueno y parecerlo,
como serlo y no mostrarlo.
El honor de una mujer,
y más mujer sin estado,
al más fácil accidente
suele enfermar, y no hay ampo
de nieve que más aprisa
aje su tez al contacto
de cualquiera: planta no hay,
que padezca los desmayos
mas presto; que sin el cierzo,
basta a marchitarla el austro.
Cuantos tus versos celebran,
cuantos tus donaires, cuantos
tu ingenio, son los primeros,
Eugenia, que al mismo paso
que te lisonjean el gusto,
te murmuran el recato,
rematando en menosprecio
lo mismo que empieza aplauso.
Y una mujer como tú
no ha de exponerse a los daños
de que parezca delito
nada, ni le sea notado
hacer profesion de risa,
que tan presto ha de ser llanto.
¿Hasta hoy en carta de dote,
Eugenia, ha capitulado
la gracia?

EUGENIA   *Quam mihi et vobis*
præstare se te ha olvidado,
para acabar el sermón
con todos sus aparatos.
Y para que de una vez
demos al tema de mano,
has de saber, Clara, que
los *non fagades* de antaño
que hablaron con las doncellas
y las demás deste caso,
con las calzas atacadas
y los cuellos se llevaron

marble monuments. I don't say
it always has to be that way,
that gallantry and courtly style
cannot be good; but we revile
them if they don't seem so. It's less   835
bad to put vice in virtue's dress
than to be perfect and not show it.
A woman's honor, and you know it,
is more fragile for one without
status; for with the slightest doubt,   840
it sickens and dies. There's no snow
can wither her skin as much; no
plant exists that will droop as fast;
the south wind, not even the blast
of the north wind, will cut her down.   845
The very same people who crown
your verses and your wit with praise
are the first, Eugenia, to raze
your modesty right to the ground
with their whispers, while they expound   850
with public flattery about
your charms, despising what they flout.
A woman like yourself must not
let anybody take a shot
at something they might think was bad   855
behavior; and don't let them add
that you have made a profession
of laughing at indiscretion.
Since when in a marriage contract
has anyone ever attacked   860
good manners?

EUGENIA   The *quam mihi et*
vobis praestare you forget.
Surely this sermon can't conclude
without that hoary platitude!
So we can end this theme once and   865
for all, Clara, please understand
that all those "thou shalt not's" which they
used to make young ladies obey,
along with starched collars and lace
stockings and all that stuff are placed   870

---

861 A common Latin sermon ending asking that God's grace "be extended to you and to me."
     (Note supplied by Daniel Williman, SUNY-Binghamton.)

a Simancas, donde yacen
entre mugrientos legajos.*
don Escrúpulo de honor
fue un pesadísimo hidalgo,
cuyos privilegios ya
no se leen de puro rancios.
Yo he de vivir en la corte
sin melindres y sin ascos
del qué dirán, porque sé
que no dirán que hice agravio
a mi pundonor; y así,
derribado al hombro el manto,
descollada la altivez,
atento el desembarazo,
libre la cortesanía,
he de correr a mi salvo
los siempre tranquilos golfos
de calle Mayor y Prado,
cosaria de cuantos puertos
hay desde Atocha a Palacio.
Uso nuevo no ha de haber
que no le estrene mi garbo:
¿Amiga sin coche? Tate;
y ¿sin chocolate estrado?
No en mis días; porque sé
que es el consejo más sano†
el mejor amigo el coche,
y él el mejor agasajo.
Las fiestas no ha de saberlas
mejor que yo el calendario:
desde el Angel a San Blas,
desde el Trapillo a Santiago.
Si picaren en el dote
los amantes cortesanos,
que enamorados de sí
más que de mí enamorados,
me festejen, has de ver
que al retortero los traigo,
haciendo gala el rendirlos,
y vanidad el dejarlos.
Todo esto quiero que tengas,
Clara, entendido; y si acaso
vieres en mí . . .

*entre mujeres, y fallos;

†que es el consejo más cano

next to the ancient manuscripts
deep in Simancas' dusty crypts.
Sir Point of Honor is a tired
and tiresome nobleman, retired
so long ago his privileges   875
are all worm-eaten at the edges.
I'm going to live here at court
without worries; I won't report
to my neighbors, because I know
that, come what may, they cannot show   880
me unchaste. Therefore, all the bolder,
I will drop my shawl to my shoulder
and with elegant, haughty gait
(which my freedom will indicate),
and safety, on the avenues   885
of tranquil ocean I shall cruise
the Prado and Calle Mayor:
a pirate, raiding that fair shore
with elegant and courtly malice
from Atocha up to the Palace.   890
No new fashion in anything
will be worn without my blessing.
A friend without a coach? No date!
A party without chocolate?
Not for me. Because I am sure   895
the best council you can secure
and the best friend, beyond reproach,
and the best party is a coach.
No one will know the festivals
or calendar of miracles   900
or saints like I, who all their names
feast, from the Angel to Saint James,
and from Trapillo to Saint Blas.
And if some suitor should be crass,
and hint about a dowry,   905
thereby showing his love for me
is much weaker than his love for
himself, watch me show him the score,
and proud to flaunt my victory,
I'll abandon him like debris.   910
So I want you to understand
that when you see all these things I've planned,
Clara, you'll . . .

---

872 Simancas: castle near Valladolid that houses Spain's National Historic Archives

887, 890 Prado, Calle Mayor, Atocha: principal streets in Madrid

902 The Angel: May 5; St. James: July 25

903 Trapillo: presumably the nickname of some saint, perhaps the Veronica: July 12; St. Blas: February 3

CLARA   ¿Qué he de ver,
                 si aún de escucharte me espanto?

[Sale don Alonso muy alegre.]

D. ALONSO   ¡Eugenia! ¡Clara!

LAS DOS   Señor.

D. ALONSO   Pediros albricias puedo.

LAS DOS   ¿De qué?

D. ALONSO   De la mejor dicha,
                 mayor bien, mayor contento
                 que sucederme pudiera,
                 después de llegar a veros.
                 Don Toribio Cuadradillos,
                 hijo mayor y heredero
                 de mi hermano, mayorazgo
                 del solar de mis abuelos,
                 llegará al punto: una posta
                 que se adelantó, me ha hecho
                 relación de que ahora queda
                 muy cerca de aquí.

EUGENIA   Por cierto
                 que pensé que había venido,
                 según tu encarecimiento,
                 algún plenipotenciario
                 con la paz del universo.

D. ALONSO   ¡Mari-Nuño!

[Sale Mari-Nuño.]

MARI-NUÑO   ¿Qué me mandas?

D. ALONSO   Aderécese al momento
                 aquese cuarto de abajo,
                 y esté aliñado y compuesto.
                 Tú, ¡Brígida!

[Sale Brígida.]

                                   Saca ropa
                 de la excusada.

BRÍGIDA   Ya tengo
                 un azafate, que pueden
                 beber su holanda los vientos.

[Vase.]

D. ALONSO   ¡Otáñez!

[Sale Otáñez.]

OTÁÑEZ   ¿Señor?

CLARA   See? How can I see,
                      when even hearing frightens me?

[Enter Don Alonso, excited.]

ALONSO   Eugenia! Clara!

THE GIRLS   Yes, my lord?   915

ALONSO   Let embraces be my reward.

THE GIRLS   For what?

ALONSO   For what? For the best luck,
                and the best fortune that has struck
                your father since this morning when
                he first laid eyes on you again.   920
                Don Toribio, who's my eldest
                nephew and doubtless will be blessed
                with all Cuadradillos one day,
                both houses and the full array
                of our family lands, will be   925
                here soon. A messenger whom he
                asked to run ahead without pause
                says he is almost here.

EUGENIA   Because
                of all the fuss you made I thought
                that perhaps good fortune had brought   930
                us some plenipotentiaries
                to give us universal peace.

ALONSO   Mari-Nuño!

[Enter Mari-Nuño.]

MARI-NUÑO   Here I am, sir.

ALONSO   Fix up that downstairs room. Make sure
                it is all straightened up and clean.   935
                You, Brígida!

[Enter Brígida.]

                          Get him clean linen
                from the clothes closet.

BRÍGIDA   It is in an
                open basket to catch the air
                and be fresh as morning, I swear.

ALONSO   Otáñez!

OTÁÑEZ   Sir?

D. ALONSO   Buscad
[Vase Mari-Nuño.] algo de regalo presto,
                    para que coma en llegando.

[Vase Otáñez.]

                    Y a las dos, hijas, os ruego
                    le agasajéis mucho. Ved
                    que es vuestra cabeza; y creo
                    que será la más dichosa
                    la que le tenga por dueño,
                    pues será escudera suya
                    la otra.

[Aparte.]   (Así inclinar pretendo
                    a Eugenia.)

EUGENIA   Yo desa dicha
                    pocas esperanzas tengo,
                    que Clara es mayor.

CLARA   ¿Qué importa,
                    si es más tu merecimiento?

EUGENIA   ¿Falsedad conmigo, Clara?

D. ALONSO   Ya en el portal hay estruendo.
                    Oíd.

[Dentro don Toribio]

D. TORIBIO   ¿Vive aquí un señor tío
                    que yo en esta corte tengo,
                    con dos hijas, por más señas,
                    con quien a casarme vengo,
                    de dos la una, como apuesta?

[Dentro]

OTÁÑEZ   Esta es la casa.

D. ALONSO   Yo creo
                    que es él sin duda. Llegad
                    conmigo al recibimiento.

D. TORIBIO   ¿Y está acá?

OTÁÑEZ   En casa está.

D. TORIBIO   Pues
                    ten ese estribo, Lorenzo.

[Sale don Toribio vestido de camino ridiculamente.]

ALONSO   Hurry and get   940
                    some fancy food that we can set
                    for him to eat when he comes in.

[Exit Otáñez.]

                    Daughters, I hope you two will win
                    his heart with courtesy. Look well,
                    for he is the head of our clan,   945
                    and lucky is the one who can
                    call him her husband; for her squire
                    the other will be.

[Aside]   (This will fire
                    Eugenia to want him.)

EUGENIA   Small chance
                    have I my fortune to advance   950
                    that way. Clara is older.

CLARA   No
                    matter: greater merit you show
                    by far.

EUGENIA   Clara, surely you jest?

[A loud knock offstage]

ALONSO   Do you hear thunder in the west?
                    Listen!

[Offstage]

TORIBIO   Does an uncle of mine   955
                    live in this house with his two fine
                    daughters? For from the note you sent
                    one of those two beauties is meant
                    to be my bride. Am I correct?

[Offstage]

OTÁÑEZ   This is the house, sir.

ALONSO   I suspect   960
                    that this must be the man. Let's go
                    and welcome him with warm hello.

[Don Toribio and Otáñez enter. The other three leave the drawing room and go to
the anteroom which is in the rear of the stage.]

TORIBIO   Is my uncle home?

OTÁÑEZ   He's inside.

TORIBIO   Here, help me dismount. What a ride!

[Don Alonso goes to meet Don Toribio; Eugenia and Clara watch through the door.]

EUGENIA	¡Jesús! ¡Qué rara figura!
CLARA	Tú tienes razón por cierto.
EUGENIA	¡Ay, que consintió mi hermana en murmuración!

D. ALONSO
                                       Contento,
sobrino y señor, de ver
que haya concedido el cielo
esta ventura a mi casa,
salgo alegre a conoceros
por mayor pariente della.

D. TORIBIO
Pues bien poco hacéis en eso;
que en el valle de Toranzos,
desde tamañito, tengo
el ser cabeza mayor
adonde quiera que llego.

D. ALONSO
Llegad: ved que vuestras primas
desean mucho conoceros,
y han salido a recibiros.

D. TORIBIO
Razonables primas tengo.

CLARA
Vos seáis muy bien venido.

D. TORIBIO
Tanto favor agradezco.

D. ALONSO
¿Cómo venís?

D. TORIBIO
                                   Muy cansado;
que traigo un macho, os prometo,
de tan mal asiento, que
me ha hecho a mí de mal asiento.

D. ALONSO
Mientras de comer os dan,
sentaos.

D. TORIBIO
                              ¿No será más bueno
el trocarlo, y que me den
de comer mientras me siento?
Pero por no ser porfiado,

[Siéntase.]
que os sentéis los tres os ruego;
que yo de cualquier manera
estoy bien.

CLARA

                              ¡Lindo despejo!

EUGENIA	Good Lord! That is a bizarre sight!	965
CLARA	Sister, you're absolutely right!	
EUGENIA	Oh! To think my sister has used her tongue to gossip!	

[Don Alonso returns with Don Toribio, dressed in ridiculous riding clothes.]

ALONSO	I'm enthused, my nephew and lord, to observe that Heaven more than I deserve has granted my house today. I am doubly pleased to certify that you're our finest relative.	970
TORIBIO	Well, that's not so superlative; for in Toranzos, ever since I was a toddler, I was prince of everything, I was the chief of every corner of my fief.	975
ALONSO	Come meet your cousins, who can't wait to greet you, to communicate the extent of their gratitude.	980
TORIBIO	A reasonable attitude.	
CLARA	You are most welcome, sir, with us.	
TORIBIO	I appreciate all this fuss.	
ALONSO	How was the trip?	
TORIBIO	Not so good, you'll be sad to hear. I rode a mule so rough of seat that it maligned my own, and I've a sore behind.	985

[They go from the anteroom to the drawing room.]

| ALONSO | While they bring out something to eat,
please sit down. | |
| TORIBIO | I'd prefer a seat
at the table, so they could feed
me while they set it. But don't read
me wrong: I'll sit down anywhere.
But you three sit as well, I swear. | 990 |

| CLARA
[Aside] | What a pretty style! | |

---

975 Toranzos: a fictitious village

EUGENIA

    ¿Esta es mi cabeza?

CLARA

                    Sí.

EUGENIA

    En aqueste instante creo,
    cierto, que soy loca, pues
    tan mala cabeza tengo.

D. TORIBIO

    Finalmente, primas mías,
    como digo de mi cuento,
    parece que sois hermosas,
    ahora que caigo en ello;
    y tanto, que ya me pesa
    que seáis a la par tan bellos
    ángeles.

LAS DOS

           ¿Por qué?

D. TORIBIO

               Porque . . .
    mas explíqueme un ejemplo.
    Escriben los naturales
    que puesto un borrico en medio
    de dos piensos de cebada,
    se deja morir primero
    que haga del uno elección,
    por más que los mire hambriento:
    yo así en medio de las dos,
    que sois mis mejores piensos,
    no sabiendo a cuál llegue antes,
    me quedaré de hambre muerto.

D. ALONSO

    ¡Oh sencillez de mi patria,
    cuánto de hallarte me huelgo!

CLARA

    ¡Buen concepto y cortesano!

EUGENIA

    De borrico es, por lo menos.

D. TORIBIO

    Mas remedio hay para todo.
    ¿No ha de traerse, a lo que entiendo,
    tío, una dispensación,
    por razón del parentesco,
    para la una?

D. ALONSO

             Claro está.

D. TORIBIO

    Pues traigan dos, que yo quiero
    dar el dinero doblado;

EUGENIA
[Aside to Clara]   Can this be   995
                              the real head of our family?

CLARA   Yes.

EUGENIA   Then I know I am insane,
                              to have a head with such a brain.

TORIBIO   Now at last, sweet cousins of mine,
                              I am sitting, by your design   1000
                              all nicely settled in my chair.
                              Say! You are an attractive pair.
                              So much so it's deplorable
                              that you are both such beautiful
                              angels.

THE GIRLS   How's that?

TORIBIO   Because . . . but let   1005
                              a parable my meaning set.
                              It's written somewhere that if you
                              place an ass halfway between two
                              feed bags of barley he will die
                              before he'll choose to satisfy   1010
                              his hunger in one of them, no
                              matter how great his pain. Just so
                              I find myself halfway between
                              the cutest feed bags that I've seen;
                              not knowing where to turn my head,   1015
                              from hunger I will soon be dead!

ALONSO   Oh, the simplicity of my
                              native land! How happy am I
                              to find you again.

CLARA   That will pass
                              for a courtly conceit.

EUGENIA
[Aside]   An ass   1020
                              seems to be the subject.

TORIBIO   I'm sure
                              that every illness has its cure.
                              Since one is my cousin, don't we
                              need a dispensation to be
                              issued, uncle, so that we can   1025
                              be married?

ALONSO   Yes, that is the plan.

TORIBIO   In that case, uncle, let there be
                              two dispensations, for I'd see

y desa suerte, en teniendo
para cada una la suya,
casaré con ambas. Pero
ansí que se me olvidaba,
¿cómo estáis, saber deseo,
vos y mis señoras primas?

D. ALONSO   Muy alegre y muy contento
de ver mi casa y mis hijas,
y a vos, para que seáis dueño
del fruto de mis trabajos.

D. TORIBIO   Eso y mucho más merezco.
Si vierais mi ejecutoria,
primas mías, os prometo
que se os quitaran mil canas.
Vestida de terciopelo
carmesí, y allí pintados
mis padres y mis abuelos,
como unos santicos de Horas.
En las alforjas la tengo.
Esperad, iré por ella,
para que veáis que no os miento.

[Sale Mari-Nuño y espántase don Toribio.]

MARI-NUÑO   La comida está en la mesa.

D. TORIBIO   ¡Ay, señor tío! ¿qué es esto?
¿Trajisteis este animal
de las Indias?, que no creo
que es hombre ni mujer, y habla.

D. ALONSO   Es dueña.

D. TORIBIO   ¿Y es mansa?

MARI-NUÑO
                                    Ingenio
cerril tiene el primo.

EUGENIA   No es,
sino tonto por extremo.

D. ALONSO   Cómo queda vuestro padre
y su casa, saber quiero.

	my money doubled, and that way,	
	with two papers, it is okay	1030
	for me to wed both. But I'll bet	
	there is one thing that I forget,	
	and I'd like to know: how are you,	
	good sir, and my sweet cousins too?	
ALONSO	I am most happy and delighted	1035
	to see my daughters, and excited	
	to be back home, and resolute	
	that you, sir, should enjoy its fruit.	
TORIBIO	All that and much more I deserve.	
	Ah, cousins, if you could observe	1040
	my letters of nobility,	
	the marvelous things you would see	
	would make you young again. They're dressed	
	in crimson velvet, and impressed	
	with pictures of my ancestors	1045
	just like saints in a book of hours.	
	As a matter of fact, my kin	
	are assembled on parchment in	
	my saddlebags. Wait, let me bring	
	them, so you won't think I'm lying.	1050

[Mari-Nuño enters and startles Don Toribio.]

MARI-NUÑO	Good sirs, dinner is ready now.	
TORIBIO	Uncle, what's this? Who is this cow?	
	Can you have brought this animal	
	from the Indies? She is too small	
	for a man, and entirely	1055
	too big for a woman, and . . . she	
	even speaks.	
ALONSO	She's a duenna.	
TORIBIO	Is . . .	
	is she tame?	
MARI-NUÑO		
[Aside to Eugenia]	This cousin has his	
	mind still back on the farm.	
EUGENIA	He talks	
	as dumb as any man who walks!	
ALONSO	Cousin, how is your father, and	1060
	your ancestral estates and land?	

1041 letters of nobility ("ejecutoria"): geneaology attesting to the family's blue blood; Asturias was never conquered by the Moors, and Asturian pride in purity of ancestry is a comic commonplace of the Golden Age

1046 book of hours: book of daily prayer, often copiously illustrated

D. Toribio	No me haga mal de hijodalgo de comedias, si me acuerdo.
Mari-Nuño	La mesa está puesta.
D. Toribio	¿Y dónde tenéis la mesa?
Mari-Nuño	Allá dentro.
D. Toribio	No sé si lo crea.
Mari-Nuño	¿Por qué?
D. Toribio	Porque la instrucción que tengo es, que no me crea de dueñas. Pero yo lo veré presto. Perdonadme, que no soy amigo de cumplimientos.

[Vase.]

Clara	¡Lindo primo, por mi vida!
Mari-Nuño	El no es galán; pero es puerco.
Eugenia	Las guardas de peste, ¿cómo entrar le dejaron dentro?
D. Alonso	¿De qué estáis tristes las dos?
Las dos	Yo de nada.
D. Alonso	Ya os entiendo. Os habrá el estilo y traje desagradado. Pues esto es lo más y lo mejor que tenéis, veréis cuán presto le mejoran corte y trato. Los más vienen así, y luego son los más agudos. Más explicaros cuán contento y alegre estoy, no es posible, de ver que vuelva a mis nietos la casa de mis mayores. Don Toribio ¡vive el cielo!, se ha de casar con la una, sin pensar la otra por eso que no ha de casar con otro como él; porque no quiero que lo que a mí me ha costado tanta fatiga y anhelos, me malbarate un mocito que gaste en medias de pelo más que vale un mayorazgo.

TORIBIO	I must be a fool in a play; if I could remember, I'd say!
MARI-NUÑO	The table is ready.
TORIBIO	Pray, where can this table be?
MARI-NUÑO	Inside there.

1065

TORIBIO	I cannot believe it.
MARI-NUÑO	Why not?
TORIBIO	Because the instructions I got were that duennas are not to be believed. However, we shall see. Please forgive my impertinence, for I hate to pay compliments.

1070

[Toribio exits.]

CLARA *[Aside]*	(Lord, this cousin is something fine!)
MARI-NUÑO	(He's no gentleman; he's a swine!)
EUGENIA *[Aside]*	(I wonder how the soldiers who guard us from plague could let him through?)
ALONSO	Tell me, why are you two so sad?

1075

THE GIRLS	It's nothing.
ALONSO	I know what. You've had a shock seeing our cousin's clothes and choice of words. You know that goes away in a week or two. Most country boys are quickly engrossed in the court. You'll see how soon his clothes are in style, and his speech is too. But let me tell you again what happy rapture I sustain to see that my ancestral lands will come into my grandson's hands. This Don Toribio, by my life, will take the one of you to wife. While my other daughter, I vow, will wed as well. I'll not allow that what has cost me such grief, toil, and worry some dandy should spoil by spending on silk hose more plate than one would pay for an estate.

1080

1085

1090

1095

1074 soldiers: stationed at the city gate to keep contagious people out

> Si viera por un sombrero
> de castor dar veinte o treinta
> reales de a ocho yo a mi yerno
> sacados de mi sudor,
> perdiera mi entendimiento;
> y así no hay que hablar, sino
> persuadiros desde luego
> que éste y otro como éste
> han de ser esposos vuestros.

[Vase.]

CLARA   Primero pierda la vida.

EUGENIA   La vida no; mas primero
               me quedaré sin casar,
               que es más encarecimiento.

If on some beaver hat I saw
any profligate son-in-law
of mine hand over ten or twenty
gold pieces of eight that with plenty
of hard work I had earned, I know   1100
that raving mad is what I'd go!
Therefore I will brook no reply,
for your marriages surely lie
with this man and another just
like him, and wed them both you must.   1105

[*Alonso exits.*]

CLARA   First I would rather lose my life.

EUGENIA   My life no; but before his wife
                 I'd be, I swear I'll never wed,
                 which is far worse than being dead.

Jornada Segunda

[Salen don Juan, don Félix, y Hernando.]

D. FÉLIX
¿Cómo habéis, don Juan, pasado
la noche?

D. JUAN
                              ¿Cómo pudiera,
don Félix, en vuestra casa,
sino muy bien, puesto que ella
de mi tristeza no tiene
la culpa?

D. FÉLIX
                              Pues ¿qué tristeza
es la que ahora os aflige?

D. JUAN
No sé cómo os la encarezca.
Desde el instante que vi
esa divina belleza
que aún en mi memoria vive
a pesar de tanta ausencia,
todas aquellas cenizas,
que entre olvidadas pavesas
aún no juzgué que eran humo,
llama han sido: de manera
que conocí que han estado
en ocioso fuego envueltas,
tibias, pero no apagadas;
calladas, pero no muertas.
No volví a verla ayer tarde,
porque no volvió a la reja;
y así, hoy con la esperanza
de que siendo hoy día de fiesta
no dejará de salir,
he madrugado por verla.
A la puerta de la calle
voy a esperar que amanezca
segundo sol para mí.
Vos haced, por vida vuestra,
puesto que no importa al caso,
que nada don Pedro entienda.

[Vase.]

D. FÉLIX
¿Habrá hombre tan necio como
el que hallar memorias piensa
en una mujer, al cabo
de tantos años de ausencia?

HERNANDO
Déjale que con su engaño
viva.

Act II

A room in Don Félix's house
[Don Félix, Don Juan and Hernando]

FÉLIX   Tell me, Don Juan, how did you sleep   1110
the night?

JUAN   How do you think, but deep
in slumber, Don Félix, because
this is your house: it did not cause
my grief, it cannot take the blame
for my melancholy.

FÉLIX   Whence came   1115
this sadness which afflicts you so?

JUAN   I am afraid I do not know
how to explain it. The moment
I saw again that monument
of beauty, who, despite her long   1120
absence, is still alive and strong
in my memory, all these old
ashes, which lay under such cold
embers I feared they were but smoke,
have sprung to fire, and they awoke   1125
so fast I knew they had been wrapped
in lazy flame whose strength was capped:
lukewarm sparks that still flickered red,
quiet, slumbering, but not dead.
The whole day I managed to see   1130
her just once, on her balcony;
and today, with the expectation
that because of the celebration
she is most certain to appear,
I got up early just to see her.   1135
Now I am going to wait by
the door until the eastern sky
glows radiantly with her light.
But you know, this is of such slight
importance that it would be best   1140
not to keep Don Pedro abreast
of it.

[Juan exits.]

FÉLIX   Can there be such a dunce
to imagine love lives on, once
the years have passed, and that still he
has a place in her memory?   1145

HERNANDO   Let him live with this mad deceit.

D. FÉLIX	Un cortesano, que era,
	decía, el engaño la cosa
	que más y que menos cuesta.
	Veamos estotro doliente
	en qué estado está, ya que esta
	casa, de locos de amor
	se ha vuelto convalecencia.

[Sale don Pedro.]

D. FÉLIX	¿Qué hay, don Pedro? Buenos días.
D. PEDRO	Fuerza será que lo sean,
	recibiéndolos de vos
	y en vuestra casa, por vuestra,
	y por la dicha de estar
	mis esperanzas tan cerca.
	No creeréis cuánto gozoso
	y ufano estoy de que sea
	vuestra vecina esta dama;
	pues con eso, cosa es cierta
	que para verla, don Félix,
	dos mil ocasiones tenga;
	y por no perder ninguna
	voy a esperarla a la puerta,
	pues sin duda que hoy a misa
	habrá de salir por fuerza.
D. FÉLIX	En ella don Juan aguarda.
D. PEDRO	Así se hará la deshecha
	mejor, paseándonos todos.
	Vos, aunque llevaros quiera
	a otra parte, no vais; pero
	de suerte que nada entienda.

[Sale don Juan.]

D. FÉLIX	¿Qué hacéis, don Juan?

[Sale Don Juan.]

D. JUAN	Esperaros
	para saber a qué iglesia
	queréis que vamos a misa.
[Aparte.]	(De aquí no hagamos ausencia.)
D. PEDRO	Lo mismo le decía yo.
	Vamos adonde os parezca.

FÉLIX	I once heard a courtly conceit
	which said: "The thing that costs the most,
	and the least, is deceit." That ghost
	of love who's in the other room 1150
	must still be sleeping, I assume.
	Such love-sick fools there are aboard,
	it seems a convalescent's ward.

[Don Pedro enters.]

FÉLIX	Well, Don Pedro, good day to you.
PEDRO	It must be so, for you outdo 1155
	yourself with hospitality
	in everything you do for me.
	And besides, the one I adore
	and hope to win lives right next door!
	You can't imagine how delighted 1160
	I find myself, and how excited
	to have that lady be your neighbor.
	For it will be an easy labor,
	Don Félix, to catch sight of her
	two thousand times a day, I'm sure. 1165
	And since I'd not waste even one
	chance to glimpse her charms, let me run
	to the doorway where she must pass
	when she leaves home to go to mass.
FÉLIX	That's where Don Juan is stationed too. 1170
PEDRO	With all of us there, we will do
	a more convincing job of proving
	our nonchalance. If he tries moving
	off with you, stay put. But do not
	let Don Juan figure out our plot. 1175

[They exit.]

A street
[Don Félix and Don Pedro enter and meet Don Juan.]

FÉLIX	Don Juan; why are you waiting here?
JUAN	For you. Where would you like to hear
	mass today?

[Aside to Don Félix]

	Don Félix, you know
	whatever he says, we can't go.
PEDRO	That's exactly what I was saying. 1180
	Let's go wherever you like praying.

[Aparte.]

No os vais, don Félix, de aquí.

FÉLIX
[Aparte.]

(Desta suerte fácil fuera
servir un hombre a dos amos,
mandando una cosa mesma.)
Vuesarcedes, caballeros
muy enamorados, ¿piensan
que no hay más que irse y llevarme
cada cual a su querencia?
Pues no, ¡vive Dios!, que hoy
se han de estar donde yo quiera;
que quiero yo enamorar
también un día en conversa.
Y así, hasta que mis vecinas
salgan y vamos tras ellas,
para ver la que me toca
festejar (pues cosa es cierta
que yo la que quiero más,
es la que tengo más cerca),
no se ha de ir de aquí ninguno.

D. PEDRO

Por mí sea norabuena.

D. JUAN

Por mí también.

D. PEDRO
[Aparte.]

                              ¡Lindamente
habéis hecho la deshecha
con don Juan!

D. JUAN
[Aparte.]

                              ¡Bien con don Pedro
desmentido habéis mis penas!

D. FÉLIX
[Aparte.]

(Más lo hago por saber
si es que es la dama una mesma.
Y si es la que de las dos;
mas no prosiga mi lengua;
que es tarde para que a mí
beldad alguna me venza.)

D. JUAN

Pues ya que queréis, don Félix,
que os asistamos, no sea
tan de balde, que no os cueste
el pagarnos una deuda
que nos debéis.

[Aside to Don Félix]

Remember, Don Félix, don't budge.

FÉLIX
[Aside]

(This is how I would not begrudge
serving two masters: if they make
me do the same for each one's sake.)   1185
Most noble gentlemen, good knights
and truest lovers: by what rights
do you think you can command me
to go with you so docilely?
By God, I shall not go! Today   1190
both of you must agree to stay
where I decide. I will approve
today only for talk of love.
So until those neighbor girls set
foot in the street, and we three get   1195
in line behind them to decide
which one I get to court (for I'd
be an idiot not to choose
a neighbor girl to be love's muse),
let no one move. That's my decree.   1200

PEDRO

That's perfectly alright with me.

JUAN

With me too.

PEDRO
*[Aside to
Don Félix]*

What a clever way
to make Don Juan decide to stay!

JUAN
*[Aside to
Don Félix]*

How cleverly you have concealed
my grief with this deceptive shield.   1205

FÉLIX
[Aside]

(I only do this to discover
if the two have a single lover,
and of the two girls, if the one . . .
I think I'd better hold my tongue;
not even a pretty girl can   1210
conquer the heart of this old man.)

JUAN

Well, Don Félix, since you would make
us wait here with you, why not take
advantage of the time to pay
a debt you owe since yesterday   1215
to the two of us?

D. Pedro   Es verdad,
y es famosa ocasión esta,
pues sólo para hacer hora
son las relaciones buenas.

D. Félix   Yo me huelgo. Pues así
hablaré un rato siquiera,
sin que a la mano me vayan
con amor, celos y ausencia.
Con el general contento,
Madrid, digno a su fineza
a su lealtad y su amor,
oyó las felices nuevas
de las bodas de su rey;
y más cuando supo que era
la divina Marïana . . .

D. Juan   Tened, que dejar es fuerza
otra vez la relación
para otra ocasión suspensa.

D. Félix   ¿Por qué?

D. Juan   Porque sale gente.

D. Félix   ¿Cuánto va que se me queda
la relación en el cuerpo,
y vienen otros a hacerla?

D. Pedro   Un criado es el que sale,
que a su amo sin duda espera.

D. Juan   Bien podéis ya proseguir.

D. Félix   Digo que en gozosa muestra
del alegría de todos;
pues todos juntos quisieran
significar los afectos
en regocijos y fiestas;
y aunque, como vos dijisteis,
caminan con su pereza
las dichas, y no es el gusto
correo a toda diligencia;
con todo eso, llegó el día
de saberse que en Vïena
el Rey desposado estaba,
remitiéndole que ejerza
sus poderes Ferdinando,
Rey de Hungría y de Bohemia,
Ferdinando, ínclito jóven,
en quien la sacra diadema
de rey de romanos, presto
hará la elección herencia.
El, pues, no del poder sólo

PEDRO   That seems good
                    to me, Félix, I wish you would.
                    For long narrations are sublime
                    only if you are killing time.

FÉLIX   I would be pleased. At least this way   1220
                    I can say what I want to say
                    without you always butting in
                    with love, jealousy, and chagrin.
                        Madrid, with general delight
                    reflecting loyalty,   1225
                    and deep respect, and love,
                    the nuptials of royalty
                        considered happy news; and more so
                    when she found the bride
                    was that divine young Mary-Anne . . .   1230

JUAN   I'm sorry in midstride
                    to cut you off, but hold your rhyme
                    to regale us another time.

FÉLIX   Why?

JUAN   Because someone's coming out.

FÉLIX   I wish my words would! But I doubt   1235
                    anything will come out today
                    except them! That's all I can say!

PEDRO   It is only a servant who
                    must have been sent outside to do
                    something.

JUAN   Why don't you go on now?   1240

FÉLIX   I'll try it, if they will allow:
                        All the court together showed
                    its pride and jubilation
                    in parties and festivities
                    and joyful celebration.   1245
                        And although, as you said, good fortune
                    never seems to scurry,
                    and while the coach that brings delight
                    is never in a hurry,
                        nevertheless, at last the day   1250
                    arrived that brought the word
                    that in Vienna our good king
                    had wed, but had deferred
                        to Ferdinand of Hungary,
                    great king, unparalleled,   1255
                    who soon will wear the diadem
                    of Rome, when they have held
                        the election. There he exercised
                    both might and gentleness,

usó, mas de la fineza:
con que sirviendo a su hermana,
hizo de la corte ausencia.
Dejemos en el camino
las dos majestades (que ésta
no es la acción que a mí me toca,
ya que vos con la agudeza
de vuestro ingenio dijisteis
el aparato y grandeza),
y vamos a que Madrid,
desvelada, fiel y atenta
al servicio de sus reyes,
que es de lo que más se precia,
en tanto que prevenía
la usada lid de sus fiestas,
convidó lo más ilustre
de la española nobleza,
para una máscara; haciendo
(fuese acaso o diligencia)
a propósito de bodas
ceremoniosa la fiesta;
porque si a la antigüedad
revolvéis humanas letras,
hallaréis como en las nupcias
aun menos ilustres que éstas,
con antorchas en las manos
corrían tropas diversas
a quien llamaban preludios,
invocando la suprema
deidad del sacro Himeneo,
a cuyas aras las teas
sacrificaban, cantando
epitalamios, en prendas
de que a aquellos casamientos
favorable a asistir venga.
Y así de la antigüedad
tomando Madrid aquella
parte festiva, y dejando
la gentílica depuesta,
usó el regocijo sólo,
mejorando ilustre y cuerda
el rito, pues que fue dando
al cielo gracias inmensas
de sus dichas, cuyas voces
variamente lisonjeras,
fueron el epitalamio
que España cantó contenta,
en música, que es confusa,
más dulce, si no más diestra.

leaving the court, he served his sister   1260
with fine courtliness.
    But let us leave their majesties
there on the road (for this
is not the story I would tell,
since with great artifice   1265
    you have already narrated
that grand and glorious scene).
Instead, let's go back to Madrid,
where plans to serve the queen
    and king (which is Madrid's great pride)   1270
kept all the court awake,
attentive to each detail
of the party they would make.
    While they readied the jousting lists
and built the royal stand,   1275
they sent out invitations
to the noblest in the land
    to come to a masked ball: for with
the wedding they would seize
the moment to put on a show   1280
of great festivities.
    If you read the ancients carefully
I'm sure that you will find
that weddings, even those which
lesser loves than these two bind,   1285
    were attended by great hoards of men
with torches in their hands
who'd gallop all around, and sing
and wave their firebrands
    invoking that most holy Hymen,   1290
god of marriage bed,
they'd sing epithalamia
and on his altar shed
    their torches, praying he would come
to bless the bride and groom.   1295
And thus from ancient rites, Madrid
their essence did exhume,
    leaving behind the pagan parts
and doubling up the joy.
Wisely, Madrid bettered those rites,   1300
electing to employ
    its voices, instruments, and hearts
in praising God's largess,
and this epithalamium
in music to express.   1305

En toda mi vida vi
tan hermosa tropa bella,
como la máscara junta,
cuando al compás de trompetas,
clarines y chirimías
empezaron a moverla
los dos polos que de España
y de Alemania sustentan
la política, bien como
dando generosas muestras
de que Alemania y España
por todo el tiempo interesan,
una en que tal prenda da,
y otra en que admite tal prenda.
Bien quisiera yo pintarlos;
pero aunque más lo pretenda,
no es posible, si no es
que la retórica quiera
en sus figuras prestarme
el uso de sus licencias,
cometiendo una que llaman
tropo de prosopopeya,
que es cuando lo no posible
bajo objeto de la idea,
o callando se imagina,
o hablando se representa.
Porque si no es que finjáis
allá en la fantasía vuestra
bajar de púrpura un monte,
arder de plata una selva,
y de selva y monte luego
formáis un monstruo, que a fuerza
de nuevo metamorfosis
todo en fuego se convierta,
no podréis imaginar
cómo aquel peñasco era
de luz y nácar y plata,
en cuya abrasada selva
fueron las plumas las flores,
y las hachas las estrellas.
Tan iguales todos juntos
y cada uno, que no hubiera
pareja que poder darles,*
si ellos mismos no se hubieran
antes convenido a ser
ellos mismos sus parejas.
Cuando del un puesto al otro
corrían las tropas, eran
disueltas exhalaciones
y dilatados cometas.

*pareja que poder darle,

In all my life I never saw
a finer troop than those
which came together in this masque;
who, when the sound arose
   from trumpets, oboes, clarinets, 1310
followed the lead of Spain
and Germany's young monarchs,
who their politics sustain
   and through their union show one heart
for Spain and Germany: 1315
the one proffers the prize, the other
takes it joyfully.
   How I would like to picture them
for you, but though I try,
it can't be, unless rhetoric 1320
should somehow magnify
   my gifts, and lend a figure from
her potent arsenal:
prosopopoeia is the trope
that makes impossible 1325
   events seem real, when ideas
clothed with form appear,
and silently fill up the eye,
or loudly fill the ear.
   Because if you cannot compel 1330
your fantasy to frame
a purple mount descending,
or a silver woods aflame,
   and, then, from woods and mountain
form a monster, and require 1335
it, through new metamorphosis,
to be sheet of fire,
   then you cannot imagine how
that pinacle was shaped,
with mother-of-pearl and silver light, 1340
a flaming forest draped
   with feathers that were flowers,
and each torch a shining star.
Each one was dressed so like the others,
all were on a par; 1345
   none could surpass in elegance
this beautiful array,
if they had not already passed
themselves in every way.
   And when swiftly the revelers 1350
from mount to mount did fly,
they seemed like fragile shooting stars,
pale comets in the sky.

Tan hermosa fue la noche,
que el día entre pardas nieblas
sucedió por muchos días
la faz de nubes cubierta,
llorando lo que llovía,
o de envidia o de vergüenza.
Hasta que desempeñada
vio su luz con la belleza
del día, que vio la plaza
para los toros dispuesta.
Porque aunque su hermoso circo
siempre ha sido heroica afrenta
de cuantos anfiteatros
Roma en ruina nos acuerda,
nunca con más causa, pues
nunca se vio su grandeza,
a fuer de dama, ni más
despejada ni más bella
pues que cuando vio que a tropas
ocupaban la palestra
de los lucidos criados
las adornadas catervas,
como a su triunfo trajeron
los grandes héroes, que en ella
la suerte han hecho precisa;
por quien ya el acaso deja
de ser acaso, pues ya
no viene a ser sino fuerza
el que ha sacado al acierto
del nombre de contingencia.
A ninguno he de nombraros,
y es justo; que no quisiera
que habiendo ya tantas plumas
pintado a sus excelencias,
los desluciesen ahora
cortedades de mi lengua.
Sólo os diré que no hubo
bruto que armada la testa,
la piel manchada, arrugado
el ceño, hendida la huella,
dilatado el cuello, el pecho
corto, la cerviz inhiesta,
de una vez escriba osados
caracteres en la arena,
como quien dice: "Esta es
o vuestra huesa o mi huesa,"
que no fuese triunfo fácil
del primor y la destreza,
del que más hidalgo bruto
soberbio con la obediencia,

This evening was so beautiful
that day, in leaden cloud,   1355
sequestered her fair face away,
because she was so proud
    that, thus eclipsed, she rained salt tears
of envy or of shame:
until that day when clouds diffused   1360
and radiant light became;
    and in the plaza, decked for bulls,
she let herself be seen
over that lovely circus
which affront has always been   1365
    to as many amphitheaters
as Roman ruins record;
but not once with greater reason
than these festivals afford,
    since not once, for any woman,   1370
did the Romans decorate
their imperial metropolis,
nor did they saturate
    her balconies and tribunals
with so fine a multitude   1375
when her heroes brought their captives
home, with pride, to be reviewed
    in that triumph chance bestowed them.
Here chance, without power, holds
no sway, for here deliberate   1380
right pageantry unfolds.
    I will not name these noble men;
which is but right, because
so many able pens have sung
their deeds with great applause   1385
    that my poor tongue would only paint
them in a lesser light.
But let me say, there was no bull
with head well armed to fight,
    with spotted hide, with wrinkled brow,   1390
with sturdy-legged attack,
with muscled shoulders, ample chest,
unbending neck and back,
    no brute whose scribal hoofs did trace
his challenge in the sand   1395
as if to say: "Here, on your tomb
or mine, I take my stand,"
    that was not easy triumph for
the gallant strength and skill
of these proud nobles who those noble   1400
brutes drove with their will;

dócil con la lozanía,
sus amenazas desprecia
al tacto del acicate,
o al aviso de la rienda;
pues ya el asta y ya la espada,
en ambas acciones diestra,
airosamente mezclaban
la hermosura y la fiereza.
Feliz acabó la tarde,
quedando Madrid contenta
con ella y con la esperanza
de que sus dichas se acercan.
Y así, sólo en prevenciones
desde entonces se desvela,
porque siendo, como es,
la corte el centro y la esfera
que ha de merecer lograrla
más suya, desaire fuera,
habiendo de paso tantas
ciudades héchola fiestas,
exceder ella en las dichas,
y las otras en finezas:
y más estando a su aplauso
las naciones extranjeras,
o de envidiosas pendientes,
o de curiosas atentas.
Y así, la prolijidad
de las horas de la ausencia
gastó sólo en disponer
aparatos que ahora es fuerza
que yo remita a mejor
pluma que nos los refiera.
Diciendo ahora solamente
que la señora condesa
de Medellín, de Cardona
ilustre familia excelsa,
a Denia fue a recibirla
como mayor camarera,
adonde esperó hasta el día
de la deseada nueva
de que ya su Majestad
(que Dios guarde) estaba en Denia.
Aquí el señor Almirante
a darla la enhorabuena
de parte del Rey salió;
y aunque salió a la ligera
fue con aquel lucimiento
digno a ser quien es; que fuera
en su excelencia muy tibia
la disculpa de la priesa.

who taming them with graceful ease,
their bellowed threats disdain
with every subtle touch of spur,
each gentle tug of rein.   1405
   For now with lance, and now with sword,
and always expertly,
they mingled graceful beauty
with their sterling bravery.
   The bullfight ended happily,   1410
and all Madrid did cheer
at it and that her happiness
would soon be drawing near.
   So ever since, Madrid has lain
awake in preparation;   1415
for as the court is center
of the world and of our nation,
   and since the world has graced
this royalty, with word and deed,
it would be shameful did the court   1420
all others not exceed;
   and even more so, since the nations
all watch eagerly
suspenseful in their envy
or their curiosity.   1425
   Madrid employed the hours waiting
for their monarchs by
preparing for their welcome in ways
which I think that I
   will let a better pen describe   1430
another time. The scene
I will describe is this: my lady,
Countess of Medellín,
   exalted daughter of Cardona
went to meet the fleet   1435
in Denia, as lady
of her chamber should, to greet
   her when the longed-for news should come
that now Her Majesty
(God keep her safe) in Denia   1440
at last would leave the sea.
   From here, my lord the admiral
to give her welcome from
the king set out, and though he parted
with a minimum   1445
   of preparation, he displayed
that shining dignity
of who he is, for haste could never
dim his nobility.

1433 Countess of Medellín: Mariana's Mistress of the Robes (Camarera mayor), a member of the powerful Sandoval and Lerma families

De deudos, criados y amigos
fue el séquito de manera,
que a no hacer particular
elección, pienso que fuera
dejar sin gente a Castilla;
que de un almirante della,
¿quién de ser deudo, o amigo,
o criado se reserva?
¡Oh felice casa, adonde
entre todas tus grandezas,
el afecto es patrimonio,
y lo bien visto es herencia!
En este intermedio pues
hizo Madrid diligencias
más afectivas en orden
a que todo se prevenga
con majestad y aparato,
para la entrada a la Reina,
asistida dignamente
del que tío la festeja,
del que esposo la merece,
del que amante la celebra,
poniendo a sus pies dos mundos;
pues como cuarto planeta,
cuanto ilumina, la postra,
cuanto dora, la sujeta,
coronándola tres veces,
esposa, sobrina y reina.
Con que hasta el felice día
que nuestros ojos la vean
entrar triunfante en su corte,
mi relación se suspenda,
divertida en la esperanza
de que generosa venga
a ser fin de nuestras ansias,
término de nuestras penas,
logro de nuestros deseos,
y a par de las dichas nuestras,
con felice sucesión
nos viva edades eternas.

D. JUAN   La relación con el tiempo
se ha medido de manera,
que acabarla y salir gente,
ha sido una cosa mesma.

D. PEDRO   Sí, mas no la que esperamos.

D. FÉLIX   No, porque es el padre dellas.

D. JUAN   No le conocí hasta ahora.
[Aparte.]   (Que en mi tiempo estaba fuera.)

His kinsmen, servants, and his friends   1450
thronged to his retinue:
so many that if he'd not chosen
carefully those who
    could go, he would have left Castille
empty from end to end: 1455
since to her admiral, who is
not kinsman, aide, or friend?
    Oh happy house, displaying grandeur
without arrogance:
its patrimony's service,   1460
duty's its inheritance.
    Madrid, then, in this interlude
used all her energy
to double her preparedness
with pomp and majesty,   1465
    to perfect every detail
for the queen's arrival here
grandly accompanied by one
who, uncle, does revere
    her; one who, husband, merits her;   1470
who, lover, celebrates
her merit, setting at her feet
two worlds; Madrid prostrates
    itself before the shining light
that gilds all her demesne,   1475
which crowns her with the triple crown
of niece and wife and queen.
    And so, until that happy day
when we will see her wend
her way, triumphant, through the court,   1480
this long tale I'll suspend;
    convinced and certain in my hope,
and sure in my belief
that she will fulfill our desires
and end our every grief;   1485
    and her good fortune and our luck
shall join eternally
by giving us an heir who'll carry
on her monarchy.

JUAN   Don Félix: your story's limits   1490
                are exactly what time permits.
                You did very well scheduling
                its close with that door's opening.

PEDRO   But they're not who we're waiting for.

FÉLIX   No. That's their father at the door.   1495

JUAN   I've not seen him before today.
[Aside]   (When I was there he was away.)

D. Pedro   Nunca hasta ahora le vi.

[Aparte.]   (Que yo siempre amé en su ausencia.)

D. Juan   ¿Quién es el que con él viene?

Hernando   Yo podré dar esa cuenta.
                 Es un sobrino asturiano,
                 con quien el padre desea
                 casar una de las dos.

[Salen don Alonso; don Toribio, vestido de negro, ridículo.]

D. Juan
                 Quiera el cielo que no sea
                 la novia la que yo adoro.

D. Pedro
                 Plegue a Dios que no sea Eugenia.

D. Félix   Pasémonos.

D. Toribio   Como digo,
                 ¿qué hacen, tío, a nuestra puerta
                 estos mocitos?

D. Alonso   ¿No están
                 en la calle? ¿Qué os altera?

D. Toribio   ¡En la calle de mis primas,
                 sin más ni más, se pasean!

D. Alonso   Pues ¿por qué no?

D. Toribio   Porque no
                 me ha de haber paseante en ella
                 ni piante, ni mamante;
                 y más estos de melena,
                 que Filenos de golilla
                 de candil, y bigotera,
                 andan cerrados de sienes
                 y transparentes de piernas.

D. Alonso   ¿Qué habemos de hacer, si son
                 vecinos?

D. Toribio   Que no lo sean.

D. Alonso   ¿Cómo, si tienen aquí
                 sus casas?

D. Toribio   Que no las tengan.

D. Félix   Fuerza es hablarle. Yo llego,
                 pues buena ocasión es ésta.*

*D. Juan: pues buena ocasión es esta

PEDRO   This is the first time I have viewed
                         him.
[Aside]   (He was away while I wooed.)

JUAN   Who is that person at his side?   1500

HERNANDO   I know. Their father notified
                         a cousin from Asturias
                         to come to Madrid to discuss
                         marriage with one of the girls.

[Don Alonso enters, with Don Toribio, dressed ridiculously in black.]

JUAN
[Aside]   (I
                         hope to Heaven it is not my   1505
                         intended. I'd never recover!)

PEDRO
[Aside]   (I hope Eugenia's not his lover.)

FÉLIX   Let's go.

TORIBIO   Tell me, what is that gang,
                         uncle? Why do you let them hang
                         around our door?

ALONSO   We cannot get   1510
                         them off the street. Why so upset?

TORIBIO   How can they soil my cousin's street,
                         parading up and down to beat
                         the band?

ALONSO   Well, why not?

TORIBIO   Well, why not?!
                         How can I let these dandies trot   1515
                         up and down the street? Damned if I'd
                         do it. These fancy, sissified,
                         bare-legged, big-collared ruffians
                         who wax their mustaches and prance
                         around give me the creeps, with their   1520
                         tiny brains and their shaggy hair.

ALONSO   But they are neighbors, what can we
                         do?

TORIBIO   Neighbors! Well, let them not be.

ALONSO   But how can we do that if they
                         have houses?

TORIBIO   Let them move away.   1525

FÉLIX   We have to talk to them. I'll go.
                         This is our chance to make a show.

Dadme, señor don Alonso,*
aunque de paso, licencia
para besaros la mano
y daros la enhorabuena
de haber al barrio venido;
que aunque excusarlo debiera
hasta estar en vuestra casa
y visitaros en ella,
el alborozo de ver
que tan buen vecino tenga,
dilatar no me permite
que a su servicio me ofrezca.

D. PEDRO   Todos lo mismo decimos.

D. TORIBIO

                ¡Qué ceremonia tan necia!

D. ALONSO   Guárdeos Dios por la merced
que me hacéis; que si supiera
la dicha de mereceros
tantos favores, hubiera
cumplido mi obligación,
visitándoos en la vuestra.
Conoced a mi sobrino
que quiero que desde hoy sea
vuestro servidor.

D. TORIBIO   ¿Yo había
de ser alhaja tan puerca?

D. ALONSO   Esta es acción cortesana.

D. TORIBIO   Más me huele a corte-enferma.

D. ALONSO   Llegad, don Toribio: ved
que estos señores esperan
conoceros.

[Llega.]

D. JUAN   En nosotros
tendréis a vuestra obediencia
hoy amigos y criados.

D. TORIBIO   Guárdeos Dios por la fineza.

D. FÉLIX   ¿Venís con salud?

D. TORIBIO   Al cielo,
gracias, ni mala ni buena,
sino así así, entreverada,
como lonja de la pierna.

*D. Félix: Dadme, señor don Alonso,

My lord Don Alonso, allow
me, sir, since we meet here, to bow
respectfully to you, to kiss   1530
your hand, and wish for you much bliss
in your new house and neighborhood;
and although I confess I should
have waited to proceed until
I found you at home, even still,   1535
my delight in finding that I
have such nice neighbors made me try
to offer assistance to you.

PEDRO   We offer our services too.

TORIBIO
[Aside]   (This ceremony is absurd!)   1540

ALONSO   May God bless you for each kind word
you have said. If I had but known
that such courtesy would be shown
me, I would certainly have met
my obligations, and my debt   1545
discharged, by visiting at your
house. This is my nephew; I'm sure
that from this moment he will be
your servant.

TORIBIO   You mean you want me
[Aside to Alonso]   to demean myself with some sort   1550
of work?

ALONSO   Of course not; but at court
[Aside to Toribio] we all talk this well.

TORIBIO   This well?! Talk
this sick you mean!

ALONSO   Nephew, pray walk
over to those good men and greet
them as you should.

[Toribio approaches them.]

JUAN   We're pleased to meet   1555
you. From today you can depend
on each as your servant and friend.

TORIBIO   God bless you for your courtesy.

FÉLIX   How is your health?

TORIBIO   Alright, praised be;
I'm not so good and not so bad;   1560
I show some health, like one who's clad
in too short trousers shows some leg.

D. Alonso   Más despacio besaré
              vuestras manos: dad licencia.

D. Félix   Vos la tenéis.

D. Alonso   Don Toribio,
              venid.

D. Toribio   ¿Aquí te los dejas?

D. Alonso   ¿Qué he de hacer?

D. Toribio   Yo lo sé.

D. Alonso   ¿A dónde
              vas?

D. Toribio   A dar a casa vuelta.

D. Alonso   ¿A qué?

D. Toribio   A decir a mis primas
              que en todo hoy no salgan fuera.

D. Alonso   ¿Han de quedarse sin misa?

D. Toribio   ¿Qué dificultad es ésa?
              Mi ejecutoria les basta
              para ser cristianas viejas.

D. Alonso   ¡Jesús, y qué disparate!
              Venid, venid: no lo entiendan
              esos hidalgos.

D. Toribio   Par Dios,
              que si por mi voto fuera,
              no habían de salir de casa,
              quisieran o no quisieran.

[Vanse.]

D. Félix   No sé cómo fue posible . . .

D. Juan   ¿Qué?

D. Félix   Que la risa detenga,
              viendo al primo.

D. Pedro   ¡Qué figura
              tan rara!

ALONSO	'Til some less hurried time, I beg your leave to kiss your hand.
FÉLIX	Of course.
ALONSO	Don Toribio, I think perforce 1565 we should be going.
TORIBIO [Aside to Alonso]	Go? And let them stay here?
ALONSO	Nephew, you forget this is a public street.
TORIBIO	I know just what to do to overthrow their plans.
ALONSO	What are you doing? Where 1570 are you going?
TORIBIO	To take good care to take care.
ALONSO	How's that?
TORIBIO	To prepare my cousins for staying inside.
ALONSO	You would leave them unsanctified by mass?
TORIBIO	There is no need for that. 1575 There's proof in my certificate of lineage that they are old Christians.
ALONSO	My God, how stupid can you get? Come, come; this gentleman doesn't need to hear this.
TORIBIO	By God, 1580 as for me, I'd not spare the rod to keep those two girls locked inside, in spite of what they might decide.

[Alonso and Toribio exit.]

FÉLIX	You know, I didn't think I could . . .
JUAN	What's that?
FÉLIX	. . . keep from having a good 1585 laugh at that cousin.
PEDRO	Strange!

1578 Old Christians: not descended from converts from Islam or Judaism;
   see note to verse 1041

D. Juan   Extraña presencia
de novio.

*[Salen doña Clara y doña Eugenia con mantos,
Otáñez delante, y Brígida y Mari-Nuño detrás.]*

Hernando   Ya las dos salen.

D. Félix   Desde aquí podremos verlas,
como acaso.

Clara   Echate el manto,
que hay gente en la calle, Eugenia.

Eugenia   ¿Qué he hecho yo para no andar
con la cara descubierta?

Otáñez   ¡Tomad! ¡Luego la faltara
a la hermanica respuesta!

Mari-Nuño   Callad, que no os toca a vos
hablar en estas materias.

Brígida   Ni a vos en éstas ni esotras,
y habláis en esotras y éstas.

D. Félix   Pasemos ahora al descuido.

D. Juan
    ¡Oh, permita amor que en ella
al verme, estén sus memorias,
ya que no vivas, no muertas!

D. Pedro
    ¡Oh, plegue a Dios que se obligue
de ver que he venido a verla!

Clara   Advierte que llega gente.

Eugenia   Y bien, la gente que llega,
¿qué se lleva por llevarse
hacia allá esta reverencia?

[Aparte.]   Mas ¡cielos! ¿Qué es lo que miro?
Don Juan es. Ya de su ausencia
debió de cesar la causa;
y no es mi duda sola ésta,
sino estar con él don Pedro.
Aquésta es la vez primera
que ha sido por ignorancia
amiga la competencia.)

JUAN   If that
                        is a bridegroom I'll eat my hat!

*[Clara and Eugenia enter, wearing veils, Otáñez in front of them and Brígida
behind, with the duenna Mari-Nuño.]*

HERNANDO   The two girls are coming out.

FÉLIX   From
                        here we can watch them as they come.

CLARA   Use your veil, Eugenia, for there   1590
                        are men in the street.

EUGENIA   I don't care.
                        What have I done to have to walk
                        all covered up?

OTÁÑEZ   You always talk
                        far too much, young lady. Now, take
                        this!

[Eugenia puts a handkerchief over her head.]

MARI-NUÑO   You be quiet! You mistake   1595
                        your business when you butt into
                        this.

BRÍGIDA   It's not your business, but you
                        make everyone's business yours.

FÉLIX   Say,
                        let's meander over their way.

JUAN
[Aside]   (Oh love, grant that when she sees me   1600
                        I'll return to her memory:
                        if not alive, at least not dead!)

PEDRO
[Aside]   (Oh God, please let her precious head
                        be filled with thoughts of me again!)

CLARA   Watch what you do. Here come those men.   1605

EUGENIA   If those men come this way, what harm
                        if I take my vivacious charm
                        over there, and meet them halfway?

[Eugenia waves the kerchief in her hand in greeting.]

[Aside]   (Heaven help me! What can I say?
                        Don Juan! There must be no need for   1610
                        him to stay away any more.
                        But that's not the worst! Do I see
                        Don Pedro with him? This must be
                        the very first time that unplanned
                        competition lends friendly hand.)   1615

D. FÉLIX   ¿Cuál es de las dos, don Juan,
               la que tanto amor os cuesta?

D. JUAN

               La del pañuelo en la mano.
               No volváis tan presto a verla;
               no advierta que de ella hablamos.
               Y porque tampoco advierta
               don Pedro mi turbación,
               voy a esperar a la iglesia.
               Quedáos vos con él.

D. FÉLIX   Sí haré.
               Don Pedro, ¿cuál es de aquéllas?

D. PEDRO   La que, en la mano un pañuelo,
               descubierta va, es Eugenia.
               No volváis tan presto; no
               conozca que hablamos della.
               Quedáos, que porque no dé
               mi amor a don Juan sospecha,
               tras él voy.

[Vase.]

D. FÉLIX

                              Ya sé, a lo menos,
               que la dama es una mesma.

CLARA   Sin pañuelo me he venido,
               el tuyo, hermana, me presta;
[Destápase.] que ir tapada me congoja.

EUGENIA   A mí el venir descubierta,
               pues por si fue encuentro acaso,
               que me hayan visto me pesa.

[Tápase. Dala el pañuelo a Clara.]

D. FÉLIX

               Ya puedo ver, pues que tengo
               nombre, seña y contraseña,
               cuál es la dama que adoran.

CLARA   No a mirar el rostro vuelvas.

FÉLIX
[Aside to Juan]   Of those two lovely girls, Don Juan,
                         I know you love one, but which one?

JUAN
[Aside to Félix]   It is the one with the kerchief.
                         Don't look at her; just take a brief
                         glance, or she'll think we talk of her.   1620
                         And since I do not want to stir
                         Pedro with my delirium . . .
[Aloud]   I'll wait in church for you to come.
[Aside]   You wait for him.

[Exit Don Juan.]

FÉLIX
                                       Alright, I will.
                         Don Pedro, I know that you thrill   1625
                         to one of them. Which one?

PEDRO
                                              The one
                         with her kerchief in hand has done
                         me in. That's Eugenia. No, don't
                         turn around to look; then she won't
                         know we're talking about her. Stay   1630
                         here. I don't want to give away
                         my feelings to Don Juan. I'll go
                         after him.

[Exit Don Pedro.]

FÉLIX
[Aside]   (At least now I know
                         that they are in love with the same
                         girl.)

CLARA
                            Eugenia, I think I came   1635
                         out without a kerchief. Let me
                         have yours awhile, so they won't see
                         my face.

[Eugenia takes the kerchief off.]

EUGENIA
                                  I'd best not go uncovered
                         either. If those two men discovered
                         me, I'd be upset.   1640

[She adjusts her veil and gives Clara her kerchief.]

FÉLIX
[Aside]   (They gave me
                         her name, sign, and countersign. She
                         must be the one they both adore.)

CLARA   Please don't look toward him any more.

EUGENIA   ¡Jesús, y qué condición!
                          Lástima es que no seas suegra,
                          según te pudres de todo.

[Vanse.]

D. FÉLIX   ¡Oh cuánto he sentido verla!
                          Que aunque estoy con el cuidado
                          de que aquesta competencia,
                          el día que se declare,
                          ha de parar en pendencia;
                          siendo la dama una misma,
                          ya para mí se acrecienta
                          ver que de las dos ha sido,
                          aunque entrambas son tan bellas,
                          la que me lo pareció
                          más, cuando la vez primera
                          vi a las dos en la ventana.
                          Pero esto ahora no es de esencia,
                          que yo acabaré conmigo
                          que mi honor a mi amor venza,
                          sino acudir a estorbar
                          que a desengañarse vengan,
                          en tanto que yo a la mira
                          discurro de qué manera
                          entre dos amigos que hacen
                          de mi confianza, deba
                          prevenir el lance, haciendo
                          a su estorbo diligencia.

[Vase.]

[Salen don Toribio y don Alonso.]

D. ALONSO   ¿A qué volvéis aquí?

D. TORIBIO   ¿A qué
                          he de volver ¡pese a mí!
                          sino a escombrarlos, si aquí
                          están los que aquí dejé?

D. ALONSO   Pues ¿qué os va en eso?

D. TORIBIO   ¿Qué más
                          queréis que a un hidalgo vaya,
                          que ver que holgazanes haya
                          adonde hay primas?

D. ALONSO   Jamás
                          tan necia locura vi.
                          En Madrid ¿quién reparó
                          si hay gente en la calle?

EUGENIA   You're the worst crab I ever saw!   1645
                    You should have been a mother-in-law,
                    the way you sour everything.

[Félix sees them after the exchange. All the women exit with Otáñez.]

FÉLIX   Oh, this is an unhappy hour!
                    It still worries me that when they
                    bring their competition one day   1650
                    into the open, it well might
                    provoke them to some bloody fight,
                    since the two of them love just one
                    girl; and what's worse, I have begun
                    to think that, even though the two   1655
                    girls are lovely, both friends pursue
                    the one who seemed the loveliest
                    to me, the one I like the best.
                    But that should not matter to me,
                    for my honor shall guarantee   1660
                    to put a finish to my love.
                    Instead, I shall work to remove
                    my good friends from the deadly threat
                    of undeception, to abet
                    their love affairs, since they confide   1665
                    in me; and to take each one's side
                    at the same time that I prevent
                    all chance of mortal accident.

[Exit.]

[Don Toribio and Don Alonso enter.]

ALONSO   What did you come back for?

TORIBIO   What did
                    I come back for? I swear to God,   1670
                    I'll give those young punks such a prod
                    that once and for all we'll be rid
                    of them.

ALONSO   What makes you care so much?

TORIBIO   You'd have a nobleman like me
                    let those ruffians be so free   1675
                    around my gentle cousins?

ALONSO   Such
                    doltish simplicity is shot
                    with lunacy. In Madrid, who
                    bothers about what people do
                    in the street?

D. TORIBIO	Yo.
D. ALONSO	Y vos ¿por qué?
D. TORIBIO	Porque sí.
D. ALONSO	Aun bien que se han ausentado, y ya nadie aquí se ve.
D. TORIBIO	Acertáronlo, porque venía determinado.
D. ALONSO	Pues ¿qué era vuestra intención?
D. TORIBIO	Sólo ver si la anchicorta, como en caperuzas, corta en sombreros de castrón.
D. ALONSO	Vos ¿qué tenéis que temer para llegar a ese extremo?
D. TORIBIO	Mucho tengo y nada temo; que desde que llegué a ver de mis primas los dos cielos, si verdad digo, señor, tengo a Eugenia tanto amor, que aún los hombres me dan celos.
D. ALONSO	Aunque esas cosas me dan enfados, he agradecido que os entréis a ser marido por las puertas de galán. Pero ha de ser con cordura; que celos no ha de tener un hombre de su mujer.
D. TORIBIO	Pues ¿de cuál? ¿de la del cura?
D. ALONSO	Dejad delirios, por Dios y baste saber de mí, si es Eugenia la que aquí os agrada de las dos, que Eugenia vuestra será.
[Aparte.]	(Que es lo que yo deseaba.)
D. TORIBIO	Con eso el rencor se acaba que el verlos aquí me da a nuestra calle volver en tanta conversación.
D. ALONSO	Pues yo la dispensación haré al instante traer. Venid ahora, que quiero ganar las albricias yo

TORIBIO   I do.

ALONSO   Why?

TORIBIO   Why not?   1680

ALONSO   Well, anyway, they have all gone.
There's nobody around here now.

TORIBIO   Lucky them! I came out, I vow,
with my determination drawn.

ALONSO   What did you plan to do with that?   1685

TORIBIO   I planned to see if this stout knife
would shorten a fancy cape's life
or make hash of a beaver hat.

ALONSO   I cannot understand why you
are so afraid.

TORIBIO   I'm not afraid;   1690
but yet I fear. Those men have made
me quake. For since I saw those two
cousins, that pair of heavenly
angels, sir, by the stars above,
Eugenia fills me with such love   1695
that all men pique my jealousy.

ALONSO   That jealous raving is a thing
that bothers me. But I'm pleased you
will enter matrimony through
the doors of gallantry. Just bring   1700
wisdom to your affairs; at least
be prudent. You'll have a calm life
if you're not jealous of your wife.

TORIBIO   Of whose wife should I be? The priest's?

ALONSO   Good God, cease your raving. Please cease.   1705
Let it be enough to remind
you that if when you choose you find
Eugenia the best, it would please
me very much if she would be
yours.

[Aside]   (Which is just what I intended.)   1710

TORIBIO   Hearing that, my anger is ended;
seeing those men is what made me
carry on so much, and make our
street buzz with so much conversation.

ALONSO   I will make sure the dispensation   1715
is requested within the hour.
Come along with me. For I must
savor the benefits of knowing

de ser la que prefirió
vuestro amor.

D. Toribio   Oíd primero.
La dispensación, señor,
¿de Roma no ha de venir?

D. Alonso   Por ella a Roma se ha de ir.

D. Toribio   Pues siendo así, ¿no es mejor
abreviarlo de otro modo?

D. Alonso   ¿Qué modo?

D. Toribio   Uno que yo sé.

D. Alonso   ¿Qué es?

D. Toribio   Desposarnos, y que
vamos a Roma por todo.

[Vanse.]

D. Félix   Yo estimo la confianza.

D. Juan   Pues habiendo reparado
que al verme el color mudado,
hizo su rostro mudanza,
que no la hizo, sospecho,
su amor, y que está constante,
porque es el rostro volante
del reloj que anda en el pecho.
Y así, pues que sólo ha sido
mi dicha el haber llegado
donde de vos amparado
sea amor tan bien nacido;
lo que habéis de hacer por mí
(puesto que entablada ya
la amistad del padre está),
es proseguir desde aquí
de suerte, que con entrar
vos en su casa, me dé
ocasión amor en que
pueda escribir, ver y hablar.

D. Félix
[Aparte.]   (¡En buen empeño de amor
estoy! Pues en lance igual,
si a un amigo soy leal,
soy a otro amigo traidor.)

D. Juan   ¿No me respondéis?

which daughter I shall be bestowing
to your loving care.

TORIBIO   Hey! I just   1720
remembered. Don't you have to go
to Rome to get a dispensation?

ALONSO   Yes. Rome must sign the proclamation.

TORIBIO   Well then, my lord, if that is so,
the process takes too long. Let's prune   1725
it.

ALONSO   How?

TORIBIO   Bring it to rapid end.

ALONSO   Yes, but how?

TORIBIO   Betroth us, then send
us to Rome for our honeymoon.

[They exit.]

[Enter Don Félix and Don Juan.]

FÉLIX   Many thanks for your confidence
in me.

JUAN   Well, I noticed that when   1730
she saw my face lose color, then
the color of her countenance
changed, which I am certain attests
to unchanging love we both feel:
since the face is the balance wheel   1735
of the clock which beats in our breasts.
How lucky for me that I drew
you for my friend, for you aid me
with such warm generosity,
love will learn gentleness from you.   1740
What you must do for me now (since
you've begun to make overtures
to that noble father of hers)
is to go on from there. Convince
him with some pretext to allow   1745
you to enter his house, which will
let me write notes to her, and fill
my eyes, and speak my lover's vow.

FÉLIX
[Aside]   (What a fix for an arbiter!
For in an affaire like this, if   1750
I am loyal to one, I miff
the other one as a traitor.)

JUAN   Well, what do you say?

D. Félix   No sé
qué os diga, don Juan, pues no
soy hombre tan bajo yo,
que ocasión procuraré
con nadie para engañarle.

D. Juan   ¿Cuál es mi amigo mayor?

[Sale don Pedro.]

D. Pedro   Don Félix, si de mi amor . . .

D. Félix

Que prosiga he de estorbarle.
A buen tiempo habéis venido,
y luego proseguiréis
lo que decirme queréis;
que quiero que prevenido
de una porfía en que estamos,
seáis juez.

[Aparte.]   (Así, vive Dios,
tengo de hablar con los dos.)

D. Pedro   El argumento esperamos.

D. Félix   Si un grande amigo os pidiera
que trabaseis amistad
con hombre de calidad,
para que fuese tercera
en su casa de su amor,
¿hiciéraislo vos?

D. Pedro   Yo sí.

D. Félix   Yo no.

D. Pedro   ¿Por qué?

D. Félix   Porque en mí
fuera escrúpulo traidor;
pues el día que llegara
de traición a otro que fuera*
mi amigo, preciso era
lo lograra o no lograra.
Si no lo lograra, ¿en qué
a mi amigo le servía?
y si lo lograra, hacía
una gran ruindad, porque
el que engañado de mi,
se daba ya por mi amigo,
ya lo era, y yo su enemigo:

*de traición a que otro fuera

FÉLIX   I don't know
                          what to tell you, Don Juan. I am
                          not the sort of man who can sham.   1755
                          Deceptive machinations go
                          against my nature. I can't lie.

JUAN   Tell me, which is the better friend?

[Enter Don Pedro.]

PEDRO   Don Félix: since you comprehend
                          my love . . .

FÉLIX
[Aside]   (I have the feeling I   1760
                          must stop him quickly.)
[Aloud]   You have come
                          at a good time, my friend; you may
                          tell me what you wanted to say
                          later. Right now you must become
                          judge in a dispute in which we   1765
                          find ourselves.
[Aside]   (This just will not do;
                          I will have to talk with these two!)

PEDRO   Well, what is this perplexity?

FÉLIX   If a good friend should request of
                          you to forge friendship with a man   1770
                          of quality, so that you can
                          advance the fortunes of his love
                          as go-between, do you suppose
                          you would?

PEDRO   I'd do it if I could.

FÉLIX   Not I.

PEDRO   Why not?

FÉLIX   My conscience would   1775
                          brand me a traitor, for it knows
                          if the day should come when one friend
                          asked me to commit treachery
                          to another, then I would be
                          a traitor, and surely offend.   1780
                          If I did not do it, then how
                          would I help the friend who requested?
                          By doing it, I'd have infested
                          myself with meanness, because now
                          the other friend, whom I'd deceived,   1785
                          who thought he could rely on me,
                          could not; because his enemy

es cierto; pues siendo así,
¿cómo es posible que yo
sea enemigo del que ya
por mi amigo se me da?
Luego si en no serlo no
es nada lo que consigo,
y en serlo consigo ser
su amigo, ¿cómo he de hacer
yo traición al que es mi amigo?

D. PEDRO   Siendo ésa vuestra opinión,
ya no tengo qué os decir.

[Vase.]

D. JUAN   Yo tampoco, y habré de ir
a buscar otra ocasión.

[Vase.]

D. FÉLIX   ¿Habrá desdicha mayor?
¿Que no me baste el no amar,
para saberme librar
de impertinencias de amor?
¿Qué haré entre uno y otro amigo,
que cada uno en su esperanza
hace de mí confianza?
Pues nada enmendar consigo,
viendo tan cerca a los dos
de la dama, ¿qué podré
de mi parte hacer? No sé
que haya medio, vive Dios,
si ya no es que a ver alcance
que las damas solas son
las que en cualquier ocasión
hacen bueno o malo el lance.
Mas ¿cómo podré atrevido
hablar en materia tal
a una mujer principal,
ni darme por entendido?
Cara a cara he de saber
si a los dos quiso o no quiso;
pero hasta dar el aviso,
un papel lo podrá hacer;
que a su opinión no se atreve
quien por salvar su opinión,
la advierte de una ocasión.
Ahora falta quien le lleve,
pero ¿ha de faltarme modo,
sin que lo llegue a fiar
de otro, de poderle dar?

I had become. So I achieved
nothing. And so I ask you, do
you think it right if I malign   1790
one who would be a friend of mine?
If I'm his enemy, do you
agree I gain no dividend?
And if I'm not his enemy,
am I not his friend? Don't you see: 1795
how can I then deceive my friend?

PEDRO   There's nothing I can say, if you
                   are so completely disinclined.

[Pedro exits.]

JUAN   Me either. I will have to find
                   some other method that will do.   1800

[Juan exits.]

FÉLIX   Can there be worse predicaments
                   than these? Even though I refuse
                   to love, I cannot disabuse
                   myself of love's impertinence.
                   What can I do, caught here between   1805
                   two friends? For each hopeful gallant
                   enlists me as his confidant.
                   I'm sure I cannot intervene
                   for myself, seeing my two good
                   friends so close to that lady. What   1810
                   can I do? What chance have I got?
                   There is no way . . . unless I could
                   manage to visit the girl and
                   let her choose for herself whichever
                   she wants; unless she wills it, never   1815
                   can any lover's requests stand
                   a chance of success. But I don't
                   see where I'll find the courage to
                   speak without giving her the true
                   picture. I am certain I won't   1820
                   find out until I ask her, face
                   to face, did she love them or not.
                   And yet, to unravel that knot
                   a written note might take the place
                   of a visit. Yes, I could give her   1825
                   a note without risking that she
                   form a bad opinion of me.
                   Yes, a note. But who would deliver
                   it? Now that I think about it,
                   I do not dare to trust my note   1830
                   to any but the one who wrote

Ahora bien, salir a todo
me toca, haciendo testigos
los cielos, que aventurar
yo un empeño, es por sacar
de otro empeño a dos amigos.

[Vase, y salen doña Eugenia, doña Clara,
Brígida, y Mari-Nuño.]

CLARA   Ten, Mari-Nuño, este manto.
¡Oh quíen en casa tuviera
capellán, para no ir fuera,
y más a concurso tanto!

EUGENIA   Mucho me holgara venir
ahora de buen humor,
para poder con mejor
título que tú, decir:
¡quién la parroquia tuviera
diez leguas, para tener
más que andar y más que ver!

MARI-NUÑO   Aténgome a la primera.

BRÍGIDA   Yo a la segunda.

MARI-NUÑO   ¿Por qué?

BRÍGIDA   Porque no he visto en mi vida
escrupulosa aturdida,
que al primer lance no dé
de ojos.

[Salen don Alonso y don Toribio.]

D. ALONSO   En tu cuarto espera,
que yo la llegaré a hablar.

D. TORIBIO   Sí haré.
                     Desde aquí escuchar
lo que responde quisiera.

[Quédase don Toribio al paño.]

D. ALONSO
[Aparte.]   (Saber que a Eugenia eligió
ha sido ventura extraña:
llévesela a la montaña,
porque lo menos que yo
en la corte he menester,

it. So be it. I will commit
the folly myself. Heaven be
my witness, I take on this task
only because my two friends ask,   1835
and thus one risk will help all three.

[Félix exits.]

[A room in Don Alonso's house]
[Eugenia, Clara, Brígida and Mari-Nuño]

CLARA   Mari-Nuño, please take my shawl.
Oh, wouldn't it be nice to have
a chaplain in our house, to save
us from going out among all   1840
those people!

EUGENIA   So say you. But my
idea is the opposite.
You love calm. I want none of it.
That is why I laugh when I cry:
Oh, wouldn't it be fine if we   1845
lived in a parish ten leagues wide,
so we could spend all day outside
looking.

MARI-NUÑO   The first one is for me.

BRÍGIDA   I'll take the second one.

MARI-NUÑO   Why's that?

BRÍGIDA   Because I've never seen a vain,   1850
scruple-parading scatterbrain
who, at first shot, did not fall flat
on her face.

[Exit Mari-Nuño and Brígida.]
[Enter Don Alonso and Don Toribio, who stays by the door.]

ALONSO   Wait in your room now,
and I will go and speak with her.

TORIBIO   I will.
[Aside]   (However, I prefer   1855
to hide here to listen to how
she answers.)

[He hides behind a curtain.]

ALONSO
[Aside]   (To think that he chose
Eugenia: what a lucky break!
How I hope he decides to take
her back to the Mountains! God knows   1860
the very last thing I need here

es una hija discreta,
retórica ni poeta,
y no de mal parecer.)
Eugenia, yo vengo a hablarte;
no tienes, Clara, que irte;

[A Eugenia.]

que albricias he de pedirte

[A Clara.]

del pésame que he de darte.

EUGENIA   ¿Albricias a mí, señor?

CLARA   ¿Pésame, señor, a mí?

D. ALONSO   Pésame y albricias, sí.

LAS DOS   ¿De qué?

D. ALONSO   Efectos son de amor.
                   Don Toribio, enamorado,
                   me ha dicho cuánto desea
                   que Eugenia su mujer sea;
                   y aunque ponerte en estado

[A Clara.]   a tí, por ser la mayor,
                   primera obligación era,
                   él elige de manera,
                   que del gozo y del dolor,
                   pésame tuyo a ser pasa.

[A Eugenia.]   Hoy tu parabién, por ver
[A las dos.]   que pierdes, y ganas, ser
                   la cabeza de tu casa.

CLARA   Aunque pérdida es penosa,
                   yo estimo que el bien posea
                   Eugenia, para que sea
                   mi hermana la venturosa,
                   feriando el pesar a precio
                   del parabién que la doy.
                   Gócesle mil años.

[Aparte.]   (Hoy,
                   sólo hizo gusto el desprecio.)

[Vase.]

D. TORIBIO
                   ¡Qué triste va de perderme
                   la escudera de su hermana!
                   Veamos ella qué ufana
                   responde de merecerme.

EUGENIA
                   Esto sólo me faltaba

	at court is a gabby, poetic,	
	indiscreet daughter, who's frenetic	
	and beautiful as well, I fear.)	
[Aloud]	Eugenia, I must talk with you.	1865
	Clara, there is no need to go.	
[To Eugenia]		
	There's good news I want you to know.	
[To Clara]		
	However, there is bad news too.	
EUGENIA	There is good news for me, my lord?	
CLARA	My lord, you have bad news for me?	1870
ALONSO	Good news and bad news too, you'll see.	
THE GIRLS	How's that?	
ALONSO	They are both love's reward.	
	Don Toribio, filled with love, has	
	told me how very satisfied	
	he would be to have as his bride	1875
	Eugenia; though you, Clara, as	
	the older of my daughters, I	
	should marry first. He made his choice,	
	asking us to mourn and rejoice	
	at the same time. So I comply.	1880
	Clara, you have my sympathy.	
	Eugenia, your new life begins.	
	One loses and the other wins	
	leadership of the family.	
CLARA	Although this loss causes me pain,	1885
	I acknowledge with genuine	
	good feeling that Eugenia win	
	this prize, that my sister attain	
	such good fortune. Therefore I'll nurse	
	my grief with my good wishes for	1890
	her pleasure.	
[Aside]	(My scorn for him bore	
	good fruit today. Oh, how much worse	
	it could have been!)	
[Clara exits.]		
TORIBIO [Aside]	(At losing me	
	how sad this squiring sister goes!	
	Let's see how the other one shows	1895
	pride at being worthy of me.)	
EUGENIA [Aside]	(So many new things have occurred	

de añadir (confusa estoy)
a las novedades de hoy.

D. ALONSO   ¿Qué me respondes? Acaba
de dudar.

EUGENIA   Que agradecida
una y mil veces, señor,
rindo por tanto favor
a tu obediencia mi vida
que aunque no me toca a mí
elegir, pues no he de hacer
nunca más que obedecer,
haré mal, si viendo en ti
gusto, en mi primo amor fiel,
no respondo agradecida.

[Aparte.]   (¡Mal haya mi alma y mi vida,
si me casare con él!)

D. ALONSO   No en vano esperaba yo
de tu mucho entendimiento,
Eugenia, ese rendimiento.

D. TORIBIO
Yo también.

D. ALONSO   El esperó
en su cuarto, y ganar quiero
con él las gracias también.

D. TORIBIO
Que a mí las gracias me den,
será más razón.

EUGENIA   Hoy muero,
pues tras mis penas, he sido
objeto de un ignorante.

[Sale don Toribio.]

D. TORIBIO
[Aparte.]   (¡Qué airoso sale un amante,
cuando está favorecido!)
Sea muy enhorabuena
el ser, prima, tan dichosa,
que merezcáis ser mi esposa.

EUGENIA
¡Esto faltaba a mi pena!

[Vuelve doña Eugenia la espalda.]

today. This is the very last
straw. God help me. I'm all aghast!)

ALONSO   Speak up. I cannot hear a word.   1900
Stop wavering.

EUGENIA   In deference,
my lord, I am so thankful for
your favors, that for evermore
I shall owe you obedience.
Since it is not for me to choose,   1905
but rather I have to obey,
dear father, everything you say,
I know that I cannot refuse,
especially since you are very
pleased that I'll be my cousin's wife,   1910
and he loves me . . .

[Aside]   (God take my life
and soul if ever I shall marry
that man!)

ALONSO   I did not hope in vain,
Eugenia, that you would consent,
given your loving temperament.   1915

TORIBIO
[Aside]   (Me either.)

ALONSO   Now I will explain
things to Don Toribio, who stayed
in his room: for I want to win
his thanks as well.

[Exit Alonso.]

TORIBIO
[Aside]   (Let him begin
by thanking me.)

EUGENIA   I am afraid   1920
that today I die, for I was
just promised to an idiot.

[Don Toribio comes out of hiding.]

TORIBIO
[Aside]   (Look at me, how proudly I strut
now that she loves me as she does.)

[Aloud]   Dearest cousin, will you allow   1925
me to recognize your just pride
at deserving to be my bride?

EUGENIA
[Aside]   (That's the last thing I needed now!)

D. TORIBIO   ¿Por qué adorándome . . .

EUGENIA
                                              ¡Ay Dios!

D. TORIBIO   . . . me desadoráis?

EUGENIA   Porque,
                  si antes con mi padre hablé,
                  ahora he de hablar con vos.
                  Señor don Toribio, yo,
                  por no responder aquí
                  resuelta a mi padre, di
                  una palabra, que no
                  he de cumplir, si supiera
                  perder mil veces, rendida
                  a sus enojos, la vida.
                  Y siendo desta manera
                  que no he de casar con vos,
                  de la elección desistid
                  que habéis hecho, y advertid
                  que estamos solos los dos:
                  y si de lo que aquí os digo,
                  algo a mi padre decís,
                  he de decir que mentís.

D. TORIBIO   ¿Cómo se habla eso conmigo,
                  escudera de mi casa,
                  ingrata, desconocida,
                  falsa, aleve y fementida?

EUGENIA   No deis voces; que esto pasa
                  entre los dos, y no es, no,
                  para que salga de aquí.

D. TORIBIO   ¿Vos no sois mi prima?

EUGENIA   Sí.

D. TORIBIO   ¿No soy vuestro esposo?

EUGENIA   No.

D. TORIBIO   Decidme, ¿no soy galante?

EUGENIA   No lo dudo.

D. TORIBIO   ¿Y entendido?

EUGENIA   ¿Pues no?

D. TORIBIO   ¿Hidalgo?

EUGENIA   Cierto ha sido.

TORIBIO	Tell me why it is you adore me . . .	
EUGENIA *[Aside, turning her back on him]*	(God!)	
TORIBIO	. . . by unadoring me.	1930

EUGENIA
Before, I was forced to agree
with my father. Not any more!
Sir Don Toribio, you should know
that because I could not deny
my father's wishes, just now I   1935
promised a thing that I have no
intention of ever fulfilling,
even if his anger should make
me lose my life. Make no mistake:
there is no way I would be willing   1940
to marry you. So please desist
in pressing your affection on
me. I won't marry you. Be gone!
Here we're alone; if you persist,
and tell my father what I've said,   1945
then be sure, Don Toribio, I
will tell him it is all a lie.

TORIBIO
Woman, are you out of your head?
How can you talk to me this way?
You treacherous squire, you ingrate,   1950
you false, wily, vile reprobate!

EUGENIA
Hush! Be quiet! This must all stay
between us. Father must not know
any of it. It must not leave
here.

TORIBIO   You're my cousin?

EUGENIA   I believe   1955
so.

TORIBIO   And am I your husband?

EUGENIA   No!

TORIBIO   Am I gallant enough, pray tell?

EUGENIA   No doubt at all.

TORIBIO   Of wise discourse?

EUGENIA   For sure.

TORIBIO   A nobleman?

EUGENIA   Of course.

D. TORIBIO	¿Airoso?

EUGENIA   Mucho.

D. TORIBIO   ¿Y amante?

EUGENIA   También.

D. TORIBIO   Pues de mis cuidados
¿en qué estriban mis desvelos?

EUGENIA   Preguntádselo a los cielos,
a los astros y a los hados,
que no inclinan mi albedrío.

D. TORIBIO   Pues en algo está el busilis.

EUGENIA   En que vos no tenéis filis
para ser esposo mío.

D. TORIBIO   ¿Cómo que filis no tengo?
¡Tal a un hombre se le dice,
que tiene un solar con más
de tantísimos de filis,
que no hay otra cosa en él,
por do quiera que se mire,
sino filis como borra?
Que aunque yo qué es no adivine,
bien lo puedo asegurar;
pues siendo algo que sea insigne,
es preciso que no deje
de estar allá entre mis timbres.
¡A mí, que filis no tengo!
¿Esto los cielos permiten?
¿Esto consienten los hados?
Prima, ved lo que dijisteis:
más filis tengo que vos.

[Sale don Alonso.]

D. ALONSO   ¿Adónde, sobrino, os fuisteis,
cuando os busco para daros
mil norabuenas felices
de que vuestra prima ya,
agradecida y humilde,
sabiendo vuestra elección,
no hay cosa que más estime?

D. TORIBIO   Mi prima (si es que es mi prima)
es una mujer terrible,
con todos sus aderezos
de sirena, áspid y esfinge.
Aquí me ha dicho una cosa,
que no pudiera decirse

TORIBIO	Genteel?	
EUGENIA	Yes.	
TORIBIO	A lover as well?	1960
EUGENIA	That's right.	
TORIBIO	Why this antipathy, then, and why this unpleasant mask?	
EUGENIA	Ask the heavens to tell you; ask the planets, or ask destiny why none of them inclined my will.	1965
TORIBIO	It can't be something that I lack.	
EUGENIA	It's that you haven't got the knack to be my husband, or the skill.	

[Eugenia exits.]

TORIBIO	What do you mean I haven't got the knack? How can you speak such rot about my ancestral estate where so many knacks congregate they fill every available nook and cranny, chair and table? I've got more knacks than I've got hay. Even if I don't know what they are, I am certain beyond doubt that I have lots of them about; if they are precious, they must be with my proofs of nobility. How can you tell me I have no knacks? How can heaven let this go? Why have the fates not struck you dead? Cousin, you can't mean what you said! I have more knacks than anyone.	1970 1975 1980 1985

[Enter Don Alonso.]

ALONSO	Tell me, cousin, where did you run when I have been looking for you to congratulate you. Your new fiancée, your cousin, has told me that her joy is manifold because you've chosen her, and she is as happy as she can be.	1990
TORIBIO	That terrible cousin of mine (if that she be) is a great swine, a horrible, ungrateful minx, worse than the siren, asp, or sphinx. Just now she told me something so awful and crude that there is no	1995

a un barquillero asturiano
de los de quite y desquite.

D. ALONSO   ¿A vos?

D. TORIBIO   En toda esta cara.

D. ALONSO   Fuerza será que me admire.
¿Qué fue?

D. TORIBIO   Que filis no tengo.
Y para que se averigüe
si los hombres como yo
tienen o no tienen filis,
por no obligarme a retarla
en extranjeros países,
haced que me compren luego
cuantos filis sean vendibles,
y cuesten lo que costaren.

D. ALONSO   Esa es locura terrible.

D. TORIBIO   ¿Tan caros son? Pues no importa.
Dónde se venden, decidme,
o yo lo preguntaré;
que volver no se permite
a su vista, hasta volver
todo cargado de filis.

[Vase.]

D. ALONSO   ¿Hay delirio semejante?
Sobrino, escuchad, oídme.

[Salen doña Clara, y doña Eugenia.]

CLARA   ¿Qué es esto? ¿Con quién das voces?

EUGENIA   ¿Con quién te enojas y riñes?

D. ALONSO   Contigo, ingrata.

EUGENIA   ¿Conmigo,
el día que más humilde
sólo trato obedecerte?

D. ALONSO   Ven acá. ¿Qué le dijiste
a tu primo, que enojado,
no hay quien con él se averigüe?

EUGENIA   ¡Yo a mi primo! En todo hoy
ni le hablé ni vi.

	way to say it, even to an Asturian ferryboatman!	2000
ALONSO	She said something to you?	
TORIBIO	Right here in my face.	
ALONSO	That seems very queer. What was it?	
TORIBIO	That I have no knack! I don't see how she can attack somebody as extraordinary as I am, someone who's the very cream of nobility, and say I have no knack! But to forestay my challenging her to a duel on some foreign battlefield, you'll just have to help me to obtain some, and hang the cost!	2005 2010
ALONSO	That's insane!	
TORIBIO	They cost that much?! Well, I don't care. If you want to help, tell me where they sell them, or I will have to ask someone else. I'm telling you, I won't visit her, or relax, until I'm loaded up with knacks.	2015

[Toribio exits.]

ALONSO	I've never seen such lunacy. Nephew, wait! Stop! Listen to me!	2020

[Clara and Eugenia enter.]

CLARA	What's this? Who are you shouting at?	
EUGENIA	Who are you angry at? What's that noise?	
ALONSO	With you, you ungrateful thing.	
EUGENIA	With me, when I do everything I can do to humbly obey?	2025
ALONSO	Come over here. What did you say to your cousin, who's so upset nobody knows what makes him fret?	
EUGENIA	To my cousin? I did not see him all day long.	

D. ALONSO   ¿Qué dices?

EUGENIA   Lo que es cierto.

D. ALONSO   ¡Vive Dios,
               si disimulada finges,
               y es verdad que le has hablado
               bachilleramente libre,
               que te he de hacer! Tras él voy,
               por si puedo reducirle
               a que no ande preguntando
               adónde se venden filis.

[Vase.]

EUGENIA   Yo a mi primo, ¿qué pudiera,
               que fuese ofensa, decirle?

CLARA   No te disculpes conmigo,
               pues sé, aunque no llegué a oírte,
               que perderás tu remedio,
               sólo por decir un chiste.

EUGENIA   Aunque eso de mi remedio
               con falsedad me lo dices,
               lo oigo yo como lisonja,
               viendo que hasta un tonto, un simple,
               aún el alma que no tiene,
               a mi vanidad la rinde.

CLARA   ¿Qué quieres decirme en eso?
               ¿Que nadie hay que a mí se incline,
               neciamente imaginando
               que a méritos me compites?
               Pues no es sino que no hay nadie
               que sin respeto me mire,
               porque sé yo hacer que todos
               de otra manera me estimen
               que a ti, siendo solamente
               lo que a las dos nos distingue,
               el verte a ti no sé cómo,
               pero a mí como a imposible.

EUGENIA   ¡Ay! que no es eso.

CLARA   Pues, ¿qué?

EUGENIA   Obligarásme a decirte
               lo que a mi primo.

CLARA   ¿Qué es?

EUGENIA   Que
               tampoco tú tienes filis.

ALONSO   How can that be?   2030

EUGENIA   I'm telling the truth.

ALONSO   God help you,
                 Eugenia, if it is not true,
                 and I discover that you were
                 babbling rudely to him, then you're
                 going to get such a . . . Now let   2035
                 me try to locate him, and get
                 him off this imbecilic track
                 of asking where to buy a knack.

[Exit Alonso.]

EUGENIA   What could I possibly tell my
                 cousin to make him vilify   2040
                 me?

CLARA   Don't waste your excuses on
                 me. I didn't have to hear one
                 word to know all about it. You'd
                 give up your future for a crude
                 joke.

EUGENIA   You disdain me when you mention   2045
                 my future with such condescension;
                 but for me it's a compliment,
                 since it means any indolent
                 simpleton surrenders his soul,
                 if he has one, to my control.   2050

CLARA   And what exactly do you mean?
                 That there is no one who is keen
                 on me, because they foolishly
                 think that you can compete with me?
                 Well, if you want to be correct,   2055
                 they all look at me with respect,
                 because I know very well how
                 to make them think the fates endow
                 me with virtues you've never seen.
                 The biggest difference between   2060
                 us is that you're accessible,
                 and I am quite untouchable.

EUGENIA   That's not it.

CLARA   Well?

EUGENIA   It's nothing; but
                 you are just like our cousin.

CLARA   What?

EUGENIA   Well, without getting personal,   2065
                 you don't have any knack at all!

[Vase.]

CLARA   No lo dirás, porque yo
a responder no me obligue,
que cuando . . . Pero ¿qué miro?
¿Quién hay que esta cuadra pise,
para estorbar el que lleguen
mis enojos a sus fines?
¿A quién buscáis, caballero?

[Sale don Félix.]

D. FÉLIX
[Aparte.]   (¡Ay amistad! pues que vine
a hacer por ti una fineza,
no a una infamia me inclines;
pues vi hermosura, a quien mal
mi libertad se resiste.)
Viendo a vuestro primo ir fuera,
a quien vuestro padre sigue,
me atreví a llegar a hablaros.

CLARA   ¿A mí?

D. FÉLIX   A vos.

CLARA   Hombre, ¡qué dices!
¿A mí a hablarme?

D. FÉLIX   Sí, señora,
porque sé que en esto os sirve
mi deseo, y no os ofende.

CLARA

            ¡Plegue a Dios, que no me obligue
una necia a que me huelgue
de qué! . . . Pero no es posible.

[Sale Eugenia al paño.]

EUGENIA

            ¿Con quién hablará mi hermana?
Desde aquí es bien que lo mire.

CLARA   ¿A mí dejadme dudarlo
mil veces,
[Aparte.]   (mal reprimirme
puedo.)
            me buscáis?

D. FÉLIX   A vos.

CLARA   Pues antes que oséis decirme . . .

[Exit Eugenia.]

CLARA   You only say that to me to
               get me to answer back to you,
               but when I . . . Say, what's that I see?
               Who is it spying there on me,   2070
               and preventing my anger from
               ruining my equilibrium?
               Good sir, who are you looking for?

FÉLIX
[Aside]   (Oh, friendship! I came to implore
               this woman on your behalf. Don't   2075
               make me do something that I won't
               be proud of. I look at her, and
               know my free will cannot withstand.)
[Aloud]   Seeing your cousin go outside,
               and that your father walked beside   2080
               him, I dared to converse with you.

CLARA   With me?

FÉLIX   With you.

CLARA   That will not do,
               sir. You would talk with me?

FÉLIX   Yes, my
               lady, for I know in this I
               serve you, and do you no offense.   2085

CLARA
[Aside]   (I hope to God the consequence
               of her foolishness won't make me
               play the fool . . . ! But that cannot be.)

[Eugenia enters and hides behind the curtain.]

EUGENIA
[Aside]   (Who is my sister talking to?   2090
               From here I can see what they do.)

CLARA   Serve me? I doubt that a thousand
               times.
[Aside]   (Things are getting out of hand.)
[Aloud]   You would serve me?

FÉLIX   My lady, yes
               I would.

CLARA   Well, before you address   2095
               me more . . .

EUGENIA

    ¡Oh si fuera algo de aquello
de posible y de imposible!

CLARA

    . . . quién sois y qué me queréis,
que os vais es bien que os suplique,
sin decirlo; que a mí nada
hay que a buscarme os obligue.

D. FÉLIX

    Sin deciroslo, me iré,
si en eso mi pecho os sirve;
mas no sin que lo sepáis;
que en este papel se escribe,
para que con esto llegue
a saberse, sin decirse.

EUGENIA

    ¡Oh si tomara el papel,
porque hubiera qué decirle!

D. FÉLIX

    Tomad, y adiós.

CLARA

               ¡Yo papel!

D. FÉLIX

    Y porque a verle os anime,
sólo os diré que el honor
vuestro en leerle consiste,
y que don Pedro y don Juan
no arriesguen y precipiten,
no digo su vida, que ese
es peligro muy humilde,
sino vuestro honor, que fuera
pérdida más infelice.

EUGENIA

    Si toma el papel, soy muerta.

CLARA

    Hombre, mira lo que dices.
Ni a ti, a don Juan, ni a don Pedro
conozco yo.

EUGENIA

             ¡Ay de mí triste!
Que todo esto sobre mí
viene, si el papel recibe.
Mas por engaño la habla.

CLARA
[Aparte.]

    (¿Qué sola una vez que quise
yo no ser yo, no he podido?)
¿Qué aguardas pues para irte?

EUGENIA
[Aside]   (Oh, if this spectacle
                    were unreal or impossible!)

CLARA   . . . and tell me who you are and what
                    you want, sir, you must depart. Cut
                    short this speech; for no courtesy   2100
                    obligates you to talk with me.

FÉLIX   If that's what you want, I will say
                    no more, and take myself away.
                    But I won't leave you ignorant,
                    for in this letter, which you can't   2105
                    ignore, it's written down. Although
                    I speak no further, you will know.

EUGENIA
[Aside]   (Oh, how I hope she takes the letter;
                    then I'll know for sure I can get her!)

FÉLIX   Take it then, and goodbye.

CLARA   Indeed   2110
                    not!

FÉLIX   To be certain you will read
                    it, I'll say, for your benefit,
                    your honor hangs on reading it.
                    That Don Pedro and Don Juan should
                    not endanger their lives, which would   2115
                    after all be only a minor
                    loss, but should risk something much finer
                    and a loss much greater by far:
                    your honor, prize most singular!

EUGENIA
[Aside]   (If she takes the letter I'll die!)   2120

CLARA   My good sir, look what you say. I
                    don't know any Pedro or Juan
                    or even you.

EUGENIA
[Aside]   (My luck is gone!
                    All this will come down on my head;
                    if she takes that letter I'm dead!   2125
                    And yet, I think his words deceive.)

CLARA
[Aside]   (The first time I wanted to leave
                    my body to become someone
                    else, I can't!)

[Aloud]   Sir, you have not gone?

D. FÉLIX

Ya que tan desentendido
vuestro decoro porfíe,
y agradecer no pretenda
la fineza de que os dije
mi empeño y el de los dos;
ya que lo que debo hice
a amigo y a caballero,
me iré. Adiós.

CLARA
[Aparte.]

No os vais, oídme.

(Sin duda que aquí hay engaño,
y así, es bien que le averigüe.)
¿Con quién presumís que habláis,
porque la fineza estime?

D. FÉLIX

¿No sois doña Eugenia?

CLARA
                                            Sí.

EUGENIA

¿Hay mujer más infelice?

CLARA

Dad ahora el papel, y adiós.

EUGENIA

Que le deje es bien que evite,
barajando el lance. Hermana . . .

CLARA

¿Qué tienes? ¿De qué te afliges?

EUGENIA

Mi padre y mi primo vienen,
y porque tú no peligres,
vengo a avisarte; que yo
ya tú ves cuánto estoy libre.
Mira lo que hemos de hacer.

D. FÉLIX

¿Quién vio empeño tan terrible?

CLARA

¿Qué se ha de hacer, sino que entren
y que todo se averigüe
para que no quedes vana
tú de que por mí lo hiciste?
¡Padre! ¡Señor! ¡Primo! ¡Otáñez!

EUGENIA

Si fuera cierto el venite,
muy buen lance hubiera echado.

CLARA

¿No hay nadie que pueda oirme?

FÉLIX   My lady, though you refuse to   2130
                    change your attitude, nor will you
                    even thank me for those fine things
                    I said, which such elegance brings
                    to my suit and that of my friends;
                    since I have said what each intends,   2135
                    I shall take leave of you. Goodbye.

CLARA   No, don't go. Listen to what I
                    have to say.
[Aside]   (There must be some trick
                    here; let me see what makes it tick.)
[Aloud]   With all that elegant confessing,   2140
                    whom did you think you were impressing?

FÉLIX   Aren't you Doña Eugenia?

CLARA   Yes.

EUGENIA
[Aside]   (Can a woman feel more distress?)

CLARA   Give me the letter then; goodbye.

EUGENIA
[Aside]   (I must keep that letter from my   2145
                    sister. I'll shuffle and redeal
                    the cards.)
[Aloud]   Sister . . .

CLARA   What makes you squeal
                    like that?

EUGENIA   My father's coming here
                    with my cousin. But have no fear,
                    I've warned you in time. So you see   2150
                    you cannot blame this mess on me.
                    You have to think what we must do.

FÉLIX
[Aside]   (Have ever things gone so askew?)

CLARA   There is nothing to do, but call
                    them in here to discover all   2155
                    that's going on. So you can't flount
                    that it was all on my account.
                    Cousin! Otáñez! Father! Lord!

EUGENIA
[Aside]   (Just imagine what a reward
                    they'd have given me if they'd come   2160
                    in fact!)

CLARA   Are you all deaf and dumb?

D. Alonso   Voces de Clara.
[Dentro.]

Eugenia
                                  ¡Ay de mí!
                   Que ya es verdad lo que dije
                   por fingimiento.

Clara   Llegad
                   todos.

Eugenia   No a voces publiques
                   que está aquí este hombre.

Clara   Sí quiero.

D. Félix   Aquí es bien que me retire,
                   por asegurar la espalda.

[Escóndese, y salen don Alonso, don Toribio, Brígida,
Mari-Nuño, y Otáñez.)

Todos   ¿Qué es esto?

Clara   Que un hombre . . .

Eugenia
                                              ¡Ay triste!

Clara   . . . dentro está de nuestra casa.
                   Yo desde aquesos jardines
                   le he visto en el corredor
                   del desván: por un tabique
                   saltó. Subid allá todos:
                   quedarse no solicite
                   a robarnos esta noche.

D. Alonso   Aquesos serán sus fines.

Mari-Nuño   En casa de indiano, ¿quién
                   duda que eso solicite?

D. Toribio   Nadie primero que yo
                   el primer escalón pise;
                   que a mí me toca el asalto,
                   si fuese el desván Mastrique.
                   Vea mi prima que tengo
                   pujanza, ya que no filis.

[*Offstage*]
ALONSO   That's Clara shouting.

EUGENIA
[*Aside*]   (Woe is me!
                   What I pretended so falsely
                   has just come true!)

CLARA   Come over here,
                   everybody!

EUGENIA   Don't let them hear   2165
                   this man is with us.

CLARA   Yes I will.

FÉLIX   I think I'll leave while I can still
                   get out of here.

[*Don Félix hides; Don Alonso, Don Toribio, Brígida, Mari-Nuño, and Otáñez
enter.*]

ALL   What is this noise?

CLARA   There is a man . . .

EUGENIA
[*Aside*]   (Now she destroys
                   me!)

CLARA   . . . somewhere inside our house. From   2170
                   the back garden I saw him come
                   into the attic corridor.
                   I saw him jump from wall to floor.
                   Run after him. Don't let him keep
                   hidden, to rob us while we sleep.   2175

ALONSO   I'm sure that's what he wants to do.

MARI-NUÑO   In an American's house, who
                   can doubt that that must be his plan?

TORIBIO   Stop! The first step is mine. No man
                   must set his foot on it before   2180
                   I. I shall be the conqueror
                   of the stairs, climb from floor to floor
                   and lead the charge, as if this were
                   Algiers! Let my cousin infer
                   my valor from this brave attack,   2185
                   even if I don't have a knack.

[*Toribio exits.*]

2184 Algiers: as if he were attacking the Moors

D. Alonso   Contigo voy.

Clara   Subid vos,
             Otáñez.

Otáñez   Ya a los dos siguen
             los filos de la Tizona.
             Conmigo van dos mil Cides.

Clara   Vosotras, desde allá dentro,
             ved que entrar no solicite
             por otra parte a esconderse.

Mari-Nuño   Un argos seré.

Brígida   Yo un lince.

Clara   Todas tus bachillerías
             mira de lo que te sirven,
             que al primer lance te pasmas,
             y al primer susto te rindes.
             Ya tienes franca la puerta,
             hombre: ya bien puedes irte.
             Déjame el papel, y adiós.

[Sale don Félix.]

D. Félix   El os guarde: y pues difícil
             no es lo que os advierto, ved
             lo que importa.

[Dala el papel.]

Eugenia
[Aparte.]   (¡Ay de mí triste!
             ¿Que no pudiese estorbarlo?)

D. Félix

             Amor, no me precipites,
             que aunque ingenio y hermosura
             todo en ella se compite,

ALONSO   I'm with you.

[Alonso exits.]

CLARA   Otáñez, you go
                  with them.

OTÁÑEZ   I will strike such a blow
                  with my "Tizona's" cutting blade
                  that he will think the Cid has laid   2190
                  into him.

[Exit Otáñez.]

CLARA   You go inside there
                  to guard the bottom of the stair,
                  just in case that rapscallion thinks
                  to hide down here.

MARI-NUÑO   I'll be a lynx.

[Exit Mari-Nuño.]

BRÍGIDA   I'll be an Argos.

[Exit Brígida.]

CLARA   All your schemes   2195
                  are not worth one whit now, it seems.
                  The first shot gives you such a fright
                  that you give up before the fight.

[She goes to where Don Félix is hiding.]
                  You'll find the door is open wide,   2200
                  good sir: it's safe to go outside.
                  But first give me the note, and then
                  goodbye.

FÉLIX   Goodbye then. But again
                  I repeat, read this note, and see
                  how it profits you.

[He gives her the letter.]

EUGENIA
[Aside]   (Woe is me!   2205
                  There was no way I could prevent
                  it.)

FÉLIX
[Aside, as he goes]   (Love, don't work your devilment
                  on me. Although beauty and wit
                  together make her exquisite

_____

2189 Tizona: the sword of Rodrigo Díaz de Vivar, Spain's medieval epic hero known as El Cid.
2194 lynx: animal known for its acute eyesight
2195 Argos: mythological creature with 100 eyes

es dama de mis amigos,
y adorarla es imposible.

[Vase.]

CLARA

¡Señor! Ya el hombre a otra casa
pasado ha; no solicites
buscarle.

[Salen todos.]

D. ALONSO

       Forzoso era,
pues no fue hallarle posible.

D. TORIBIO

Nigromántica es su dicha,
pues me le ha hecho invisible.

CLARA

Digo que pasó a otra casa,
que yo le vi sano y libre.

D. ALONSO

Con todo eso, a verla toda
vamos.

D. TORIBIO

     Y ahora, ¿qué dices?
¿Tengo o no filis?

[Vanse.]

EUGENIA

        No sé,
que ahora no estoy para filis.

CLARA

Esto, necia, presumida,
he hecho, para que mires
que tener valor y ingenio,
es tenerle y no decirle;
y vete de aquí, que quiero
ver lo que el papel me dice.

EUGENIA

No sosegaré (¡Ay de mí!)
hasta ver lo que la escribe.

[Vase.]

CLARA

De aquí la envié, porque
si este hombre este engaño finge
para escribirme a mí, ella
no lo entienda, ni imagine.

indeed, she is the lady of
my best friends; so I cannot love
her.)   2210

[Exit Félix]

CLARA
[Shouting]   My lord, I just saw the man
run across the street, so you can
stop looking for him.

[Don Alonso and Don Toribio enter.]

ALONSO   We had to
stop, for we could not find a clue   2215
to his whereabouts.

TORIBIO   He must be
a magician for, you see, he
has vanished completely.

CLARA   I said
I saw the man escape. He sped
across the street.

ALONSO   Well, nonetheless,   2220
I think it would be best to press
on with the search. Let's go.

TORIBIO   Now, do
I have the knack or not?

[Exit Alonso.]

EUGENIA   I'm through
with that knack stuff. Leave me alone!

[Toribio exits.]

CLARA   I did all this so you'd be shown   2225
once and for all, you idiot,
you presumptuous ninny, what
real valour and wit can be:
actions, not proud verbosity.
Run along while I read this note   2230
and see what the gentleman wrote.

EUGENIA
[Aside]   (Alas! I know I cannot rest
'til I see it, I'm so obsessed.)

[Exit Eugenia.]

CLARA   I sent them off, because if this
man is using an artifice   2235
to write to me instead, I'm sure
I should keep it secret from her.

[Lee.]

No se atreve a vuestro honor,
quien por vuestro honor se atreve
a presumir que os obliga
con lo mismo que os ofende.
Y así, en esta confianza
de pensar que errando acierte,
lo que hay que culparme vaya
por lo que hay que agradecerme.
Don Juan, más enamorado
que fue de vos, de vos vuelvo,
y don Pedro os sigue, más
fino cuanto más ausente.
Que dejen de declararse
no es posible, ni que dejen
de remitir al acero
la competencia, de suerte
que a dar escándalo pase;
y pues podéis facilmente
remediarlo con mandar
a don Pedro que se ausente,
o a don Juan que se retire,
quedándoos vos dueño siempre
del desdén y del favor,
quitad el inconveniente;
que a mí el aviso me toca,
procediendo desta suerte
con vos, conmigo y con ellos,
caballero, amigo y huésped.

¡Válgame Dios! Que de cosas
tan varias, tan diferentes,
en un punto me combaten,
y en un instante me vencen!
En lo que dice y no dice,
es muy cierto que me ofende
este papel: es verdad,
que si aqueste papel viene
a Eugenia, cuando pensaba*
que el papel para mí fuese,
solicitando aquel medio
que me ha obligado a leerle,
he sentido que no sea
su intento aquel, sino éste.
¿Cómo puedo yo decirlo,
si no es ya que en mí reviente
no sé qué callada mina
que amor en el alma enciende?
¿Amor dije? Pues no siento,
sino haber tan neciamente

*a hacer, que cuando pensaba

[She reads.]

"I'll not make bold with your honor,
though for it I shall make bold
to presume that what offends you   2240
obligates a hundred-fold.
    Though I err, the help I give you
well may file a counterclaim,
and the thanks that you shall give me
cancel out all of my blame.   2245
    Don Juan now loves you even more
than when he went away;
Don Pedro's passion, even when
he's absent, swells each day.
    There is no way to stop them from   2250
incessantly declaring
their love for you, and so I fear
their swords they'll soon be baring
    in open conflict, which will cause
a loud and awkward scandal.   2255
Yet you have the ability
this rivalry to handle:
    just tell Don Pedro to retire,
or make Don Juan refrain.
You still will have complete control   2260
of favor and disdain,
    and thus the problem you will solve,
and I my errand end,
with you, with them, and with myself,
host, gentlemen, and friend."   2265

How many varied things unite,
God have mercy on me!, to fight
with me simultaneously
and in one moment conquer me.
Both in its words and silences   2270
everything that this letter says
offends me. I am confident
that this letter was really meant
for Eugenia, even though I
thought for a time it might apply   2275
to me. And since he found the way
to make me read, to my dismay,
those terrible words, I know his
affections, and where his heart is.
Yet how can I even speak of   2280
this, unless some hot spark of love
has exploded the silent mine
that underlies my heart's design?
Did I say love? Well, I don't feel
a thing, save regret for the zeal   2285

>
> persuadídome que a mí
> me buscase: y es de suerte
> la vanidad de una dama
> persuadida a que la quieren,
> que aunque la ofenda el amor,
> más el engaño la ofende.
> Y más cuando está a la mira
> una necia, una imprudente,
> una loca . . .

[Al paño Eugenia.]

EUGENIA   Esta soy yo.

CLARA   De tan vanas altiveces,
que presume que ella sola
todo cuanto mira vence.
¡Oh envidia, oh envidia! ¡Cuánto
daño has hecho a las mujeres!
Pues por vengarme de Eugenia,
diera . . .

[Sale doña Eugenia.]

EUGENIA   ¿En qué Eugenia te ofende,
para pensar a tus solas
el cómo della te vengues?

CLARA   Este papel te lo diga.
Que acaso a mis manos viene
por las tuyas.

EUGENIA   Ya lo sé.

CLARA   Pues si lo sabes, y tienes
tan a riesgo tu opinión,
que estriba sólo en que lleguen
a declararse dos hombres;
mira si es justo que piense
cómo he de vengar, ingrata,
falsa, atrevida y aleve,
la ocasión en que . . .

EUGENIA   Oye, aguarda,
que para que consideres
tanta amenazada ruina
cuán fácil remedio tiene,
me huelgo de haber venido
a esta ocasión.

[Llega a la ventana.]

CLARA   ¿Pues qué emprendes?

which I mustered up to convince
myself, though without evidence,
that he meant me. What vanity
we women use, convincingly,
to persuade ourselves they love us.   2290
Hope of love is injurious,
but self-deceit is even worse.
And all the more when that perverse
ninny might by spying on me:

[Eugenia says, from behind the curtain,   2295
as an aside]   (That's me.)

CLARA   She is so haughty in her pride:
she thinks all men are gratified
by her looks and her looks alone.
Oh envy, oh envy! How prone
we women are to your sharp sting!   2300
I know I would give anything
to avenge myself on her.

[Eugenia enters.]

EUGENIA   Tell
me what I have done to compel
you to talk of revenge on me?

CLARA   This note, with crystal clarity,   2305
will tell you what you want to know.
By chance I read it, even though
it belongs to you.

EUGENIA   I know it.

CLARA   If you do, how can you permit
such a threat to your reputation,   2310
letting two men make declaration
of their love? And you ask me how
can this be just, and why I vow
—you false traitor, you reprobate—,
to take my vengeance.

EUGENIA   Listen, wait.   2315
Before you threaten me with such
mayhem or ruin, there's a much
easier solution, I'm sure.
Just watch me, how quickly I cure
your disease.

[Eugenia goes over to the window.]

CLARA   Now what?

EUGENIA
    ¡Señor don Pedro!

CLARA
              ¿Qué haces?

EUGENIA
    Hablar un instante breve
a un caballero, que está
en la calle.

CLARA
             ¿A esto te atreves?

EUGENIA
    Sí, que en su cuarto mi padre
está ya con su accidente
de la gota, que hoy le ha dado,
y don Toribio no puede
ver desde el suyo esta reja;
y así he de satisfacerte.
¡Señor don Pedro!

[Llega por dentro don Pedro a la reja.]

D. PEDRO
              Bien fue
menester oír dos veces
mi nombre, para que alguna
creyera que dél se acuerde
vuestra memoria; que un triste
no cree su bien facilmente.

EUGENIA
    No prosigáis, que esta reja
es de otras tan diferente,
cuanto hay de no serlo a ser
ahora de las paredes
de mi padre; y si allí pudo
la seguridad hacerme
usar de algunas licencias,
mi honor prisionera tiene
su libertad ya, y tan otra
habéis de ver que procede,
cuanto hay de que otros me guarden
a guardarme yo. Así, hacedme
merced de volveros luego
donde otra vez no os encuentre
ni en mi calle ni en mi reja,
suplicándoos que prudente
deis de mano a una esperanza
que no hay sobre qué se asiente.

D. PEDRO
    Oíd.

EUGENIA
        Perdonad, que no puedo.

EUGENIA
[*Shouting*]   Hello, sir!   2320
                    Hey! Don Pedro!

CLARA   What's all this stir?

EUGENIA   Calm down, I just want to talk for
                     a brief moment with this señor
                     who's there in the street.

CLARA   You would dare
                     do that?

EUGENIA   Of course, Father is where   2325
                     he can't hear us; with an attack
                     of gout he is flat on his back.
                     And Don Toribio, from his room
                     can't see this window, I presume.
                     So I will give you satisfaction.   2330
                     Don Pedro!

[*Don Pedro enters, and comes up to the window.*]

PEDRO   You see my reaction
                     is slow, though you called my name twice,
                     because I can't believe you're nice
                     enough now to remember me
                     even once. Such felicity   2335
                     comes hard to one who grieves.

EUGENIA   Don't go
                     on, please; the bars of this window
                     are from those windows where we met
                     as different as they can get.
                     And if there my knowing that I   2340
                     was secure made me satisfy
                     you much more freely than I should,
                     the honor of my maidenhood
                     now holds me prisoner. You'll see
                     me behave now as differently   2345
                     as is the difference between
                     one who finds herself overseen
                     by other people and one who
                     guards herself. So, therefore, will you
                     please remove yourself to some place   2350
                     where I will never see your face
                     again at my window or in
                     my street. Right now you must begin
                     to forget, and your hopes retract,
                     for they have no basis in fact.   2355

PEDRO   Listen . . .

EUGENIA   I cannot, for your sake.

D. Pedro   Cuando por veros . . .

Eugenia   Haréisme
                ser, sobre ingrata, grosera.

D. Pedro   ¿Vos?

Eugenia   Sí.

D. Pedro   ¿Cómo?

Eugenia   Desta suerte.

[Cierra la ventana.]

Clara   Y al otro ¿qué has de decirle?

Eugenia   Haz cuenta que si le viere,
                le diré lo mismo al otro,
                Clara; porque las mujeres
                como yo, puestas en salvo,
                si se esparcen y divierten,
                es para aquesto no más;
                que amor bachiller no tiene
                más fondo que sólo el ruido.
                Aquel emblema lo acuerde
                del perdido caminante,
                a quien de noche acontece
                que avisado del estruendo*
                con que del monte desciende
                pequeño arroyo, le asusta,
                le perturba y estremece;
                y huyendo dél, da en el río:
                porque a todos les parece
                que es manso cristal aquel
                que aún las guijas no le sienten
                y en su agua perecen. Pues
                que no tiene riesgo advierte
                la ruidosa, porque el riesgo
                el agua mansa le tiene:
                y así, fue del agua mansa
                lo mejor guardarse siempre.

[Vase.]

Clara   ¿Qué escucho, ¡cielos! qué escucho?
                "Que no tiene riesgo advierte
                la ruidosa, porque el riesgo
                el agua mansa le tiene:
                y así, fue del agua mansa
                lo mejor guardarse siempre."
                Sin duda (¡ay de mí!) que oyó
                cuanto dije, o lo parece,

*que alumbrado del estruendo

PEDRO   If I could only see . . .

EUGENIA   You'll make
                   me seem worse yet if I dismiss
                   you rudely.

PEDRO   You?

EUGENIA   Yes.

PEDRO   How?

EUGENIA   Like this!

[Eugenia closes the window.]

CLARA   What will you tell the other one?   2360

EUGENIA   If I see him, he'll be undone,
                   Clara, just like this one. Because
                   women like me, if no one draws
                   the line, seem loose, and to enjoy
                   themselves, but yet they don't destroy   2365
                   themselves. It's all a game. This kind
                   of puppy love, let me remind
                   you, is nothing but a lot of
                   noise. A good emblem for this love
                   is that of the lost traveler,   2370
                   who late at night hears a great stir
                   of crashing water that descends
                   the mount, and he misapprehends
                   the noise, trembles, and is afraid;
                   and wildly fleeing the cascade,   2375
                   he falls in the river, which all
                   perceived to be tranquil crystal
                   because they cannot even see
                   its current move, and cruelly
                   they perish there. The noisy stream   2380
                   warns it is what it does not seem:
                   completely safe; it is the still
                   waters that are likely to kill.
                   That's why all mothers warn their daughters:
                   "Always be wary of still waters."   2385

[Exit Eugenia.]

CLARA   Good heavens! What is this I hear?
                   That the noisy waters appear
                   risky but are safe, because still
                   waters are the waters that kill;
                   and thus all mothers warn their daughters: 2390
                   "Always be wary of still waters."
                   No doubt, alas!, my sister heard
                   what I said, every single word,

según el concepto habla
de lo que mi pecho siente.
Pues ya que el acaso hizo,
en las respuestas que ofrece,
lo que el cuidado debiera;
ya que por ella me tiene
el caballero que trajo
el papel, lograr intente
la ocasión, que con su nombre
amor a mi amor ofrece;
porque con más verdad pueda
decir que riesgo no tiene
la ruidosa, porque el riesgo
el agua mansa le tiene:
y así, fue del agua mansa
lo mejor guardarse siempre.

since she has so neatly expressed
everything I feel in my breast.   2395
But even though I answered him
by chance, with a capricious whim,
I gave the answers just as though
I had planned. Since he does not know
who I am, but takes me for her,   2400
then let chance make me luckier
still, so that I win, with her name,
love as bright as my own love's flame.
That way the old proverb will be
truer still, and they all will see   2405
that there's no risk in noisy rill,
for true danger lies with the still
stream: and thus, to avoid a slaughter,
one has to beware of still water.

Jornada Tercera

[Salen Clara y Mari-Nuño.]

CLARA
Esto pasa, y sólo a ti
lo dijera.

MARI-NUÑO
          Ya tú tienes
experiencia de lo mucho
que fiar de mi amor puedes.
Pero deja que me admire
de oir que a tal extremo lleguen
los despejos de tu hermana.

CLARA
Dos caballeros pretenden
su favor, y a mí me toca
que el escándalo remedie,
ya que llegó a mi noticia;
y así es fuerza hablar a este
que me dio el aviso. Y para
hacer que el daño se enmiende,
tú has de darle un papel mío
en su nombre, porque llegue,
ignorando que soy yo,
a hablarme más claramente
esta noche, y . . . Pero luego
proseguiré; que parece
que anda gente ahí fuera: mira
quién es.
          Bien de aquesta suerte
con la verdad se ha engañado
Mari-Nuño, que ha de hacerme
lugar para conseguir
hablarle de noche y verle,
ya que mi pena . . .

[Sale a la puerta don Toribio, y quiere entrar, y Mari-Nuño lo impide.]

MARI-NUÑO
                Esperad,
que no es bien que nadie entre,
sin avisar, a este cuarto.

D. TORIBIO
Dos veces para mí eres
dueña hoy.

MARI-NUÑO
          ¿De qué manera
se entiende eso de dos veces?

D. TORIBIO
Una en lo que estorbas, y otra
en lo que un cuarto defiendes.

Act III

[Clara and Mari-Nuño]

CLARA
That's what it is. You know I would   2410
tell only you.

MARI-NUÑO
    I am a good
friend of yours, and you can trust me
now, as before, unfailingly.
But I must tell you I am shocked
to discover just how half-cocked   2415
your sister is in her affairs.

CLARA
Each of two young gentlemen swears
his passion for her. I must put
things right since I know what's afoot.
That's why I must talk to the man   2420
who told me about it. I can
remedy the damage if you
will give him my letter; but do
it in her name: so that he, not
knowing who I am, or my plot,   2425
will come here and speak to me more
frankly . . . But someone's at the door.
I'll tell you the rest later. Go
see who it can be.

[Mari-Nuño exits.]

    And, just so,
I employ the truth to mislead   2430
Mari-Nuño, who will proceed
to arrange things for me to see
him tonight and talk, and for me
to tell him how I suffer.

[Don Toribio tries to get in, and Mari-Nuño stops him.]

MARI-NUÑO
    Wait!
You have no right to violate   2435
her privacy. You must knock first.

TORIBIO
That's twice at the same time I'm cursed
by you, you duenna.

MARI-NUÑO
    Just what does
that pretend to mean?

TORIBIO
    The first was
when you depressed me with your gloom;   2440
next when you defended her room.

2438 duenna: the enmity between squires and duennas was a comic commonplace of the
    Golden Age stage

MARI-NUÑO   ¿Será justo, si no están
               decentes, que a verlas lleguen?

D. TORIBIO   ¿Pues cómo pueden no estar
               siempre mis primas decentes?

CLARA   ¿Qué es eso?

D. TORIBIO   Que esa estantigua
               a mí el paso me defiende.

CLARA   Hace muy bien, porque aquí,
               sin mi padre, nadie puede
               entrar.

D. TORIBIO   Sí puede, y ya sé
               de qué ese ceño procede,
               y así no quiero enojarme,
               porque sé también que tienen
               licencia las desvalidas
               de llorar amargamente.

CLARA   Yo confieso que lo estoy;
               y pues la dichosa en este
               cuarto no está, no tenéis
               que hacer en él: brevemente
               dél os id, o yo me iré,
               porque de mí no se piense
               que me vengo en estorbaros,
               cuando hay más en que me vengue.

D. TORIBIO   Eso es poco y mal hablado.

CLARA   Ven, Mari-Nuño. (Que tienes
               que hacer por mí esta fineza.)

[Vase.]

MARI-NUÑO   Tuya soy y seré siempre.
               Pero aguárdate, veré
               quién llama.

[Llega a la puerta.]

D. TORIBIO   ¡Cielos, valedme!
               Que este remoquete, sobre
               aquella sospecha fuerte,
               que áspid del pecho, a bocados
               todo el corazón me muerde,
               es, ahora que caigo en ello,
               un bellaco remoquete.

MARI-NUÑO	Would it be right, if they're not yet decent, for you to barge in?
TORIBIO	Get one thing straight, and no argument, my cousins are always decent.

2445

CLARA	What's going on?
TORIBIO	This old scarecrow has halted me here like a foe.
CLARA	She does well. Because unless my father says so, no one dares try this door.

TORIBIO	Well I dare. And I'll bet, I know what's got you so upset with me. So I'll try to contain myself, for well I know the pain which causes you such sad distress and makes you cry with bitterness.

2450

2455

CLARA	Well, I confess that I am sad. But the one of us who is glad is not here, so you should not be here either. You must go, quickly, or I shall leave. For I will not have anyone think that I got my vengeance keeping you at bay when I have a far better way than that.

2460

TORIBIO	Hey, that's no way to talk.
CLARA	Mari-Nuño, come here.

[Aside to Mari-Nuño]

Don't balk
at doing this business for me.

2465

MARI-NUÑO   You know I am yours, faithfully.
[A knock is heard.]

But wait. Let me see who is at
the door.

TORIBIO	God help me. This old bat, this hag, this scrawny bag of bones is worse than a witch among crones: she is an asp at my breast who murders me with each foul chew. And, far worse than all of that, she is a hag-faced monstrosity.

2470

2475

Cuando buscamos la casa,
vi . . . Lengua mía, detente:
no lo digas, sin que antes
te haya dicho yo que mientes.
Vi que detrás de la cama
de Eugenia ¡oh malicia aleve! . . .
estaba detrás . . .

[Vuelve Mari-Nuño.]

MARI-NUÑO   Señora,
albricias, que este billete
con coche y balcón . . .

D. TORIBIO   Mujer,
en lo que dices advierte;
que balcón, billete y coche,
sobre dueña, me parece
es traer todo el yerro armado.

MARI-NUÑO

Mal encuentro fuera éste,
si importara. Mi señora . . .

D. TORIBIO

Memoria, no me atormentes.

MARI-NUÑO   ¿Aquí no estaba?

D. TORIBIO   Aquí estaba
un poco antes que se fuese.

MARI-NUÑO   A buscar a entrambas voy
con este papel.

D. TORIBIO   Detente,
que antes he de verle yo
que ellas.

MARI-NUÑO   ¿Qué llama verle?
Que aunque no importara nada,
no le he de dar, por no hacerle
tan dueño de casa ya.

D. TORIBIO   ¿Qué va . . .

MARI-NUÑO   ¿Qué?

D. TORIBIO   . . . que de un puñete
te abollo sesos y toca?

MARI-NUÑO   ¿Qué va que no es mayor que éste?

[Dale una puñada.]

D. TORIBIO   Los dientes debieron de irse,
pues he perdido los dientes.

When looking through their house I saw . . .
But I had better lock my jaw:
I must not speak, for even I
would suspect that my own words lie.
I saw, behind Eugenia's bed,   2480
—oh treachery most foul, most dread!—,
there, behind her bed . . .

[Mari-Nuño, rushing in]

MARI-NUÑO   My lady,
good news, for this letter you see,
with coach and balcony . . .

TORIBIO   Woman,
watch what you say, for nothing can   2485
be worse; since a balcony, coach,
letter, and a duenna approach
the very quintessence of sin.

MARI-NUÑO
[Aside]   (I hate to see our talk begin
like this.)

[Aloud]   I wonder where she went . . .   2490

TORIBIO
[Aside]   (Memory, why this harsh torment?)

MARI-NUÑO   Wasn't my lady here?

TORIBIO   I say
she was, before she went away.

MARI-NUÑO   I'm going to look for them to
give them this note.

TORIBIO   You shall not do   2495
that, I swear, because I must read
it first.

MARI-NUÑO   No, you shall not succeed
in that, for even though it be
of no importance, you won't see
it. You are not the master here.   2500

TORIBIO   What if I . . .

MARI-NUÑO   What?

TORIBIO   . . . I punch your ear,
smash your head and knock off your hat?

MARI-NUÑO   You can't punch me harder than that!

[She gives him a punch.]

TORIBIO   Ow! You've given me such a clout
that half my teeth have fallen out!   2505

MARI-NUÑO   ¡Ay, que me matan! ¡Señores,
                 acudan a socorrerme!

D. TORIBIO   Sólo me faltaba ahora
                 ser ella la que se queje.

MARI-NUÑO   ¡Que me matan!

[Da voces.]
[Sale doña Eugenia, doña Clara, don Alonso, y Brígida.]

D. ALONSO   ¿Qué es aquesto?

CLARA   ¿Qué ha sucedido? ¿Qué tienes?

MARI-NUÑO   Don Toribio, mi señor,
                 colérico e impaciente,
                 porque no le quise dar
                 aqueste papel, que viene
                 para las dos, puso en mí
                 las manos.

LAS DOS   ¡Jesús mil veces!

D. ALONSO   Por cierto, señor sobrino,
                 vuestro enojo, sea el que fuere,
                 es muy sobrado. ¡A criada
                 de mis hijas desta suerte
                 se ha de tratar!

D. TORIBIO   ¡Vive Dios!
                 que soy yo . . .

D. ALONSO   No habléis.

D. TORIBIO   . . . quiene tiene
                 de qué quejarse . . .

D. ALONSO   Ya basta.
                 Dadme vos, dadme el billete;
                 que quiero ver la ocasión
                 que tuvo para ofenderse.

EUGENIA
                 ¡Ay de mí, si fuese acaso
                 de alguno de los ausentes!

CLARA
                 Quiera el cielo que no sea
                 que algo de tus cosas cuente.

D. ALONSO
[Lee.]   *Sobrinas mías, yo tengo balcón en*
                 que esta tarde veáis la entrada de la Reina
                 nuestra señora: el coche va por vosotras,

MARI-NUÑO	Help, help! He's murdering me! He's killing me! Come and help me, please!
TORIBIO	That's the last thing I needed now, for this old hag to raise a row.
MARI-NUÑO	He's killing me!

[Eugenia, Clara, Don Alonso and Brígida enter.]

ALONSO	What's going on?	2510
CLARA	What's happened here while I was gone?	
MARI-NUÑO	Sir, Don Toribio is the cause. Angry and impatient, because I would not let him see this note, which is for the two girls, he smote me with his hands.	2515
THE GIRLS	Jesus Christ and all his saints!	
ALONSO	I must reprimand you, cousin. For your anger, no matter how justified, is so excessive that I am dismayed. How could you treat my daughters' maid in such a fashion!	2520
TORIBIO	By God, I am the one . . .	
ALONSO	Quiet!	
TORIBIO	. . . who should cry foul, since . . .	
ALONSO	That's enough from you! Give me that letter. Give it to me. I want to see what made her upset enough to cause this stir.	2525
EUGENIA *[Aside]*	(Oh, woe is me! I hope that it's not from my absent favorites!)	
CLARA *[Aside to Eugenia]*	Heaven help us if it declares the truth about your wild affairs.	2530
ALONSO *[Reading]*	"Dear nieces: on my balcony this afternoon you can watch the entrance of our lady the queen. A coach will come	

que no dudo que mi primo . . .

Ahora de nuevo vuelvo
a enojarme y ofenderme
de que escrúpulo haya habido
en vuestro juicio. En aqueste,
doña Violante, mi prima,
hijas, os dice que quiere
que con ella vais adonde
veáis la entrada excelente
de la Reina, cuya vida
el cielo por siglos cuente.

Tomad, leedle vos; veréis
cuán necio, cuán imprudente,
habéis pensado otra cosa;
que no quiero que se ausenten,
hasta que vos le leáis.

[Toma el papel.]

D. TORIBIO   Mostrad. Dice desta suerte:
Sobrinas mías, yo tengo
balcón . . . Tío, finalmente,
¿hasta que yo lea, no han de ir?

D. ALONSO   No.

D. TORIBIO   Pues muy bien me parece;
que no irán de aquí a dos años.

D. ALONSO   ¿Por qué?

D. TORIBIO   Porque no sé leerle,
y esos habré menester
para aprenderlo.

D. ALONSO   ¿Que llegue
a tanto vuestra ignorancia?

D. TORIBIO   ¿Pues qué defecto es aqueste?
Como desos leer no saben,
y lo saben todo. Esténse,
hasta que lo aprenda, en casa,
y entonces irán.

D. ALONSO   Mal pueden,
si hoy es la entrada.

D. TORIBIO   ¿Habrá más
de que la entrada se quede,
hasta que yo sepa leer?

for you; I have no doubt that my cousin . . ."   2535

Once more I find myself angry
and offended most grievously
that your judgment is so impaired.
In this note, about which you cared
to make such a fuss, my cousin   2540
Doña Violante, daughters, in
so many words invites you to
visit her balcony where you
can watch the glorious entrance
of the queen in her elegance.   2545

[To Toribio]   Here, read it for yourself. You'll see
how wrongly, how imprudently,
you believed that it was something
else. Daughters, you are not going
until his own eyes have read it.   2550

TORIBIO   Let me see it.
[He takes the note.]   It says, to wit:
"Dear nieces: on my balcony
this afternoon . . ." Do you agree,
uncle, that until I have read
it they can't go?

ALONSO   That's what I said.   2555

TORIBIO   That's good, for they won't leave in two
years.

ALONSO   Why?

TORIBIO   Since I haven't a clue
about how to read. And it will
take me two years to learn.

ALONSO   I still
can't believe what a simpleton   2560
you are.

TORIBIO   What's wrong with being one?
Look how many know-it-alls don't
know how to read. My cousins won't
leave here until I learn to read.
Then they can go.

ALONSO   Then they won't need   2565
to, you idiot; the entry
is today.

TORIBIO   Until I read, the
entry can wait for me as well.

D. ALONSO   Hijas, aquesto sucede
                 una vez en una edad:
                 verlo es justo. Brevemente
                 os poned los mantos, y id,
                 o pésele o no le pese
                 a don Toribio; que yo,
                 a causa de mi accidente,
                 no saldré de casa, y basta
                 que vuestra voz me lo cuente,
                 cuando volváis.

CLARA   A tu gusto
                 humilde estoy y obediente.

EUGENIA   Si me das licencia a mí,
                 contigo es bien que me quede.

D. ALONSO   No, hija, ambas habéis de ir.

BRÍGIDA   Aquí ya los mantos tienen.

CLARA   Ponme, Mari-Nuño, el mío.
                 Toma, y lo que digo advierte.

[Dala un papel.]

EUGENIA
                 Sola esta vez salgo triste,
                 porque ninguno no me encuentre
                 destos dos necios amantes.

[Vase.]

CLARA
                 Sola esta vez salgo alegre,
                 por si en las fiestas, por dicha,
                 a este caballero viese.

[Vase.]
MARI-NUÑO
                 Ve segura, y fía de mí.

D. TORIBIO
                 Aunque desairado quede,
                 me huelgo, que quedo en casa,
                 entre la Reina o no entre,
                 por si puedo averiguar
                 a mis solas esta fuerte

ALONSO   Daughters, this has no parallel
                in our age. You must see it to   2570
                believe it. Quickly, both of you,
                get your mantillas; then you can
                go, if it please our countryman
                Don Toribio or not.

[Brígida exits.]   Since my
                attack, it is better that I   2575
                not leave the house. You can tell me
                about it when you get back.

CLARA   We
                are pleased to do as you command.

EUGENIA   Please give me permission to stand
                here beside you instead.

ALONSO   No, no,   2580
                my daughters, both of you should go.

[Brígida returns.]

BRÍGIDA   Here are the mantillas.

CLARA   Mari-
[Aside to   Nuño, help me with mine, please.
Mari-Nuño]   See
                this note: take it and do just what
                I say . . .

[She gives her a note and speaks softly with her.]

EUGENIA
[Aside]   (One of those two will spot   2585
                me for sure. This is the first time
                I'm sad to go out.)

CLARA
[Aside]   (Oh! If I'm
                lucky enough to see him! This
                is one time I go out with bliss!)

MARI-NUÑO
[Aside to Clara]   Enjoy yourself. You can be sure   2590
                of me.

TORIBIO
[Aside]   (Though my discomfiture
                is great, still I am pleased to stay
                home. Let the queen enter today
                or not, as long as I find out,

sospecha, que en vivos celos
amor en el alma enciende.

[Vanse.]
[Salen don Félix y Hernando.]

HERNANDO   ¿Sin ver la fiesta te vienes,
              señor, hasta casa?

D. FÉLIX   Sí,
              que no hay fiesta para mí
              donde no hay gusto.

HERNANDO   ¿Qué tienes,
              que estás tan triste, señor?

D. FÉLIX   ¿Qué más tu lengua quisiera
              de que yo te lo dijera?

HERNANDO   Ya me has dicho que es amor,
              con sólo eso.

D. FÉLIX   ¿Por qué?

HERNANDO   Porque obligarte a callar,
              sólo puede ser estar
              enamorado.

D. FÉLIX   No sé
              cómo te diga que sí,
              y que una rara belleza
              es causa de mi tristeza:
              tan imposible, que vi
              en el primero deseo
              el primero inconveniente.

HERNANDO   ¿Cómo?

D. FÉLIX   A quien don Juan ausente
              ama, y a don Pedro veo
              venir siguiendo, es la dama
              que mi libertad robó;
              y aunque siempre he de estar yo
              de la parte de mi fama,
              aún no estriba mi cuidado
              en esta especie de celos,
              sino que de sus desvelos
              uno y otro me han fiado
              el secreto; de manera,
              que obligado a embarazar
              su empeño estoy, y a callar.

here by myself, if what I doubt   2595
is fact. For love kindled in me,
I fear, a raging jealousy.)

A room in Don Félix's house
[Don Félix and Hernando]

HERNANDO   Without staying to see the show,
                my lord, you come back home?

FÉLIX   That's right,
                for I don't want any gay sight   2600
                where there's no joy.

HERNANDO   What makes you so
                sad now, my lord?

FÉLIX   Are you certain
                you'd have me unburden myself
                and tell you?

HERNANDO   My lord, you yourself
                have confessed that it is love when   2605
                you say as much as that.

FÉLIX   How does
                that follow?

HERNANDO   Because this desire
                to keep silent reveals the fire
                of love that burns in you.

FÉLIX   I was
                afraid you would see through me and   2610
                find out that a beauty most rare
                is the cause of my sad despair;
                my love's hopeless as it is grand.
                For even with my first desire
                I saw the first impediment.   2615

HERNANDO   How's that?

FÉLIX   The same girl that, absent,
                Don Juan loves, and who lights the fire
                of passion in Don Pedro, she
                it is who steals my soul away.
                And though I must always display   2620
                the honor of my family,
                I do not have to go so far
                as to allow their jealousy
                to have any effect on me.
                Both told me their secrets. Both are   2625
                my friends; so I must do my best
                to carry out all their instructions,
                and without protest or obstructions.

[Llama a la reja Mari-Nuño.]

MARI-NUÑO   Señor don Félix.

D. FÉLIX   Espera.
                   ¿A quién han llamado?

MARI-NUÑO   A vos.

D. FÉLIX   ¿Pues qué es lo que me mandáis?

MARI-NUÑO   Doña Eugenia, que leáis
                   aqueste papel, y adiós.

[Arrójale un papel y vase.]

D. FÉLIX
[Lee.]   *Agradecida al aviso que me disteis,*
                   he empezado ya a obedeceros; y para ejecu-
                   tarlo mejor, me importa hablaros. Venid
                   esta noche, que yo os estaré aguardando. El
                   cielo os guarde.

                   ¿Quién vio confusión mas fiera,
                   puesto que ni ir ni dejar
                   de ir puedo ya excusar?

[Sale don Juan.]

D. JUAN
                   ¡Cielos! ¿Qué haré?

HERNANDO
                                        Considera
                   que viene don Juan aquí.

D. FÉLIX   ¿Si vio arrojar el papel?

HERNANDO   No.

D. JUAN
                                 ¡Qué sospecha tan cruel!

D. FÉLIX   Don Juan, pues ¿qué hacéis aquí?
                   ¿No sois de fiestas?

D. JUAN   No sé
                   lo que os diga . . .

D. FÉLIX
[Aparte.]   (¡Muerto quedo!)

D. JUAN   Que ni hablar ni callar puedo.

D. FÉLIX   ¿Callar ni hablar?

[Mari-Nuño, from the street, calling through the window grill.]

MARI-NUÑO   Don Félix.

FÉLIX   Wait. Was that addressed
               to me or to you?

MARI-NUÑO   To you.

FÉLIX   Why   2630
               do you want to talk to me?

MARI-NUÑO   It's
               Doña Eugenia, who remits
               this for you to read; and goodbye.

[She throws him a note and exits.]

FÉLIX
[Reading]   "Most thankful for the notice you
               gave me, I've begun to serve you;   2635
               and to do so even better, I need to talk
               with you. Come this evening, for
               I will be waiting. May God keep you well."

               Who has seen confusion worse than
               this, for I can neither go nor   2640
               keep myself away from her door.

[Don Juan enters.]

JUAN
[Aside]   (Heavens, what shall I do?)

HERNANDO
[Aside to Don Félix]   That man
               Don Juan is coming in. Take care.

FÉLIX   Did he see her throw me the note?

HERNANDO   No.

JUAN
[Aside]   (What suspicions choke my throat!)   2645

FÉLIX   Don Juan, why is it you're not there
               where the parades are taking place?

JUAN   I don't know how to say . . .

FÉLIX
[Aside]   (I'm dead!)

JUAN   I can't keep silent, yet I dread
               to speak.

D. Juan   Sí.
D. Félix   ¿Por qué?

D. Juan   Porque os ofendo en hablar,
              y en callar me ofendo a mí:
              con que es preciso que aquí
              no pueda hablar ni callar.

D. Félix   No os entiendo.

D. Juan   Yo tampoco;
              mas si entenderme queréis,
              como licencia me deis
              (propia dádiva de un loco),
              diré el dolor que me aqueja.

D. Félix   Sí doy.
[Aparte.]   (¡Empeño cruel!)

D. Juan   Pues enseñadme un papel
              que os dieron por esta reja.

D. Félix   Sólo eso en el mundo hubiera,
              siendo quien somos los dos,
              que yo no hiciera por vos;
              y no haciéndolo, quisiera
              que el crédito de mi fe
              os debiese creer de mí
              que soy vuestro amigo.

D. Juan   Así
              lo creo; mas ¿no podré
              (viendo que habéis excusado,
              con pretexto de otro honor,
              ser tercero de mi amor,
              y que habiéndome llamado
              Eugenia en el coche ahora,
              muy enojada me diga
              que ni la vea ni siga
              más), no podré (¿quién lo ignora?)*
              entrar en temor de que
              vuestra excusa y su crueldad
              nacen de otra novedad?
              Y más viendo que llegué
              a tiempo que daros vi

---

*mas, don Félix, quien lo ignora?

FÉLIX   How's that?

JUAN   I cannot face   2650
                    you, for to speak is an offense,
                    and keeping silent offends me.
                    So that is the reason, you see,
                    for this awkward ambivalence.

FÉLIX   I don't understand.

JUAN   Nor do I,   2655
                    but if you want to understand
                    me, give me license to expand
                    my reasons (which will certify
                    me as crazy); so let me tell
                    you of my pain.

FÉLIX   Yes, go ahead.   2660
[Aside]   (Oh, cruel request!)

JUAN   You just read
                    a note that someone threw you. Well,
                    let me see it.

FÉLIX   There is but one
                    thing, even though we have been friends
                    and there is a good chance this ends   2665
                    it, I will not do. And not done,
                    you must realize, seeing how
                    much our friendship has always meant,
                    that I do this with the intent
                    of staying friends.

JUAN   I will allow   2670
                    you that; but shall I not suspect
                    (seeing that you have just refused,
                    claiming that you must be excused
                    by greater honor, to effect
                    my wishes, and since I was just   2675
                    visited by Eugenia, who
                    angrily instructed me to
                    leave her completely alone), must
                    I then not leap to the conclusion
                    that your cruel excuses stem   2680
                    from some other cause. I know them
                    for what they are. My disillusion

por esa reja un papel,
y que los secretos dél
tanto recatáis de mí,
que turbado le escondáis,
habiendo yo el nombre oído
de Eugenia, y que ella ha sido
la que os dice que leáis.

D. Félix
[Aparte.]

(¡Válgame el cielo! ¿Qué haré?
Que el papel me llama a mí,
y si me disculpo aquí,
a don Pedro culparé.)

D. Juan   ¿Qué me respondéis?

D. Félix   Ya os tengo
respondido con saber
que soy, don Juan, y he de ser
amigo, y callar prevengo.

D. Juan

Confieso que sois mi amigo,
y que vuestro huésped soy;
pero el empeño en que estoy,
vos le sabéis: y así, os digo
sólo que me aconsejéis
en este lance, por Dios.
¿Qué hicierais conmigo vos?

D. Félix

Aunque contra mí tenéis
alguna razón, si yo
en el empeño me viera,
que eráis mi amigo creyera,
y no os apurara.

D. Juan   No
es tan fácil de tomar
como de dar un consejo,
y así de admitirle dejo,
volviéndoos a suplicar
que me enseñéis el papel.

D. Félix   Si otra causa no tuviera
que la vuestra, yo lo hiciera.

D. Juan   Pues ¿hay otra causa en él
más que ser suyo y venir
a vuestra mano?

D. Félix   Sí hay,
pues la causa que le tray
es la que no he de decir.

came when I saw someone give you
a letter through that window grill,
and though I have begged you, you still   2685
secret its contents from my view.
But Don Félix, you know I heard
Eugenia's name, and I assure
you I know what's going on. Your
lies won't do. I heard every word.   2690

FÉLIX
[Aside]

(Good heavens! How can this be solved?
The note named me. If I evade
by telling the truth, I'm afraid
that Don Pedro will be involved.)

JUAN   How do you answer?

FÉLIX   I answered   2695
you already, Don Juan, because
I am still your friend, and the laws
of friendship guarantee my word,
and my silence, too.

JUAN   I confess
I am your guest and you are my   2700
friend; yet suspicions crucify
me. Can't you tell? In my distress
I only ask that you advise
me what in God's name I should do.
So if you were I, what would you   2705
do with me?

FÉLIX   Though I recognize
you have reason to be upset,
I think if I were in your shoes
I would trust the friendship, and choose
not to push me more.

JUAN   I regret   2710
that it's not as easy to take
advice as to give it. I must
reject your suggestion to trust
you, and one last time I must make
my request. Please show me the note.   2715

FÉLIX   If I did not have another
cause than yours I would not demur.

JUAN   What other cause can this promote
but your own; because the note was
from her, and to you?

FÉLIX   I swear there   2720
is another, but I forbear
to reveal it to you.

D. JUAN   ¿No fiáis de mí un secreto?

D. FÉLIX   Sí, mas no aquéste.

D. JUAN   Mirad
                 que puede nuestra amistad
                 dilatar en mí el efeto
                 de verle, mas no excusalle.

D. FÉLIX   Pues mirad cómo ha de ser,
                 porque no le habéis de ver.

D. JUAN   Saliéndonos a la calle.

D. FÉLIX   Guiad donde quisiéreis vos,
                 que a guardarle estoy dispuesto.

[Sale don Pedro.]

D. PEDRO   ¡Don Juan, don Félix! ¿qué es esto?
                 ¿Dónde vais así los dos?

D. FÉLIX   Paseándonos vamos.

D. PEDRO   No
                 es la deshecha bastante
                 a desmentir el semblante;
                 y habiendo llegado yo
                 a tiempo que ya empuñadas
                 de ambos las espadas ví,
                 no habéis de pasar de aquí.

D. JUAN   Prevenciones excusadas
                 son las vuestras, vive el cielo.

HERNANDO   No son, que mi amo y don Juan
                 a reñir, don Pedro, van.

D. FÉLIX   Calla, pícaro.

D. PEDRO   ¿Qué duelo
                 hay, que entre amigos lo sea
                 que no se pueda ajustar,
                 Félix, antes de llegar
                 al último trance? Vea
                 yo que hacéis esto por mí,
                 y sepa la causa.

JUAN   That does
                    no good at all. Won't you trust me
                    with a secret?

FÉLIX   Yes, of course, but
                    not with this one.

JUAN   Consider what   2725
                    this means, Don Félix. Because we
                    have been friends, I will accept not
                    seeing it, but I can't allow
                    this affront.

FÉLIX   Then let it be now,
                    right now, and in whatever spot   2730
                    you like.

JUAN   The street.

FÉLIX   That is alright
                    with me. You will find me ready.

A street
[Don Pedro enters and meets Don Félix, Don Juan, and Hernando
as they leave the house.]

PEDRO   Gentlemen, what is this I see?
                    Where are you going? You're all white!

FÉLIX   We are going to take a walk.   2735

PEDRO   In spite of what you say, the way
                    you both stand there serves to betray
                    the calm which you feign with your talk.
                    And since I arrived here, indeed,
                    when you were about to draw your   2740
                    swords, you must both of you assure
                    me to stop right here.

JUAN   There's no need
                    to warn us not to fight, by God!

HERNANDO   They were about to fight a duel,
                    Don Pedro. But then surely you'll   2745
                    prevent them.

FÉLIX   Hold your tongue, you clod.

[Hernando exits.]

PEDRO   How can there be a fight between
                    two friends, Félix, that another
                    can't put an end to, or defer,
                    before it comes to blows? I mean,   2750
                    do this for me, and let me know
                    what caused the quarrel.

D. Félix   Yo
no he de decirla, que no
me está a mí bien.

D. Juan   A mí sí,
que no quiero que se diga
que sobre la obligación
de huésped, es sinrazón
la que a este trance me obliga.
Y pues que sois caballero,
que nos dejaréis reñir,
la ocasión he de decir . . .

D. Félix   No diréis; porque primero
yo . . .

D. Pedro   Tened.

D. Félix
                              ¡Oh quién pudiera
su discurso suspender!

D. Juan   Que quiero con vos hacer
lo que con otro no hiciera.
Yo, don Pedro, he fiado
de don Félix que estoy enamorado
de una dama; y habiéndome valido
dél, no sólo ayudarme ha pretendido,
pero contra su honor, contra su fama,
sé que festeja aquesta misma dama.
Ved si es justa mi queja,
pues dándole un papel por esta reja . . .

D. Pedro
[Aparte.]   (¡Qué es lo que escucho, cielos!)

D. Juan   Oí (que oyen mucho contra sí los celos)
que dijo la tercera
que el dueño suyo doña Eugenia era.
Su nombre dije, poco habrá importado
el haberla nombrado,
siendo quien sois.

D. Félix
                              Con nuevas penas lucho.

D. Pedro   Esperad, que no importa, sino mucho,
porque aquese desvelo
me toca a mí con ambos, ¡vive el cielo!
con vos, pues habéis sido
de Eugenia amante, que es la que he seguido;
y con él, pues de vos a oír he llegado
que está don Félix de ella enamorado:

FÉLIX   I won't tell
you, for it does not do me well.

JUAN   I'll tell you then, for I'll have no
                       one say of me that not only   2755
                       did I behave the way a guest
                       should not, but that I lodged protest
                       for no reason at all. Now be
                       both a good gentleman and friend.
                       For since you are, and since you will   2760
                       let us duel, then I'll fulfill
                       your request and tell you . . .

FÉLIX   Suspend
                       your words, for first I'll . . .

PEDRO   Stop!

FÉLIX
[Aside]   (If I
                       could only make him stop before . . .)

JUAN   Don Pedro, let me tell you more   2765
                       than I'd tell anyone else. Why
                       I trusted my secrets of love
                       to Félix I don't know. I told him of
                       my passion for a lady, and when I
                       relied on him, not only did he try   2770
                       to assist me, but to the detriment
                       of his name and honor, Don Félix went
                       and courted her himself. That's why I'll kill
                       him, for at this window grill . . .

PEDRO
[Aside]   (Heavens! What is this I hear?)   2775

JUAN   She gave him a note, and I heard (the ear
                       of jealousy is so keen)
                       that Eugenia had sent the go-between.
                       I have told you her name; well, I don't care,
                       Don Pedro, for everywhere   2780
                       your honor is known.

FÉLIX
[Aside]   (New problems arise!)

PEDRO   Hold on. You should care more than you surmise,
                       since this affair involves me
                       with the two of you in one destiny:
                       with you, because it seems you   2785
                       have loved Eugenia, whom I followed too;
                       and with him, because I just heard you tell
                       me that Don Félix adores her as well.

	de suerte que en los dos vengar prevengo la razón que tenéis y la que tengo.
D. Juan	Si vos os declaráis de Eugenia bella amante, cuando yo muero por ella, ya con vos es mayor empeño el mío, pues ya son dos de quien mis penas fío, y dos los que me ofenden.
D. Félix	Dos son también los que agraviar pretenden mi amistad, presumiendo que, siendo yo quien soy, a ambos ofendo, cuando en mi valor hallo que al uno por el otro su amor callo, y excusar el empeño solicito, pasando la fineza a ser delito.
D. Juan	¿Fineza es, cuando impío . . .
D. Pedro	. . . cuando ingrato . . .
D. Juan	. . . con falsa fe . . .
D. Pedro	. . . con fementido trato . . .
Los dos	ofendéis mi amistad?
D. Félix	Oidme primero, pues a los dos satisfacer espero.
D. Juan	Pláticas acortemos, y puesto que tenemos nuestro duelo empezado, venid conmigo.
D. Pedro	Habiendo yo llegado a tiempo que he sabido que los dos me ofendéis, ¿como he podido dejar de ir con los dos?
D. Félix	Y ¿cómo puedo yo dejar que los dos con tal denuedo presumáis que traidor puedo haber sido?
Los tres	De ambos está ofendido mi valor.
D. Félix	Por mi honor volver espero.
D. Juan	Calle la lengua pues, y hable el acero.

[Riñen los tres, y dice don Toribio dentro.]

| D. Toribio | ¡Pendencia hay a la puerta de mi casa! |

| | So I stopped you from taking vengeance for your affront which is my own even more! | 2790 |

JUAN   You're right that I have been trying to woo
              Eugenia, and I love her more than you;
              so I've a far greater complaint to take
              up, for I confided my lover's ache
              to two friends who both abuse   2795
              me.

FÉLIX   In fact, both of you, as well, misuse
              my friendship when you pretend
              though you know who I am, that I offend
              you both, when it took valor
              to keep both lovers' secrets, as I swore,   2800
              from the other. I'm not guilty, though I'm
              afraid my scruples are seen as a crime.

JUAN   You call those scruples! You cheat . . .

PEDRO   You ingrate . . .

JUAN   You false friend . . .

PEDRO   You consummate . . .

PEDRO AND JUAN   Abuser of our friendship!

FÉLIX   Hear me first,   2805
              while I attempt to satisfy your worst
              suspicions.

JUAN   Let's cut this short,
              for now our only resort
              is to go ahead and fight.
              Come with me.

PEDRO   Since I arrived at the right   2810
              time to learn that the two of you offend
              me, you know I will attend
              you.

FÉLIX   And how can I permit
              the two of you to make a fight of it
              when both assume that I have been a cad?   2815

ALL THREE   That's enough. Both of you add
              insult to injury.

FÉLIX   Now I must seek
              revenge.

JUAN   Enough talk, now let our swords speak!

[The three fight.]

[Offstage]
TORIBIO   Come quickly! There's a duel here in my street!

[Salen don Alonso y don Toribio con espadas desnudas.]

D. ALONSO   ¿Cómo entre tres amigos esto pasa?

D. JUAN   Guárdeos Dios, que ya el duelo está acabado.

[Vase don Juan.]

D. ALONSO   Esperad, porque habiendo yo llegado,
                   ofendéis mi valor . . .

D. PEDRO   Nada esto ha sido.

                   (Seguir quiero a don Juan, pues ya se ha ido.)

[Vase.]

D. TORIBIO   Tenedlos, tío; que para ajustarlo,
                   sobre mi ejecutoria han de jurarlo.
                   Aguardad; que ya vengo,
                   mientras voy a sacarla; que la tengo
                   metida en las alforjas, como vino,
                   porque no se me ajase en el camino.

D. ALONSO   Merezca yo saber qué furia airada
                   os ha obligado aquí a sacar la espada.

D. FÉLIX   Nació esta competencia
                   sobre una diferencia
                   que en el juego los tres hemos tenido;
                   y habiendo vos venido
                   a tan buena ocasión, no fuera justo
                   que entre amigos durara este disgusto.
                   Perdonadme, señor, y dad permiso
                   que los siga.

[Vase y quédase don Toribio suspenso.]

D. ALONSO   Será muy cuerdo aviso.
                   Id, don Félix, con Dios, que sabe el cielo
                   que siento no cumplir hoy con el duelo,
                   habiéndome aquí hallado.

[Aparte.]   (Pero es tal mi cuidado,
                   que no entre don Toribio en mi sospecha,
                   que más con él me importa la deshecha.)

[Don Alonso and Don Toribio enter with drawn swords.]

ALONSO   How's this? Three friends as good as you compete   2820
            with swords?

JUAN   God keep you, sir. It's finished now.

[Juan exits.]

ALONSO   You dare walk out on me like this? I vow
            you touch my honor.

PEDRO   But this was nothing
            serious.

[Aside]   (Where can Don Juan be going?)

[Pedro exits.]

TORIBIO   Uncle, you can resolve this. Make all three   2825
            swear on my letters of nobility.
            Wait, I'll come in a moment.
            Just let me go and get the document;
            it's tucked in my saddlebag where I stowed
            it to keep it clean and safe on the road.   2830

ALONSO   I'd like to know what blind rage
            made you take out your swords here to engage
            in a duel.

FÉLIX   This small fight
            began because of a slight
            difference we three had over a card.   2835
            But since we have such regard
            for you, Don Alonso, the moment you
            came we could not continue.
            Forgive me, sir, and please give me your leave
            to follow them.

ALONSO   That's alright, I believe.   2840
            Go with God, Don Félix, and believe me
            I'm sorry I couldn't do my duty
            in your duel, though I was there.

[Don Félix exits.]

[Aside]   (But now I must take great care
            that Don Toribio not know my suspicion,   2845
            for with him it's better to have discretion.)

[Don Alonso exits.]

Eugenia's room in Don Alonso's house
[Don Toribio enters, all upset, dragging Don Alonso by the arm.]

D. Alonso   ¿De qué tan pensativo
                   habéis quedado?

D. Toribio   Imaginando vivo,
                   si nuestra solariega sangre acierta
                   en que riñendo, tío, a nuestra puerta,
                   se vayan atufados
                   sin ir los dos muy bien descalabrados,
                   y aún los tres.

D. Alonso   ¡Qué notable desvarío!
                   Pues ¿qué nos toca su disgusto?

D. Toribio   ¡Ay, tío!
                   ¡Si hablara yo . . .!

D. Alonso   ¿De qué es el sentimiento?

D. Toribio   De mucho.

D. Alonso   Pues hablad.

D. Toribio   Estadme atento.
                   Cuando yo iba a buscar filis
                   y fuisteis vos a traerme,
                   desengañado de que
                   burla de mi prima fuese,
                   siendo hablilla que las damas
                   decir por donaire suelen;
                   al volver a casa, oímos
                   voces, diciendo impaciente
                   Clara que un hombre había en ella.

D. Alonso   Es verdad, y yendo a verle,
                   no le hallamos, aunque toda
                   la anduvimos.

D. Toribio   Pues de aquese
                   examen que en ella hicimos
                   todo mi dolor procede,
                   todas mis penas se causan,
                   y todos mis celos penden.

D. Alonso   ¿Por qué?

D. Toribio   Fáltame el aliento,
                   la voz duda, el labio teme.
                   Porque como no dejamos
                   nada por ver diligentes,
                   detrás de la cama (¡ay triste!)
                   de Eugenia . . .

D. Alonso
                           ¡Cielos, valedme!

ALONSO   What has made you so pensive,
      Don Toribio?

TORIBIO   How can our blood forgive
      us, how can our entitled blood allow
      those men outside our door to raise a row   2850
      and all cocky walk away
      without our smashing two of them 'til they
      can't walk, or maybe even all three?

ALONSO   You
      must be mad. What can their fight have to do
      with us?

TORIBIO   If I begin . . .

ALONSO   What do you mean? 2855

TORIBIO   A lot.

ALONSO   Speak then.

TORIBIO   Listen to what I've seen.
      When I went to look for a knack,
      and then you came to bring me back
      all undeceived to learn it was
      one of those jokes my cousin does,   2860
      one of those things the ladies say
      to pass the hours of the day.
      When we came into the house we
      heard Clara say impatiently
      that she was sure there was a man   2865
      inside.

ALONSO   That's true, and when we ran
      to find him he was nowhere in
      the house.

TORIBIO   That was the origin
      of all my sorrow. It began
      while we were looking for that man;   2870
      and all my pain and jealousy
      derives from that sad scrutiny.

ALONSO   How's that?

TORIBIO   I'm out of breath, my lips
      tremble, and what voice I have slips
      away. Because we did not leave   2875
      any corner unsearched (I grieve
      to say), behind Eugenia's bed
      I saw . . .

ALONSO
[Aside]   (Heaven help me, I dread
      to hear . . .)

D. Toribio   vi . . .

D. Alonso   ¿Qué? ¿Al hombre?

D. Toribio   ¡Más nonada!
                    ¿Verle y no darle la muerte?
                    ¿No bastó ver . . .

D. Alonso   Proseguid.

D. Toribio   . . . una clara seña, un fuerte
                    indicio de que a deshora
                    en el cuarto salga y entre?

D. Alonso   Ved, sobrino, qué decís:
                    No algún engaño os empeñe
                    a decir . . .

D. Toribio   ¿Cómo que engaño,
                    si lo vi mas claramente
                    que cinco y cinco son diez,
                    y diez y diez serán veinte?

D. Alonso   Pues ¿qué visteis?

D. Toribio   Una escala
                    que Eugenia escondida tiene.

D. Alonso   ¿Escala escondida?

D. Toribio   Sí,
                    y de hartos pasos, con fuertes
                    cuerdas y hierros atada.

D. Alonso   ¡Vive Dios, si verdad fuese,
                    que había . . . !

D. Toribio   ¿Cómo verdad,
                    si sólo porque la vieseis,
                    os traigo aquí, cuando solo
                    está el cuarto? Un punto breve
                    esperáos: veréis cuán presto
                    aquí la miráis patente.

[Vase.]

D. Alonso   ¡Ay de mí! No en vano, cielos,
                    previne ausentar prudente
                    de la corte a Eugenia. Pero
                    si ya don Toribio tiene
                    tan vivas sospechas, ¿cómo
                    es posible que la lleve?
                    Pues ya . . .

TORIBIO   I saw . . .

ALONSO   What? A man?

TORIBIO   How
                      silly! See a man, and allow   2880
                      him to live? It was enough to
                      see . . .

ALONSO   Don't stop now. Go on.

TORIBIO   . . . a clue,
                      a clear indication that some
                      man, I know, must certainly come
                      to her room.

ALONSO   Be careful, cousin;   2885
                      could it be you were taken in
                      by something?

TORIBIO   No. How could I be
                      taken in? I saw it clearly,
                      as clear as one and one make two
                      and two are four I'm telling you.   2890

ALONSO   Well, what did you see?

TORIBIO   A ladder
                      that Eugenia hid behind her
                      bed.

ALONSO   A hidden ladder?

TORIBIO   With lots
                      of iron steps, and many knots
                      to fasten it, and wires and hooks.   2895

ALONSO   By God, if this is what it looks
                      like, I'll . . .

TORIBIO   Of course it is, but so
                      you can see it yourself, I'll go
                      and bring it to you here. It's where
                      I left it; so you just stand there   2900
                      for a moment, and you'll see how
                      quickly I get it for you now.

[Exit Toribio.]

ALONSO   Woe is me! It was not in vain,
                      Heaven, that I planned to contain
                      Eugenia by taking her from   2905
                      court. But if he can't overcome
                      his dire suspicions, then how can
                      my cousin Don Toribio plan
                      to take her?

[Vuelve con un guardainfante.]

D. TORIBIO   Mirad si es verdad . . .
Con más de dos mil pendientes
de gradas, aros y cuerdas.

D. ALONSO   ¡Necio, loco, impertinente!
¿Esa es escala?

D. TORIBIO   Y escala
que si se desdobla, debe
poderse escalar con ella,
según las revueltas tiene,
la torre de Babilonia.
Esto es para quien lo entiende.
No la sé armar.

D. ALONSO   ¡Vive Dios,
que no sé cómo consiente
mi cólera no deciros
mil pesares! Porque ese
es guardainfante, no escala.

D. TORIBIO   ¿Guarda . . . qué?

D. ALONSO   ¡Qué impertinente!
Guardainfante.

D. TORIBIO   Peor es eso
que esotro. ¿Qué infante tiene
mi prima, que éste le guarde?

D. ALONSO   Hablar con vos es hacerme
perder el juicio. No entienda
aquesto nadie: volvedle
donde estaba, y estimadme,
bárbaro, y agradecedme
que no os digo mil locuras.

[Vase.]

D. TORIBIO   Escalado seas mil veces,
guardainfante de mi prima,
quienquiera que fuiste y fueses:
¡bueno me han puesto por ti
de bárbaro impertinente! . . .
Y hasta saber el oficio
que en cas de mis primas tienes,
no he de parar.

[Dentro.]
VOCES   Para. Para.

[Don Toribio returns, carrying a farthingale.]

TORIBIO   Here. You see? It's true.
                        It's got a thousand pieces, too,   2910
                        and crossbars and laces and knots,

ALONSO   Another one of your wild shots.
                        you dolt. That's a ladder?

TORIBIO   I know
                        it is: unfolded, you could go,
                        considering the number of   2915
                        parts, up to heaven, or above,
                        or climb up the tower of Babel.
                        That is, you could, but I'm not able:
                        I can't put it together.

ALONSO   God
                        assist me, you are such a clod!   2920
                        And I'm so angry I don't know
                        why I don't give you such a blow . . . !
                        That's a farthingale, not a ladder.

TORIBIO   A farthing . . . what?

ALONSO   You're a much sadder
                        case that I thought. A farthingale.   2925

TORIBIO   Worse! To think a father would scale
                        her wall on that! A married man!

ALONSO   I'm sorry, cousin; my ears can
                        stand no more of this. Nobody
                        can decipher your lunacy.   2930
                        Take that thing back where you found it,
                        and then give me thanks, you nit-wit,
                        that I don't call you something far
                        worse.

[Alonso exits.]

TORIBIO   Well then, whatever you are,
                        you farthingale, let anyone   2935
                        at all climb you to have his fun.
                        You are why my uncle defames
                        me with "nit-wit" and all those names.
                        But until I find out just what
                        you're doing here, I will not shut   2940
                        my eyes once.

[Offstage]
Voices   Hello! Hello! We're
                        home.

2909 farthingale: a hoop framework for expanding a woman's skirt

D. Alonso   Pues que ya mis hijas vienen,
             poned luces en su cuarto.

[Sale Mari-Nuño.]

Mari-Nuño   ¡Ay de mí! Que en él hay gente.
            ¿Quién es?

D. Toribio   Yo soy, que no es nadie.

Mari-Nuño   ¿Qué haces aquí desta suerte,
            con aquese guardainfante?

D. Toribio Aquí, si saberlo quieres,
            me estaba pensando cosas . . .

Mari-Nuño   Sitio habrá donde las pienses.
            Suelta, y mira no te hallen
            aquí dentro cuando lleguen,
            que ya vienen.

D. Toribio   Mira tú
            no me obligues a que vengue
            el pasado mojicón.

Mari-Nuño   Mejor será, si lo adviertes,
            no quieras que te dé otro.

[Dala una puñada don Toribio.]

D. Toribio ¿Qué va que no es mayor que éste?

            ¡Ay, que me han muerto! Señores,
            acudid a socorrerme!
            ¡Ay, que me matan!

[Sale doña Eugenia, doña Clara, don Alonso, y Brígida.]

D. Alonso   ¿Qué es esto?

Clara   ¡Qué voces!

Eugenia   ¿Qué ruido es éste?

D. Toribio Mari-Nuño, mi señora,
            estando en este retrete,
            porque la dije no más
            que buenas noches tuviese,
            puso las manos en mí.

Mari-Nuño   Mas me dijo . . .

                              Pues pretende
            que le favorezca yo,

[Offstage]

ALONSO   It seems my daughters are here.
                        You go upstairs and light their light.

[Mari-Nuño enters.]

MARI-NUÑO   Oh! There's someone here. What a fright!
                        Who is it?

TORIBIO   It's nobody, it's   2945
                        me.

MARI-NUÑO   You scared me out of my wits.
                        What are you doing here with her
                        farthingale?

TORIBIO   Well, if you prefer
                        to know, I'm thinking about things.

MARI-NUÑO   Well, you can take your ponderings   2950
                        someplace else. Let go! And don't let
                        them catch you in here when they get
                        upstairs.

TORIBIO   You watch yourself. Don't make
                        me take vengeance on you and break
                        your head for that punch you gave me.   2955

MARI-NUÑO   You watch out yourself, or you'll see
                        me give you one that's harder still.

[He gives her a punch which she returns.]

TORIBIO   Try to beat this one if you will.

                        Help! She's killing me. Everyone
                        come see what this monster has done.   2960
                        Help, I'm dead!

[Eugenia, Clara, Don Alonso and Brígida enter.]

ALONSO   What is this racket?

CLARA   What's this shouting?

EUGENIA   Why so upset?

TORIBIO   My lady Mari-Nuño, who
                        walked in on me in this room, to
                        my politest salutation   2965
                        and wishes for good health, has run
                        amuck, laying her hands on me.

MARI-NUÑO   But he said . . .

*[Aside to Don Alonso, which
Don Toribio overhears]*
                                  . . . he wants me to be
                        his paramour. I heard him swear

porque dice que no quiere
señora de guardainfante,
y trae por testigo éste,
de quien está haciendo burla.

D. TORIBIO   ¡Qué testimonio tan fuerte!

MARI-NUÑO   A un traidor dos alevosos.

D. ALONSO
[Aparte.]

Advertid vos que no lleguen.
a entender nada las dos.

que de vuestras sencilleces,
o ignorancias o locuras,
estoy cansado de suerte. . . .
Pero hablemos de otra cosa,
no sean delirios siempre.

¿Cómo en la fiesta os ha ido?

EUGENIA   Como a quien viene, señor,
de ver el triunfo mayor
que nuestra España ha tenido
desde que su monarquía
a ser la mayor llegó.

D. ALONSO   Ya que no lo he visto yo,
de algún consuelo sería
oírlo de las dos aquí.

EUGENIA   Yo señor, te contaré
lo que me acuerdo.

[Aparte.]   (Veré
si desvelar puedo así
la pena en que me ha tenido
la competencia crüel
que vio Clara en su papel.)

CLARA
[Aparte.]

¿Viste a Félix?

MARI-NUÑO   Y advertido,
no dudo que venga.

CLARA   Pues
véle a abrir.

MARI-NUÑO   ¿Cómo, si aquí
todos están?

	no farthingalliwag was fair	2970
	enough to be his wife. And this	
	thing he dragged out for emphasis;	
	so I'm convinced he's mocking us.	
TORIBIO	Good Lord, what a preposterous	
	tale!	
MARI-NUÑO	Set a thief to catch a thief.	2975

ALONSO
[Aside to Mari-Nuño]
> I don't want to give any grief
> to the girls; take care what you say.

[Aside to Toribio]
> I am so tired of your display
> of inane imbecility
> or ignorance or lunacy,   2980
> that . . . But let's talk about something
> else beside your crazy ranting.

[To the girls]
> Tell us, did you have a good time?

EUGENIA
> Like one who's just returned, my lord,
> from seeing the greatest reward   2985
> Spain has given since her sublime
> monarchy has grown to become
> the greatest in the universe.

ALONSO
> Then because I could not immerse
> myself in the delirium   2990
> directly, you can describe it.

EUGENIA
> My lord, I'll tell you everything
> I remember.

[Aside]
>   (Perhaps I'll bring
> salve to my grief; I'll benefit
> if I can, by this gay narration,   2995
> forgetting the note I saw and
> the treachery my sister planned.)

CLARA
[Aside to Mari-Nuño]
> You saw Don Félix?

MARI-NUÑO
>   His elation
> signifies he'll come.

CLARA
>   Then you go
> and open the door for him.

MARI-NUÑO
>   Now?   3000
> Everyone's here.

CLARA   Mira, así,
como atento nos estés.

Lo que ella olvide, señor,
yo acordárselo pretendo.
¿Entiéndesme?

MARI-NUÑO   Ya te entiendo.

EUGENIA   Oirás la fiesta mayor
que habrás oído en tu vida.

CLARA   Y vos oíd también.

D. TORIBIO   ¿Pues no?

CLARA

Ve por él, mientras que yo
les doy con la entretenida.

[Vase Mari-Nuño.]

EUGENIA   Llegó el día que trocando
la divina Marïana
en felices posesiones
perezosas esperanzas,
de Madrid amanecieron,
para su dichosa entrada,
en felices aparatos
cubiertas calles y plazas,
todas las vimos, porque
transcendiendo por las vallas
fingidas de jaspe y bronce,
llegamos adonde estaba
en el Prado un arco excelso
que a las nubes se levanta.

CLARA   Aquí en el nacional traje
Madrid de su antigua usanza,
esperó a su nueva Reina,
vestida de blanco y nácar;
y para significar
de sus afectos las ánsias
con que liberal quisiera
poner el mundo a sus plantas,
ya que no la puso el mundo,
puso, por lo menos, tantas
significaciones dél,
que en este arco y los que faltan
representó de sus cuatro
partes las coronas varias
que en él amante la ofrece

CLARA   I'll show you how.

[To Don Alonso]

While you hear us describe that show,
my lord, I was just instructing
her the tasks she should do meanwhile.

[To Mari-Nuño]

You understand?

MARI-NUÑO   I see your guile.   3005

EUGENIA   Now you will listen to something
finer than you have ever heard.

CLARA   You listen to us too.

TORIBIO   Why not?

CLARA
[Aside to   And you go for him while I've got
Mari-Nuño]   them hanging on my every word.   3010

[Mari-Nuño exits.]

EUGENIA   At last the day arrived when our
Mariana, divine queen,
exchanged her laggard hopes
for her possessions most serene.
    To greet her majesty with pomp   3015
Madrid awoke at dawn,
and all her streets and plazas
artful ornaments put on.
    We saw them all, for crossing
in between the gilded fences   3020
of painted bronze and jasper,
we came to the residences
    of the monarchs in the Prado
where a mammoth arch was raised.

CLARA   Here all Madrid decked out in costumes   3025
worn in former days,
    awaited their new queen in clothes
of mother-of-pearl and white;
Madrid herself was so excited
to show her delight   3030
    and that she'd like to place the world
at her fair Monarch's feet,
that though she could not put the world,
she put the world's conceit,
    erecting on this arch, the first   3035
of many in the park,
on its four sides the crowns
which her new husband and monarch

                    quien la mereció monarca;
                    y así esta parte fue Europa,
                    como principal estancia,
                    donde sus imperios tienen
                    las demás por tributarias.

EUGENIA   Querer pintar que en él vimos
                    en casi vivas estatuas
                    a Castilla y a León,
                    por los reinos; Alemania
                    por la cuna, y por la fe
                    de la religión a Italia,
                    sin otras muchas señales,
                    imposible es ya, pues basta
                    que en este arco y los demás
                    apelemos a la estampa,
                    cuando lo expliquen sus letras
                    latinas y castellanas.

CLARA   Sólo por mayor diremos
                    que a las cuatro dilatadas
                    partes del mundo, en quien tuvo
                    dominio el planeta de Austria,
                    correspondieron los cuatro
                    elementos, siendo en claras
                    significaciones, doctos
                    reversos de sus fachadas:
                    y así a Europa se dio el aire,
                    por ser en quien más templadas
                    sus influencias se gozan
                    dulces, süaves y blandas.

EUGENIA   Y como del aire es
                    el águila remontada
                    emperatriz, cuyo nido
                    favorable aspira el aura,
                    el águila coronó
                    este elemento, adornada
                    de jeroglíficos que
                    todos del aire se sacan.

CLARA   A esta puerta pues, la Villa
                    (la ceremonia acabada
                    del besamano) empezó
                    (haciendo al compás la salva,
                    no sólo de los clarines,
                    las trompetas y las cajas,
                    sino de la voz del pueblo,
                    que es la más sonora salva)

    as lover gives to woo the bride
that he deserves as king.   3040
Thus the first side portrayed Europe,
which rules over everything.

EUGENIA   It's hard to paint the nearly living
statues that we saw,
of León and Castilla,   3045
nor have I the tongue to draw
   the effigy of Germany,
her cradle, or the one
of Italy, her chapel, each
figure the paragon   3050
   of artistry, but they have been
depicted in a book
with both Latin text and Spanish,
so you all can take a look.

CLARA   Hear only how the world's four parts   3055
that fate has relegated
to Hapsburg crowns, and which the Austrian
star has dominated,
   have linked to the four elements,
whose corresponding signs   3060
were carved upon the obverse sides
in intricate designs.
   And thus to Europe fell the air,
for of the continents
she feels most sweet and thoroughly   3065
her dulcet influence.

EUGENIA   And since the soaring eagle
is the air's emperatrice,
and since her nest is first to drink
the dawn's rosy increase,   3070
   the eagle crowned this element
with bold, imperious flair,
adorned with hieroglyphics,
each a symbol of the air.

CLARA   From this gate, then, Madrid set forth   3075
(when all had kissed her hand),
the tempo set by cannon's roar,
which with the royal band
   of drums and horns and clarinets
was joined by joyous throng   3080
of folk who cheered her with one voice,

3052 book: one of the many contemporary accounts of the wedding festivities; perhaps Bishop
    Mascarenhas' *Viage de la Serenisima Reina* (Madrid, 1650)

a caminar con el palio,
con tanto aplauso, con tanta
majestad, que no se vio
en términos de vasalla
nadie con más causa humilde,
ni soberbia con más causa.

EUGENIA   De aquí pues a la carrera
de San Jerónimo pasa,
donde no menos vistoso
la recibió el triunfo de Austria.

CLARA   De sesenta y dos coronas
que en la India rinden a España
feudo, los bultos de algunas
significaron las ansias
de servir su buena Reina
con dones y empresas cuantas
mide este imperio al Oriente,
donde su poder alcanza.

EUGENIA   Y como Asia es la mayor
parte del mundo, que abraza
Ganges, Nilo, Eufrates, Tigris,
señora de tierras tantas,
fue su elemento la tierra,
en quien se vio coronada
la melena del león,
como su mayor monarca.

CLARA   Llegó pues el Sol, del Sol
a la Puerta, en cuya estancia
Africa en el triunfal arco,
a vista suya se planta.
Y así, todas sus pinturas
fueron las fuerzas y plazas
que España en Africa goza,
desde que dos reinas santas,
política una en Madrid,
victoriosa otra en Granada,
arrancaron las raíces
desta venenosa planta.
A Africa correspondiendo
el fuego, o por su abrasada
Libia, o porque ha de ser hoy
La Puerta del Sol su estancia,
el sol, planeta de fuego,
entre pirámides altas
se vio colocado, bien
como exaltado en su casa.

        saluting her along;
          each man enthralled with his new queen,
        none sad to be her vassal,
        each humble as a serf and proud   3085
        as high lords in a castle.

EUGENIA   This bright procession passed
        to Saint Jerome's broad avenue,
        and there triumphant Austria
        received the retinue.   3090

CLARA   And of the two and seventy crowns
        the Indies pledge to Spain,
        the figured presences of some
        thereby did entertain
          to demonstrate their eagerness   3095
        to serve their favored queen
        with gifts and mottos from the East,
        as rare as earth has seen.

EUGENIA   Since Asia forms the largest part
        of terra, and embraces   3100
        the Tigris, Ganges, Nile, Euphrates
        and other diverse places,
          just so her element was earth,
        and she was proudly crowned
        with flowing lion's mane, a ruler   3105
        known the world around.

CLARA   Then came the Sun, resplendent,
        to the Plaza of the Sun,
        where Africa stood on triumphal
        arch, second to none.   3110
          And all her paintings were the forts,
        and cities held by Spain
        in Africa, since our two queens
        auspiciously did reign
          victorious in Granada   3115
        and triumphant in Madrid,
        when Spain forever of this vile
        and noxious vine they rid.
          Since fire belongs to Africa
        for Lybia's hot sand,   3120
        or since the Plaza of the Sun
        is where Africa stands,
          the sun, the fiery planet, sits
        on pyramids that rise
        up to the sky, exalted,   3125
        of the zodiac the prize.

3108 Plaza of the Sun: La Puerta del Sol in central Madrid

EUGENIA   Siguióse la Platería,
                 de tal manera adornada,
                 que sólo un arte tan noble
                 así pudiera ilustrarla;
                 pues casi desde este arco
                 se corrieron dos barandas
                 de bichas y de columnas,
                 que empezándose desde altas
                 pirámides, prosiguieron,
                 hasta que en otras rematan,
                 poblando sus corredores,
                 por una y por otra banda,
                 aparadores cubiertos
                 de diamantes, oro y plata.

CLARA   La América en otro arco
                 a Santa María estaba,
                 en cuyo templo el fiel culto
                 el *Te Deum laudamus* canta
                 fueron divinas empresas
                 cuantas dio el agua a sus aras
                 siendo perennes milagros
                 Manzanares y Jarama.

EUGENIA   En la Plaza de Palacio
                 animados en dos basas,
                 que de Himeneo y Mercurio
                 sostenían las estatuas,
                 dos triunfales carros vi,
                 de cuya fábrica rara
                 fue la significación
                 si es que me atrevo a explicarla,
                 que Mercurio, de los dioses
                 embajador, su jornada
                 a la vista de Palacio
                 feneció; y así, acabada
                 la fatiga del camino,
                 a Himeneo se la encarga,
                 porque uno su culto empiece
                 donde otro su culto acaba.

CLARA   Con este acompañamiento,
                 al compás de voces varias,
                 que del esposo, y la esposa
                 decían las alabanzas . . .

EUGENIA   En un bruto que parece
                 que sabía que llevaba
                 todo un cielo sobre sí,

EUGENIA   The gate of silversmiths came next,
adorned in such a way
that no one but an artist
could its noble style portray: 3130
     for two verandas from this arch's
pyramids reached out,
whose surfaces did twisted columns
and rare creatures sprout,
     whose glistening sideboards every person's   3135
gaping eyes did hold:
for they were set with diamonds,
with silver and with gold.

CLARA   America stood on the arch
of the church of Saint Mary,   3140
where sonorous Te Deums
echoed from the sanctuary
     and from her altars flowed two founts
that made the panorama
most meaningful, the wondrous   3145
Manzanares and Jarama.

EUGENIA   In front of the king's palace
two great statues did I see:
one was Hymen, god of marriage,
and the other Mercury,   3150
     both erected on triumphal carts,
as rich as I have been.
And though I am not a critic,
let me tell you what they mean:
     first Mercury, the messenger   3155
who serves the gods, in sight
of Phillip's palace, shed his load,
exhausted, to invite
     young Hymen to take charge of her
according to their plan;   3160
and thus one cult did reach an end,
and thus one cult began.

CLARA   The queen rode on with Hymen
as gay music filled the air
which praised the bridegroom and the bride   3165
beyond poet's compare.

EUGENIA   She rode up on a brutish beast
which seemed to know that he
bore on his saddle Heaven itself,

3140 Saint Mary: Madrid's oldest parish, near the west end of the Calle Mayor
3146 Manzanares: Madrid's river; Jarama: a river just south of Madrid

        según la noble arrogancia
        con que obedecía soberbio
        al impulso que le manda,
        llegó nuestra invicta Reina
        a las puertas de su alcázar.

D. ALONSO   Tal la relación ha sido,
        que aunque el no verlo de enojos,
        el deseo de los ojos
        se suple con el oído.

D. TORIBIO   No a mí, que aquese deseo
        nunca tuve.

D. ALONSO   ¿Por qué no?

D. TORIBIO   Como esas bodas vi yo.

D. ALONSO   ¿Dónde?

D. TORIBIO   En Cangas de Tineo,
        cuando los concejos todos
        se juntan para llevar
        las novias a otro lugar,
        entonando varios modos
        de bailes y de cantares,
        que es una fiesta bien rara.
        Si de alguno me acordara,
        se os quitaran mil pesares.

D. ALONSO   Dejad locuras, por Dios.
        Brígida, a alumbrarme ven,
        que ya recogerme es bien.

[Vase.]

CLARA   ¿Por qué no os recogéis vos?

D. TORIBIO   Porque para recogerme,
        falta salir de un cuidado.

CLARA   ¿Que cuidado?

D. TORIBIO   No he cenado;
        y tras esto, otro ha de hacerme
        perder el juicio.

CLARA   ¿Qué es?

D. TORIBIO   Vos dijisteis que había en mí
        más en que vengaros.

CLARA   Sí.

	he pranced so pridefully	3170
	beneath his sovereign, that he was	
	so privileged as to bring	
	our proud unconquered queen home to	
	her palace and the king.	

ALONSO   You describe everything so well   3175
            that, though I'm sad not to have seen
            it, everything my eyes were keen
            to see my ears have heard you tell.

TORIBIO   You may be keen, but I don't care
            one little bit.

ALONSO   Why?

TORIBIO   I've seen much   3180
            better weddings than this one.

ALONSO   Such
            a thing can't be. Where were they?

TORIBIO   Where?
            In the village of Cangas, when
            everyone who is on the town
            council meets to take some bride down   3185
            to the next village; all the men
            sing with delightful harmony
            and dance so well that it's a fine
            party. You can tell how divine
            it is with just one melody . . .   3190

ALONSO   Enough madness. Brígida, you
            come with me now to light my way.
            I'm going to call it a day.

[Don Alonso and Brígida exit.]

CLARA   Perhaps you should retire now too.

TORIBIO   I would, but I still have one care   3195
            weighing on me.

CLARA   What can that be?

TORIBIO   I must eat supper first, you see.
            And another, harder to bear,
            drives me insane.

CLARA   Well?

TORIBIO   You said how
            you wanted revenge on me for   3200
            something else, too.

CLARA   Yes.

3183 Cangas: Cangas de Onís, a town in Asturias

D. TORIBIO   Decidme la causa pues.

CLARA
[Aparte.]   La causa es que a Eugenia, a quien
                    (Dél asegurarme quiero
                    para la ocasión que espero.)
                    vos decís que queréis bien,
                    a otro favoreció.

D. TORIBIO   ¡Ay cielos!

CLARA   Si averiguarlo queréis,
                    bien facilmente podéis . . .

D. TORIBIO   Si esto oyeran mis abuelos,
                    ¿qué dijeran?

CLARA   Pues estando
                    un rato en ese balcón,
                    oiréis la conversación
                    que tiene en la calle, hablando
                    con un hombre por la reja
                    de su cuarto.

[Abre la ventana.]

D. TORIBIO   ¿Cómo qué?
                    En el balcón me estaré,
                    si acaso el dolor me deja,
                    sin chistar, de penas lleno.

[Vase.]

CLARA
[Aparte.]   (Ya éste no me estorbará,
                    pues cerrado se estará
                    toda la noche al sereno.)
                    Eugenia.

[Aparte.]   (Bueno será
                    engañarla.)

EUGENIA   ¿Qué me quieres?

CLARA   Avisarte cuánto eres
                    infeliz.

EUGENIA   ¿En qué?

CLARA   En que está
                    mi padre tan sospechoso
                    (pues no sé qué, que ha pasado,
                    Mari-Nuño le ha contado
                    acerca de que celoso

TORIBIO   I implore
        you to tell it to me, right now.

CLARA
[Aside]   (I have to make absolutely
        certain of him for what is to
[Aloud]   come.)   It's that my sister, whom you   3205
        claim to adore, is making free
        with somebody else.

TORIBIO   God forbid!

CLARA   If you want to find out for sure,
        all you have to do is procure . . .

TORIBIO   If my ancestors heard she did   3210
        this, what would they say?

CLARA   Just wait here
        on this balcony for a while
        and you'll hear my sister defile
        your love with another. You'll hear
        her woo her lover on the street   3215
        through this window grill.

TORIBIO   How do you
        like that! I'll wait right here to view
        her cause my pain and my defeat,
        as silent as I'm filled with grief.

[He opens a door to the balcony, goes out, and shuts the door.]

CLARA
[Aside]   (Now he cannot get in my way.   3220
        He'll spend all night and half the day
        out there, waiting in disbelief.)
[Aloud]   Eugenia!
[Aside]   (Let me see if I
        can deceive her as well.)

EUGENIA   What do
        you want?

CLARA   Oh, how unlucky you   3225
        are.

EUGENIA   In what way?

CLARA   It's just that my
        father is so suspicious now . . .
        I confess that I don't know what
        Mari-Nuño said to him, but
        I am quite sure she told him how   3230

          uno y otro amante tuyo
          hoy a esta puerta riñeron),
          que sus sospechas le hicieron
          desvelar, según arguyo,
          que no se acuesta. Por Dios,
          que si tienes que temer,
          me lo digas, para hacer
          como hermana.

EUGENIA   Si a los dos
          en el coche y en la reja
          viste que los despedí,
          y que no ha quedado en mí
          ni aun el ruido de la queja,
          ¿qué más de mi parte puedo
          haber hecho, ni saber
          puedo ahora qué he de hacer?

CLARA   Yo sí.

EUGENIA   ¿Qué es?

CLARA   Perder el miedo,
          puesto que inocente estás,
          y cerrada en mi aposento,
          desvelar tu pensamiento;
          que yo, desvelando más
          tu inocencia, allá entraré,
          diciendo que estás dormida,
          y mostrándome ofendida
          a su enojo, le diré
          muy bien dicho que no tiene
          razón, si en sospechar da
          de quien tan segura está.

EUGENIA   Mi vida, hermana, previene
          tu amistad; y porque más
          de mí asegurarse quiera,
          ciérrame tú por defuera.

[Entrase, y cierra doña Clara.]

CLARA   ¿Eso había de hacer?

                    Ya estás
          conmigo en campaña, Amor.
          Aquésta es la vez primera
          que te vi el rostro: no quiera
          vencer tan presto el rigor
          de tus iras. ¡Mari-Nuño!

[Sale Mari-Nuño.]

both of your suitors were so zealous
in their love they began to fight
outside your door. I think tonight
our poor father will be so jealous
that to watch you he won't go to   3235
bed at all. If you've got any-
thing to hide, sister, just tell me
so I can help you.

EUGENIA   But if you
saw me say goodbye to them, one
at my window, and one in his   3240
coach, and you can see that this is
the end, that I'm over and done
with them, what more would you have had
me do, Clara? I want to know
what to do now. Where shall I go?   3245

CLARA   I'll tell you what.

EUGENIA   What?

CLARA   Don't be sad,
don't be afraid. You're innocent,
and locked up in my room you can
be vigilant. Meanwhile, I plan
to employ every argument   3250
to show your innocence. I will
march in saying you are asleep.
If they are angry, then I'll keep
on the offensive, and I'll still
their objections, saying that they   3255
err in suspecting a person
like you, who is a paragon
of virtue.

EUGENIA   You know the best way
to protect me, sister. But so
you can be sure I won't misguide   3260
you, please lock the door from outside.

[She goes in.]

CLARA   I certainly will.

[She locks it.]   Now I know
that we are locked in battle, Love.
This is the first time I have seen
your face this close. I'd not demean   3265
you, by forcing you to remove
your troops too soon. Mari-Nuño!

[Mari-Nuño enters.]

CLARA	¿Dónde está aquel caballero?
MARI-NUÑO	En mi aposento, señora, rato ha que oculto le tengo, mientras que la relación a todos tenía suspensos.
CLARA	Esto por Eugenia hago.
MARI-NUÑO	Por eso yo te obedezco.
CLARA	Dile que salga a esta cuadra.
MARI-NUÑO	Voy.

[Vase, y sale don Félix.]

D. FÉLIX	Aunque rendido vengo a serviros, es mayor mi pena que el rendimiento.
CLARA	¿De qué?
D. FÉLIX	De ver que mi aviso ni vuestra cordura han hecho el efecto que esperamos, sino tan contrario efecto, que los dos conmigo hoy a vuestra puerta riñeron; y saliendo vuestro padre y vuestro primo a este tiempo. Queriendo acudir a todo, a nada acudí, supuesto que ni a uno ni otro alcanzar pude; y estoy con recelo de que se hayan encontrado, puesto que ninguno ha vuelto, siendo ambos huéspedes míos. Y aunque por ellos lo siento, lo siento por vos con más ventajas, pues si os confieso una verdad, me debéis vos mayor fineza que ellos.
CLARA	¿Yo mayor fineza?
D. FÉLIX	Sí.
CLARA	¿Cómo?

CLARA   Say, where did that gentleman go?

MARI-NUÑO   He's in my room, my lady, hid
                 safely inside, the way you bid   3270
                 me. He stayed there in turbulence
                 while you held the crowd in suspense
                 with your description.

CLARA   You know I
                 do this for Eugenia.

MARI-NUÑO   That's why
                 I obey you.

CLARA   Tell him to come   3275
                 out here.

MARI-NUÑO   I will.

[Don Félix enters.]

FÉLIX   Though I am numb
                 from waiting for you, I declare
                 I ache worse than from waiting there.

CLARA   Why is that?

FÉLIX   Because neither your
                 wisdom nor my warning could lure   3280
                 those two men away, and despite
                 our intentions they picked a fight
                 with me today outside your door.
                 Your father came out to deplore
                 the ruckus, and then your cousin   3285
                 came charging outside to butt in.
                 And though I wanted to take care
                 of everything, to my despair
                 I could do nothing, because I
                 couldn't get close enough to try.   3290
                 I'm sorry they rushed to attack,
                 because neither one has come back
                 home yet, and they are both my guests.
                 My great concern for them attests
                 to my true feelings, but I feel   3295
                 worse for you, and I can't conceal
                 the truth of that. For you owe me
                 an even greater courtesy
                 than they do.

CLARA   Are you certain?

FÉLIX   Yes.

CLARA   How's that?

D. Félix   Perdonad, os ruego,
                      porque no puedo decirlo,
                      aunque ya dicho lo tengo.

Clara   ¡Dicho lo tenéis, y no
                      podéis decirlo! No entiendo
                      tan nuevo enigma.

D. Félix   Yo sí.

Clara   Declaraos más.

D. Félix   No puedo,
                      que si el sentimiento es
                      por ser mis amigos, cierto
                      será, por ser mis amigos,
                      el callar mi sentimiento.

[Ruido dentro.]

D. Juan   ¡Válgame el cielo!

D. Félix   ¿Qué voces
                      son las que estamos oyendo?

Clara   En el jardin fue.

[Sale Mari-Nuño.]

Mari-Nuño   ¡Señora!

Clara   ¿Qué hay, Mari-Nuño? ¿Qué es eso?

Mari-Nuño   Por las tapias del jardín
                      se ha arrojado un hombre dentro,
                      a cuyo ruido, tu padre
                      baja ya de su aposento.

Clara   ¡Triste de mí! ¿Qué he de hacer,
                      si os ven aquí?

D. Félix   Buen remedio:
                      yo por aqueste balcón
                      saldré a la calle primero
                      que me vea.

Clara   No le abráis.

D. Félix   ¿No es mejor?

[Abre un balcón, y halla a don Toribio.]

D. Toribio   Estense quedos,
                      no hagan ruido, que ya el hombre

FÉLIX   I'm sorry, I confess   3300
                    I cannot tell you any more,
                    even though I've said it before.

CLARA   You say you've said it before, and
                    you can't now? I don't understand
                    this enigma at all.

FÉLIX   I do.   3305

CLARA   Please explain.

FÉLIX   I can't. And I rue
                    the fact that it is my feelings
                    for my friends, nothing less, that brings
                    me to the point where I must hide
                    my own true feelings deep inside.   3310

[There is a noise offstage.]

[Offstage]

JUAN   God help me!

FÉLIX   What voices are those?
                    What's that shouting, do you suppose?

CLARA   It was in the garden.

[Mari-Nuño enters.]

MARI-NUÑO   Lady!

CLARA   What's that? Mari-Nuño, tell me,
                    what is it?

MARI-NUÑO   I saw a man fall   3315
                    from the highest part of the wall
                    into the garden, and then your
                    father came downstairs to ensure
                    that all was well.

CLARA   Alas! What can
                    I do? If they find you . . .

FÉLIX   I plan   3320
                    to be gone by then. Let me leave
                    through this window. We can deceive
                    them that way.

CLARA   No! Don't open it.

FÉLIX   That's the best way.

[Félix opens the balcony door.]

TORIBIO   Will you please quit
                    talking? I say be quiet. That   3325

a la reja llega, y quiero
oír lo que habla.

D. FÉLIX   Hombre, ¿quién eres?

D. TORIBIO   ¿Quién os mete a vos en eso?
¿Métome yo en quién sois vos?
Agradecedme que tengo
que hacer aquí, que si no,
a fe que había de saberlo.

D. FÉLIX   ¿Quién vio tan extraño lance?

MARI-NUÑO   Ya en el jardín se oye estruendo.

CLARA   Apartémonos de aquí.

[Retíranse las dos, y sale don Pedro.]

D. PEDRO   Viendo mis rabiosos celos
que abriendo la puerta entró
mi enemigo hasta aquí dentro
sin poderlo yo estorbar,
que llegar no pude a tiempo,
por las tapias del jardín
a entrar me atreví resuelto
a vengar. . . . Pero ¡qué miro!
que es su padre, vive el cielo,
y brioso, con otro hombre
riñendo sale a este puesto.

[Sale don Alonso riñendo con don Juan y llega después don Félix.]

D. ALONSO   Al esfuerzo de mi brazo,
de mis iras al aliento,
pues me han hecho dos agravios
tu voz y tu atrevimiento,
los dos vengaré . . . ¡Ay de mi!,
que van mis penas creciendo,
pues cuando pensé de uno,
dos de quien vengarme tengo.

D. FÉLIX   Tened la espada, don Juan.
Don Alonso, detenéos.

D. JUAN   Mira si traidor amigo
eres, pues aquí te encuentro.

man's coming over here to chat
with her now. I want to hear.

FÉLIX   Who
do you think you are?

TORIBIO   Who told you
to butt in like this? Do I make
you say who you are? For Pete's sake,   3330
be thankful I'm busy, or else
I'd give you a couple of belts!

[He closes the door on himself.]

FÉLIX   Who ever heard of such a thing?

MARI-NUÑO   In the garden I hear shouting.

CLARA   Let's go now, please.

*[Clara and Mari-Nuño open the door where Eugenia exited, and they leave. Don
Félix hides himself on another balcony the way Don Toribio did.]*

[Don Pedro enters.]

PEDRO   My jealousy   3335
was such, that when my enemy
just opened her front door and went
right in, and I could not prevent
it because I got here too late,
I knew that I had to frustrate   3340
him by scaling the garden wall
to avenge . . . What's that I see? All
is lost! Her father comes, and he
is arguing ferociously.

[Don Alonso enters, struggling with Don Juan.]

ALONSO   By the power of this right arm   3345
and my righteous anger, you harm
me doubly with your rude boldness
and your rough words. And this excess
shall be avenged! Oh woe is me,
my sorrows grow so rapidly!   3350
Revenge against one will not do:
I must avenge myself of two!

[Don Félix enters from the balcony where he was hidden.]

FÉLIX   Don Juan, put away your sword. And
you, Don Alonso, back off. Stand.

JUAN   Look who shows up now? My false friend,   3355
butting in to God knows what end.

D. Félix   Oid, sabréis que enemigo
                  no soy, ni suyo, ni vuestro.

D. Alonso   ¡Dentro de mi casa dos
                  enemigos!

D. Félix   Deteneos.

[Don Toribio sale a la reja.]

D. Pedro

                  Aunque estorbar aquí deba
                  de don Alonso el empeño,
                  primero venganza pide
                  lo rabioso de mis celos.

                  Si por aquese balcón
                  te pasó el atrevimiento
                  de aquesa ingrata a mis ojos,
                  en ti he de vengar primero
                  los celos con que te busco.
                  Baja abajo, o vive el cielo
                  que esta pistola . . .

[Saca una pistola.]
D. Toribio

                                          ¿Pistola?
                  Hombre del diablo, está quedo,
                  que no es eso lo que yo
                  te dije. Pero ¡qué veo!
                  ¿Qué es esto, tío?

[Sale al tablado.]

D. Alonso   A mi lado
                  os poned.

[Don Pedro, que hasta aquí ha estado junto a la reja, llega donde está don Juan, don Félix, y don Alonso.]

D. Pedro

                              Pues que le abrieron
                  la ventana, llegaré
                  a matarle; que no temo,
                  ya que estoy muerto a su dicha,
                  quedar a sus manos muerto.

D. Juan   Traidor, tras ti . . . Mas ¿qué miro?
                  ¿Por la ventana resuelto
                  así os entráis?

D. Pedro   ¿Qué os admira?
                  Si tanto ruido me ha puesto
                  en obligación de entrar
                  a saber lo que es.

Félix	Listen, you know I am not your false friend, nor his, you can be sure.
Alonso	Here in my house, two enemies!
Félix	Stop arguing, I beg you, please. 3360

PEDRO
[Aside]

(Though I ought to try to frustrate
what Don Alonso wants, the state
of my furious jealousy
instead demands vengeance of me.)

[To Don Félix, who has stopped in front of the balcony where Don Toribio is hidden.]

And you: if that woman, whom I   3365
hate now with all my heart, is why
you're standing on that balcony,
I will avenge her treachery
first on you. Come down here right now,
or by all that's holy, I vow   3370
that this pistol . . . !

TORIBIO   *[coming out on the balcony]*
                                         This pistol? Hey,
you demon, get that thing away
from me! That's not what I told you
to do. But what's going on? Who
can tell me? Uncle?

ALONSO   Stand here by   3375
me.

PEDRO
[Aside]

                 (Since the window's open, I
will follow him and kill him, for
because I am dead by her score
anyway, it's all the same; and
who cares if I die by his hand?)   3380

JUAN   I'll get you, you traitor. But what
is this? Since the window's not shut,
you just climb right in?

PEDRO   Well, of course.
All those loud noises inside force
me to break in like this to find   3385
out what is going on.

D. ALONSO   Suspenso
en repetidos agravios,
no sé a cual he de ir primero.

D. FÉLIX   Teneos, señor don Alonso,
que trances de honor, el cuerdo
los venga con su prudencia
antes que con el acero:
y si me escucháis, no dudo
quedéis honrado y contento.

D. ALONSO   Uno entró por mi jardín,
otro por mi reja; pero
vos que aquí dentro os halláis,
¿por dónde entrasteis primero?
Que haciéndome el mismo agravio,
me venís a dar consejo.

D. TORIBIO   Entraría por la escala,
que escala había para ello.

D. FÉLIX   Yo soy tan interesado
en este lance, que pienso
que vine a serviros más
a todos, que no a ofenderos,
que fue a excusarle; mas ya
que conseguirlo no puedo
de una manera, de otra
lo intentaré: estadme atentos.
Doña Eugenia me ha tenido
en aqueste cuarto, a efecto
de estorbar entre los dos . . .

[Dentro doña Eugenia.]

EUGENIA   ¿Qué escucho? Dejar no puedo
de salir, al oir mi nombre.

[Dentro.]

CLARA   Tente, no salgas.

[Salen doña Clara y doña Eugenia.]

EUGENIA   Si quiero,
que ya me importa saber
qué es aqueste fingimiento.
¡Yo te he tenido (¿qué dices,
hombre?) en mi cuarto!

D. FÉLIX
                                          Teneos,
que yo doña Eugenia he dicho,
no vos.

[Señala a Clara.]

ALONSO   My mind
reels with such diverse offense.
I can't decide where to commence.

FÉLIX   My lord Don Alonso, please wait:
for in affairs of honor, great   3390
wisdom seeks its vengeance with words
of prudent counsel, not with swords.
If you'll just hear my argument
you'll be both honored and content.

ALONSO   One entered by the garden wall,   3395
one through the window grill. And all
offend me, especially you,
who seem to think that it's your due,
since you're here first by some device,
to stand there and give me advice!   3400

TORIBIO   He must have climbed up the ladder,
for a ladder there was, I'm sure.

FÉLIX   I'm so concerned in this business
myself, that my attentiveness
was to serve, my interference   3405
was to help, not to cause offense.
I tried to solve things. But if I
can't put things right with my first try,
let me see if I can appease
you some other way. Hear me, please.   3410
Doña Eugenia had locked me
in that room over there, where she
thought perhaps that I could prevent . . .

[Offstage]

EUGENIA   What's that I hear? I think he meant
me! Now I have to go out there.   3415

[Offstage]

CLARA   Wait! Don't go out!

[Clara and Eugenia enter.]

EUGENIA   Let go! I swear
you can't keep me from finding out
what this masquerade's all about.
Tell me, sir, how you can presume
to say I hid you in my room.   3420

FÉLIX   [Pointing to Doña Clara]
Hold on. I said Eugenia, not
you.

D. Alonso   ¿Cómo, cómo es eso?
                 ¿Luego tú eras la que un hombre
                 escondido tenías dentro?

Eugenia   ¿Luego tú con nombre mío,
                 Clara, la traición has hecho?

D. Toribio   ¿Luego tú por eso a mí
                 me tenías al sereno,
                 hecho avestruz del amor?

Los tres   ¿Qué es esto, ingrata? ¿Qué es esto?

Clara   Esto es que por estorbar
                 de Eugenia yo los empeños,
                 no pude estorbar el mío;
                 y pues que sois caballero,
                 no en el riesgo me dejéis,
                 cuando a otra sacáis del riesgo.

D. Félix   ¿Qué es dejaros? Con mil vidas
                 habéis de ver que os defiendo;
                 pues no amando la que es dama
                 de mis amigos, bien puedo.

D. Juan   Pues supuesto que ya quedan
                 desvanecidos mis celos,
                 yo os ayudaré.

D. Pedro   Yo y todo.

D. Alonso   ¿Hay tan grande atrevimiento?

D. Toribio   ¡Quién tuviera aquí un lanzón
                 de tres que en mi casa tengo!

D. Alonso   A mis ojos y en mi casa,
                 nadie a mis hijas (¡ay cielos!)
                 defenderá que no sea
                 su esposo.

D. Félix   Si basta eso,
                 yo lo soy suyo.

Clara   Y yo suya.

D. Alonso   ¿Quién creyera que en el hierro
                 mayor, fuera quien cayera
                 la mesurada más presto?

D. Toribio   ¿Quién no lo creyera? Pues
                 siempre en el mundo lo vemos,
                 que las aguas mansas son

ALONSO   What's that? Did you hatch this plot,
Clara? How could you dare to hide
this man, so secretly, inside
our house?

EUGENIA   Was it you, to our shame,   3425
who did this thing under my name?

TORIBIO   You were the one who made me stand
out there with my head in the sand
just like an ostrich! How could you?

ALL THREE   Ingrate! Clara, what did you do?   3430

CLARA   You know, I was trying so hard
to make myself Eugenia's guard
that I forgot to take care to
guard myself. But Don Félix, you
are a gentleman, don't leave me   3435
stuck here to set someone else free.

FÉLIX   How could I ever leave you? I
will always defend you, all my
life, since I love a lady who
is not my friends' love, I can do   3440
that easily.

JUAN   Well, now that my
jealous thoughts no longer apply,
I will help you.

PEDRO   I am willing.

ALONSO   Who has ever seen such a thing?

TORIBIO   If I had only brought my lance   3445
with me, that I left home by chance!

ALONSO   Here in my house and in my sight
nobody, by God, has the right
to defend my daughters, unless
it is their husbands.

FÉLIX   I confess   3450
that if that's all, I am hers.

CLARA   And
I am his.

ALONSO   I can't understand
how it is that the moderate
one was the first to perpetrate
such a thing.

TORIBIO   What's to understand?   3455
It is that way in every land,
that the waters that run most still

de las que hay que fiar menos,
y tienen mayor peligro
porque sin duda por eso,
guárdate del agua mansa
dijo un antiguo proverbio.

EUGENIA   Pues yo, señor, a tus plantas
humildemente te ruego
me des estado a tu gusto;
que yo con mi primo quiero
irme a la montaña, donde
te asegure por lo menos,
de que nunca delincuentes
fueron mis esparcimientos.

D. TORIBIO   ¿A la montaña? Eso no,
porque allá llevar no quiero
ni filis ni guardainfantes:
y así, con mi alforja al cuello,
donde está mi ejecutoria,
habéis de ver que me vuelvo
sin casar.

D. ALONSO   Ni yo tampoco;
que no tengo de dar dueño
tan bruto a una hija mía
a quien más atención debo,
sino darla a quien su madre
la había dado en casamiento,
y esperando mi licencia,
se quedó hasta ahora suspenso.

D. JUAN   A vuestras plantas humilde
os digo que soy el mesmo,
pues soy don Juan de Mendoza.

D. ALONSO   Con esto es del mal el menos.

D. PEDRO   Pues quedo sin esperanza
de mi amor, lograrla intento
en pedir que perdonéis
de nuestras faltas los yerros.

D. TORIBIO   Porque con la moraleja
del *Agua mansa* y su ejemplo,
dando principio a serviros,
fin a la comedia demos.

are the ones that do the most ill;
still waters are most dangerous
and that's why it is obvious   3460
that since the proverb says "Beware
of still waters" you should take care.

EUGENIA   Well then I, my lord, at your feet
with great humility entreat
you to elect the man you please.   3465
Because, if my cousin agrees,
I want to go home with him to
the mountains, where I will show you
I was never a sinful child,
though I confess I was quite wild.   3470

TORIBIO   Take you to the mountains? I will
not, because I don't want to fill
my house with farthingales or knacks.
And so I'll take my saddle packs
and letters of nobility   3475
and go back home. You will not see
me get married.

ALONSO   That's right, I won't.
My daughter deserves more; I don't
want to see her marry a brute
like you who is an absolute   3480
ninny. I will give her instead
to the man that her mother wed
her to before she died. They were
just waiting for me to concur.

JUAN   Here at your feet, humbly, I say   3485
that very man is here today:
Don Juan de Mendoza's my name.

ALONSO   There's only joy now, no more blame.

PEDRO   Well then, since my love has no chance
at all, I hope this dissonance   3490
you will relieve: my sadness halts,
if you will but pardon our faults.

TORIBIO   So, with the moral of "Beware
of still waters" do we declare
that your pleasure was all that we intended.   3495
And now, dear friends, the comedy has ended.

DATE DUE			